DEATH IN THE GARDEN CITY

DEATH IN THE GARDEN CITY

Jeanne M. Dams

This first world edition published 2019
in Great Britain and 2020 in the USA by
SEVERN HOUSE PUBLISHERS LTD of
Eardley House, 4 Uxbridge Street, London W8 7SY.
Trade paperback edition first published
in Great Britain and the USA 2020 by
SEVERN HOUSE PUBLISHERS LTD.

British Library Cataloguing in Publication Data
A CIP catalogue record for this title is available from the British Library.

ISBN-13: 978-0-7278-8913-3 (cased)
ISBN-13: 978-1-78029-655-5 (trade paper)
ISBN-13: 978-1-4483-0353-3 (e-book)

All Severn House titles are printed on acid-free paper.

Severn House Publishers support the Forest Stewardship Council™ [FSC™],
the leading international forest certification organisation.
All our titles that are printed on FSC certified paper carry the FSC logo.

Typeset by Palimpsest Book Production Ltd.,
Falkirk, Stirlingshire, Scotland.
Printed and bound in Great Britain by
TJ International, Padstow, Cornwall.

AUTHOR'S NOTE

This book is set in and around Victoria, British Columbia, Canada – affectionately referred to as The Garden City – and I owe a great debt to many kind people there. First of all, the book would never have been possible without the kindness of Barry and Moira Carlson. Moira and I met through email and became friends, and she and her husband then became my wonderful hosts for a delightful week in Victoria and environs. She is an artist and he a computer specialist – lovely people. They took me everywhere, made sure I saw everything, and answered hundreds of questions then and for weeks afterward via email. At the last, they were patient and gracious enough to read the manuscript and point out countless mistakes I made in dealing with Canadian English and with details of the Vancouver Island environment. Blessings be upon them!

Staff Sergeant Craig Harper, a detective with the Victoria Police Department, has been of enormous help in sorting out for me the complications of policing in an area with multiple munici-palities, sets of laws, and police forces.

The guides who lead the walking tours of Victoria are delightful people who were patient with my many questions and would never, never act as my fictional one did.

Finally, I am extremely grateful to my friend Teresa Betz for allowing me to use her name. Let the reader be assured that the only resemblance between the real Teresa and my fictional one is that both are very nice women.

I hope that readers who are not fortunate enough to know Victoria and the rest of Vancouver Island will get an opportunity to visit. It is honestly as beautiful and charming as I have painted it. All the pleasant people in the book are drawn from life; the nasty ones were created in my own disordered mind.

ONE

The phone call woke me from a pleasant afternoon nap, a habit I've grown entirely too fond of in recent years. A terrible waste of time, but so delightful, especially on a warm May day with the scent of hyacinths and the cheerful songs of birds wafting in through the window. Anyway, a woman my age surely deserves some down time, right?

I groped for the phone, knocked it off the bedside table, and finally managed to answer just as it stopped warbling.

Drat. Now I needed my glasses to read the caller ID. Was it worth the trouble? If it was important they'd call back or leave a message.

I lay back down and tried to recapture my dream, but I knew it was no use. Once I was awake, my brain started spinning, reminded me of all the things I should be doing. We needed groceries, especially cat food. Esmeralda trotted in at that exact moment – I swear she can read my mind – and jumped up, settling her solid bulk on my chest and reaching for my face with an insistent paw.

Sighing, I sat up, dislodging Emmy, and reached again for the phone and my glasses.

Oh. Judith Montcalm. Well, I couldn't imagine why she'd be calling, but it would be nice to talk to her. We hadn't had a lot of contact since very early in the year, when Alan and I had served as godparents at the christening of her son, who would one day be Sir Joseph Montcalm, Bart.

Emmy had already started out the bedroom door, looking back to make sure I was following. I might, after all, have forgotten the way to the kitchen, where her empty food bowl was in urgent need of attention. As I went down the stairs, I clicked on the buttons that would return the call.

'Judith? Dorothy, returning your call. Sorry I didn't answer. I couldn't get to the phone in time.' No need to mention why.

'Oh, I'm sorry if I called at a bad time. You were probably napping, and quite right, too, on such a sleepy afternoon.'

Judith got to know me very well during that brief visit to Suffolk, months ago.

'Everything here is fine,' she went on, 'so don't start worrying. Joseph is growing by leaps and bounds, and the girls are both doing well in school. Edwin's away just now, doing something obscure with a start-up company in Tanganyika, of all places. No, the reason I called is a bit complicated.'

I had been busy filling Emmy's bowl, and then of course Samantha rushed in, speaking loudly in her Siamese voice, and I had to placate her, too, as well our beloved mutt Watson, who thought he deserved his share.

'Sorry about the racket. The animals are demanding a meal. Their third today, if I've counted properly. Now! That's done. Tell all.'

'I'm a little embarrassed about it, but the fact is, I need your help, yours and Alan's. Or actually, it's my uncle who needs help, and I've terrible cheek even to ask, but he sounded so desperate, and I thought it would be just up your street, even though it's so far away.'

'What's so far away?'

'Oh, I haven't explained, have I? To tell the truth, I'm really quite worried about him. He lives in Victoria, and he's deeply troubled, but . . . well, I'll begin at the beginning.'

I switched on the kettle, spooned some instant coffee into a cup, and prepared for a saga.

'His name is John McKenzie, and he's my mother's brother. I remember him from way back when; we all lived near Toronto then, and used to get together for family occasions, holidays and birthdays and all that. He was my favourite uncle. Well, still is, for that matter. He joined the Mounties straight out of university, and loved being a policeman.'

A picture of Nelson Eddy on a horse appeared in my mind. Handsome as all get-out, wearing a devastating uniform and singing to Jeannette MacDonald one of the silliest songs ever written. 'Ooh, a Mountie! How exciting.'

'Not really. They're still called the Royal Canadian Mounted Police, but they don't actually ride horses anymore, except for parades and things. And they don't wear that gorgeous uniform much, either. They're responsible for enforcing federal and national law throughout the country, and in a lot of the provinces they're the main police force.'

My vision faded. Shoot. Another illusion gone.

'Anyway, when his wife, Aunt Margaret, died, Uncle John decided he wanted to move to a milder climate, and he was so lucky to find a good job in Victoria. That's in British Columbia, you know.'

'No. I'm afraid the things I know about Canada are terribly limited. I always was a dunce about geography. I know where Ontario is, and Quebec, and Prince Edward Island – that's because of *Anne of Green Gables*, of course. But the rest . . .' I waved a hand, foolishly, because Judith couldn't see it.

'Okay, BC is the westernmost province of Canada. It stretches all the way from the Pacific to the Rocky Mountains, and from the continental US border up to Alaska. Victoria is in the south, on Vancouver Island, which is actually just a bit north of Seattle.'

'Oh, I've heard of Vancouver,' I said brightly.

'That's the city. And it's not on Vancouver Island, just to confuse people. It's on the mainland. The island, and the city of Victoria, are perfectly beautiful places, and they have an almost-perfect climate, warm and sunny most of the time, enough rain in winter to keep the reservoirs filled, almost no snow; it's an ideal place to live. The standard of living is high, and there's very little crime. It's known as The Garden City, no less . . .'

'Then . . . I'm afraid I don't quite understand why your uncle is troubled. Does he have too little to do, the crime rate being what it is?'

'No. It isn't that. Anyway he's been retired for a few years now. But of course he still keeps a finger on the pulse of the community, and that's what's bothering him. Something is badly wrong.'

'But . . . I'm sorry, I'm not following you.' I ran my fingers through my hair in another futile gesture. 'Judith, just *what* is wrong?'

'That's just it. That's the point. He doesn't know. He can't put a finger on it. Odd things have been happening, but they don't make a pattern, and they don't make sense.'

'For instance?'

'Well, some plants have been stolen. Some aconites from the Butchart Gardens, for a start. Do you know about the Butchart Gardens?'

'Never heard of them, but that can wait. What else?'

'No, but you need to know a little about the gardens. They're huge, and really famous. Japanese tourists come all those thousands of miles to see the Japanese garden, and . . . well, anyway, they're fabulous, with amazing collections of plants, and the thing is, they're very well guarded. So the theft of plants is extremely unusual. The aconites aren't particularly valuable though, so it isn't a super big deal. But then the next thing, the next one Uncle John noticed, anyway, was somebody's oleander, a prized specimen kept in a pot and brought inside for the winter. The whole bush, pot and all, just taken away in the middle of the night.'

The coffee was beginning to take hold. 'Aconite,' I repeated. 'Oleander. You said there wasn't a pattern, but I'm seeing one here. You do know that those are two extremely poisonous plants.'

'Yes, I knew that, and so does Uncle John, of course. But the thing is, the thefts happened months ago, and there haven't been any cases of poisoning. No unexpected deaths of any kind. A few addicts overdosed on fentanyl, but sadly, that's not unexpected.'

'He's sure of that? I mean, that they were ODs and not other sorts of poison.'

'Believe me, he knows what an OD looks like. Fentanyl is a scourge, and Victoria is no more immune than anywhere else. But as for alkaloid poisonings, it's a smallish community, Dorothy, and Uncle John has contacts all over the place. He would have heard if anyone had been given monkshood or oleander. Someone stole those plants and then . . . I don't know, threw them away, I suppose. They don't seem to have been planted anywhere. A few aconites in someone's garden wouldn't be noticed, perhaps, but a potted oleander?'

'Taken to the States, maybe? Or no, I suppose customs officials check for plant material in someone's car or luggage.'

'They thought of that. The plants could have been boxed up and shipped to almost anywhere in the world, for that matter, not just the US – but why, when they can be bought at any nursery? Why steal them at all and then do nothing with them?'

'Beats me. But surely it's not all that serious, not enough to cause your uncle so much alarm.'

'Oh, but that's just the beginning. Then there began to be letter bombs.'

'Good heavens! That's altogether a different kettle of fish. That's really serious! Was anyone killed?' Surely not, I thought, or it would have made the news, even here. Canada was, after all, a Commonwealth country, and Mother England was interested in her welfare.

'No one was killed. No one was even badly hurt. Because they weren't really bombs at all. They were just fireworks rigged to go off when the letter was opened. They were sent to various offices: a lawyer, a doctor, and an IT firm. One man got a burn on his hand, and another one was nearly hit in the eye, but fortunately not quite. The envelopes were filled with some powder, too, and that had everyone excited for a while – but it was talcum powder. Just ordinary bath powder, with quite a nice scent, Uncle John said.'

'Judith, that makes no sense at all!'

'No. Just malicious mischief. Like the theft of the plants. Like the vandalism here and there – somebody's mailbox battered, a porch light broken (hit by a brick), a toilet seat hoisted up onto Queen Victoria's statue.

'And there's been damage to tents. Victoria has rather a large homeless population, and they've been living in tents in various parks. It's created a good deal of ill feeling on both sides of the issue, the neighbours wanting them to go somewhere else, the tent-dwellers feeling bullied. They do, on the whole, try to keep their precarious communities clean and tidy, and when a lot of the tents were smeared with paint, and I'm afraid worse, the tensions escalated.'

'I think I begin to see why your uncle is uneasy. Just general nastiness, isn't it?'

'That's what it looks like. But the police haven't been able to come up with a single clue as to who might be doing all these things. You can see the problem. None of these incidents, by itself, is a serious crime. There's been nothing that warrants a full-scale investigation. And the RCMP and the Victoria police are chronically understaffed, just like police forces all over. And yet the net effect of all this is to undermine the morale of the whole area. Greater Victoria has always been a peaceful, pleasant place. Oh, they have their problems, like anywhere else, but on the whole everyone seems to rub along quite smoothly. But now . . .'

Her voice trailed off, and I thought I could hear the hint of tears. 'My dear girl! This means a great deal to you, doesn't it?'

A sniff. 'Silly of me, isn't it? I've only visited Victoria once, before the children were born. Edwin had business in Vancouver, and it kept on raining and raining, and someone said it almost never rained in Victoria in the summer. Something about a rain shadow and the mountains. I didn't understand, but I hired a car and drove to Victoria. It took a long time, because a lot of it was by ferry, but I loved the trip, and I loved the island. It was all true. The sun shone and the air was warm and the gardens were beautiful and the people were friendly. I had a lovely time, even though I was by myself. So when Uncle John moved there, Edwin and I decided we'd take the children and visit, as soon as Joseph was a little older. It's been a dream for us, and now it looks like turning into a nightmare.' She sniffed again.

I let the pause lengthen for a bit. 'And you're asking for our help, Alan's and mine. What is it you want us to do?'

'I feel most awfully brazen even to ask. But . . . well, it is a lovely place, and in spring and early summer I'm told it's unbelievably beautiful, and of course we'd pay for everything . . .'

She drifted off, and if I sighed, it was inwardly. 'You'd like Alan and me to go to Victoria and see what we can find out.'

'That's it. Do you mind terribly?'

'I'll have to talk to Alan, of course. But no, I don't mind your asking. Why would I? Isn't that what friends are for? I'll talk to him as soon as he gets home, and call you back. And Judith, try not to worry too much.'

TWO

I t was a long trip. Edwin and Judith had insisted on paying for a business-class fare, so it was less uncomfortable than it might have been. And we broke the journey in Toronto, where Judith's family gave us a warm welcome and put us up for the night. But international travel, with its attendant jet lag, is always exhausting, and the older I get, the more it seems to affect me. The last lap, Vancouver to Victoria, was in a very small plane indeed, and my tolerance for discomfort had been steadily diminishing. By the time we arrived at the tiny Victoria airport, I was ready for nothing but bed – and it was, in Victoria, early afternoon.

Judith's Uncle John met us at the airport and understood completely. 'You're still running on English time, aren't you? I'm going to take you home, feed you a very light meal with a small glass of wine, and settle you down for a brief nap. Brief, mind you! Then we'll go for a walk, as the weather's so nice, have a bite of supper, and then bed. You'll sleep well, and in the morning you should be nicely adjusted to life eight time zones away from home.'

I had to exercise my best manners to avoid nodding off on the ride into Victoria, but Alan, for some reason more alert than I, kept pointing out something of special beauty or interest along the way, and I managed to stay conscious. The salad and wine, though, did it. I think I was asleep even before my head hit the pillow in our pleasant and comfortable room.

Waking was torture, of course, but I admitted I felt somewhat refreshed, especially after a cool shower and a change of clothes. 'Among the living, my dear?' asked Alan as we went downstairs to join our host.

'More or less. I could easily have slept right through till morning, though.'

'But you wouldn't have. You'd have waked in the middle of the night and been disoriented and out-of-synch for a week. Buck up, old thing. You're not in Kansas anymore.'

'Nor in Oz,' I snapped.

But really, when we set out on our walk, there did seem to be some Oz-like features. If our long journey had seemed to be largely grey, at least in spirit, Victoria was certainly in Technicolor.

John McKenzie lived in a pleasant neighbourhood of family homes, not elaborate, but well maintained. The houses gleamed with fresh paint, mostly white, but with pastels mixed in. And every house – *every* house – had its front garden. Some were simple plots of annuals, in the vivid colours of June. Some were much more elaborate, with incredible roses and flowering shrubs. I became frustrated because I couldn't see any of the back gardens for the high fences surrounding them.

John explained. 'You see, we have a deer problem. When we walk down near the gorge, we'll probably see one or two. They have almost no fear of humans, and they are very fond of many garden plants. So we build fences, and try to avoid planting some of their favourites. The trouble is, their favourites are often ours, as well. When we visit Butchart Gardens, you'll see some of the elaborate defences they've devised. Of course, they also have a huge staff of gardeners who can replant anything that gets devastated.'

I wondered if the deer ever ate oleander or monkshood, and if so, whether they died, but decided this wasn't the time to bring it up.

'We've heard a good deal about the Butchart Gardens,' said Alan blandly. 'We're going to see them?'

'Yes, and other gardens as well. I'm giving you the grand tour.'

We had, by that time, wandered into a small park. John gestured toward an inviting bench. 'You're probably ready for a respite, all things considered. And we need to talk.'

I was glad to sit. Parts of our walk had been uphill, and I'm not as young as I used to be. Not to mention befuddled by too much travel too fast.

'Judith says she's told you about my worries?' John said, making it a question.

'Some of them, at least,' I replied. 'The plants that have been stolen, the letter bombs, the vandalism.'

'Yes. There's been all that, and more. I daresay, Alan, that as a policeman you understand the petty nature of all the incidents.'

'Petty, yes, as individual episodes. As a group, I can see that they could be worrisome.'

'And more than worrisome.' He paused, looking out to a body of water visible through the trees. River? Inlet? I couldn't tell.

He sighed. 'This is a peaceable place. I need you to understand that, so that you will understand how its peace is being steadily undermined by these events. I believe you're planning to stay on the island for a couple of weeks?'

'Our plans are flexible,' said Alan. 'Judith and Edwin kindly booked our tickets with an open return date. It was hard, from so far away, to know how long we might need to ferret out any answers to your problem. If indeed we are able to do that at all, when you, here on the spot, haven't found satisfactory answers. Of course we don't expect to trespass on your hospitality. I'm sure there are hotels—'

'Don't even think about it,' said John firmly. 'I want you to have the freedom of living on your own, but certainly not the expense of a hotel.'

'Judith and Edwin—' I began.

'I know they've volunteered to underwrite your expenses, which is kind of them, but even they don't have unlimited funds. I've made other arrangements, subject to your approval, of course. I have a good friend, Amy Hartford, whose daughter Sue is off studying in Brazil just now. Her condo – the daughter's, I mean – is sitting unoccupied, and Amy has offered it to you for as long as you want. There's also a car, if you care to use it. Are you comfortable driving on the right?'

I smiled. 'Far more comfortable, to tell the truth, than on the left. Judith will have told you I'm American by birth, so most of my driving life was spent on the right. But really, does your friend's daughter want to trust both her home *and* her car to total strangers?'

'You won't be strangers to Amy for very long. She's coming to dinner with us tomorrow night. In any case,' he paused and cleared his throat, 'she and I hope to be married soon. So it's all in the family, so to speak.'

'In that case,' said Alan, glancing at me, 'we accept gratefully. You're right; freedom of movement will make things much easier for us.'

'Can we drive here legally, though? I mean, we only have English driving licenses.'

'That'll work. I've bought some maps for you, and the car has GPS, so you shouldn't get lost. And for the first few days I'll be driving you, so you can get a feel for the area.'

'Except I never pay attention when I'm being driven anywhere. But Alan has a pretty good bump of direction.' I was interrupted by a yawn that nearly cracked my jaw. 'Oh, I'm sorry! I'm not bored, truly.'

'You're exhausted, and no wonder. And it's getting chilly, so let's head for home and supper.'

And after that, a comfortable bed and blessed oblivion.

We woke very early, as was to be expected. Our bodies were still pretty much operating on English time. But five thirty in June in British Columbia is full daylight. Birds in John's garden were twittering madly, and I thought I could smell . . .

'Coffee? Or am I imagining things?'

'If you are, I am, too.' Alan yawned, stretched, and looked around the room. 'What did we do with our dressing gowns last night, do you remember?'

'No. I don't think I even unpacked anything except pyjamas and toothbrushes.' I sat up, spotted our suitcases sitting open on chairs in the corner, and padded over to Alan's. 'Here.' I tossed him his robe, then found mine and shrugged into it. 'Brrr! I didn't bother with slippers; socks will have to do.'

'You don't think we need to dress properly?'

'To go down for coffee at the crack of dawn? Unless I've read him all wrong, John isn't that formal. Anyway, we'll find out. If he's wearing actual clothes, tomorrow we can do the same.'

John was sitting at the kitchen table in his robe and slippers, reading the paper with a mug of coffee in front of him. 'Good morning! I hope I didn't wake you. I always get up early, but I didn't mean—'

'Jet lag,' I replied. 'And the birds. We couldn't sleep any longer. And when I smelled coffee, nothing could have kept me away.'

John grinned and got up to pour us some. 'Wonderful stuff, caffeine.'

'My drug of choice,' I said, adding cream and sugar. 'I'm forever grateful that it's legal.'

'Mmm.' John buried his face in his cup.

We imbibed our morning wake-up in silence for a few minutes, John offering a second cup when our mugs were empty. Then he stood and said, 'Breakfast. Eggs, bacon, toast? Cereal, porridge?'

'Ordinarily just toast and coffee,' said Alan, 'or cereal. We splurge occasionally with eggs and bacon, but not as a general rule.'

'Cholesterol worries, I suppose,' said John with another grin. 'Me, too. But we've rather a full day ahead of us, with a good deal of exercise – if you like, of course – so let's throw caution to the winds for once. How do you like your eggs?'

I'm afraid I made a pig of myself that morning. Not only did John make perfect scrambled eggs, soft and fluffy, but the bacon was American-style, thin, crisp, and smelling like heaven. When John offered me more, my protest was a token one.

'I haven't had that kind of bacon in years,' I said when I finally pushed my plate away. 'I'd expected the English kind, more like ham.'

'We have that, too. We call it back bacon, or Canadian bacon.'

'Oh, yes, I remember that from when I lived in Indiana. Now, can I help you clean up?'

'Nothing much to do, just bung everything into the dishwasher. But let me tell you what I've planned for today.' He moved about the kitchen with the smooth efficiency of long practice. 'The most important thing is a visit to Butchart Gardens. They're easily the most famous site on Vancouver Island; they get visitors from all over the world, and if you like plants and flowers at all, you'll love them. They are extensive, though, which is why I mentioned exercise. Do you both like to walk?'

I sighed. 'I'm not as good for distance as I used to be. But yes, we're both reasonably good walkers, considering that we're no spring chickens anymore.'

'There are lots of benches for taking breaks. And a coffee shop for a longer break.'

'And,' said Alan in his down-to-business voice, 'a place to investigate a theft.'

John stopped smiling. 'Yes. And that of course is one reason I'm taking you there. But only one. Yes, it's important that you see where the aconites were stolen. But it's also important that you absorb the atmosphere of the gardens, because in a way it's a pattern for the whole of the Victoria area. It's the ambience that is so precious to us, and that we stand to lose if the trouble doesn't stop. We must stop it!'

We went soberly to dress for the day.

THREE

'They don't open till eight forty-five.' John was back to his cheerful self. 'And it won't take us much more than half an hour to get there. So I propose to drive you around, to get a feel of Victoria and the surrounding area – and point out some traffic regulations that will probably be unfamiliar. Here's a map to help you get oriented. Ready to go?

'The first thing you need to know,' he said as he drove us down a busy street, 'is that greater Victoria, that is, the city and surrounding area, is divided into several municipalities. You'll see them on your map. We're in Esquimalt now, headed into Victoria proper.' He pronounced the unfamiliar word 'Es-kwai-malt'.

I looked at the map. 'Looks a lot like the French word for Eskimo, Esquimau, only that's pronounced the same as in English.'

'It is a First Nations word, a transliteration of course. The Esquimalt peoples lived here long before the white settlers came. British Columbia has a high population of indigenous people, and we latecomers are becoming more and more aware of their importance, and their rights. Look.'

John slowed the car and pointed to the right, and Alan and I craned our necks at an impressive totem pole in a little park.

'That one's a copy, though the original was where this one is now. They're carved from cedar trees to resist weathering, but they do eventually rot. You'll see a good many of them as you travel around the area, and the Royal BC Museum has a great First Peoples exhibit that tells the history. It's not always pretty. White settlers did all they could to wipe out indigenous culture in the early days. It's only within the past sixty or seventy years that attitudes have changed. Now we're crossing the famous Blue Bridge into the city.'

'I see,' said Alan in his driest tone.

'You see that it isn't blue.' John chuckled. 'I forget why they decided not to paint it blue when they rebuilt it, not long ago. But they shine blue lights on it at night to preserve the tradition.

On your left is the Upper Harbour, on your right the Inner Harbour. There's quite a bit of boat travel between, so the bridge opens. It's quite a sight, as the entire roadway tilts up, in one piece. Now we're officially in Victoria. We've turned the wrong direction to get to Butchart, but you had to see the city, and early morning is a good time, before it gets too crowded.'

We drove along the harbour. John pointed out the Visitor Centre, the ferry terminal and then, when we were about to turn inland, the British Columbia Legislature.

'Victoria is the capital of BC,' John said. 'Most people, Canadians as well as Americans, don't realize that. Vancouver is very much bigger, but Victoria was settled first, and has remained the capital. There's the Royal BC Museum and the Empress Hotel, which you'd enjoy if money were no object. I won't say you have to be Bill Gates to stay there, but it wouldn't hurt to have a healthy bank balance.'

I shrugged. 'One hotel room is very much like another. And all you do is sleep there. If money were no object, I can think of things I'd rather spend it on.'

'You'd like their afternoon tea, though.'

Alan laughed. 'You've hit upon my wife's weakness. She'd do almost anything for a truly magnificent afternoon tea.'

'I admit it. But having had tea at the Ritz, can life hold any more?'

John glanced at his watch. 'Tomorrow, if you're up to it, we'll take a guided walking tour of the city. There are several every day, leaving from the Visitor Centre, and the guides are knowledgeable and interesting. I want you to see Chinatown, what's left of it, and Beacon Hill Park, and any number of other high points. For now, though, we'd best head for the gardens.'

There is no point in trying to describe the Butchart Gardens. If you surf the net, there is an excellent website which, for once, doesn't exaggerate. Actually the real thing is far more incredible than anything you can imagine just from seeing pictures. Perhaps the most amazing fact is that this magnificent beauty spot arose from a played-out limestone quarry, through the vision of one woman, over a hundred years ago. We were told that, at one point near the beginning of the project, Jennie Butchart herself swung from a bosun's chair, planting ferns in the crevices of the sheer rock wall.

We walked for miles, sitting frequently to rest, to take in yet another gorgeous view, to talk. We oohed and aahed over the heritage roses, the exuberant summer annuals, the serene Japanese garden, the amazing fountain that changed from one pattern to another in seemingly unending variation.

It wasn't until we were settled in the café for coffee and a scone that I reluctantly brought up the unpleasant subject. 'John, I hate to talk about it, but when were the aconites stolen from the garden? And where were they? I didn't see any, though of course among thousands of plants, I might have missed them. Or haven't they been replanted?'

'They have, shortly after their loss was discovered last October. You wouldn't have noticed them today, as they're not in bloom yet. They grow in several spots; the ones that were stolen were close to one of the gazebos. Our theory, insofar as we have one, is that the thief came in close to closing time, which in October is four o'clock, and then hid until he, or she of course, could get out without being seen.'

'But . . . isn't security pretty good? Even on a day like today, when there aren't a lot of visitors, there were employees all over the place.'

'Yes, of course security is good. But we're not talking about a military installation or a defence plant. One person wearing dark clothing and carrying a small parcel could defeat them. Obviously did, in fact.'

'And Dorothy, my dear, the "how" in this case interests me much less than the "why".' Alan finished his coffee. 'I can imagine no reason why someone would go to all that trouble to steal plants that could be bought at any nursery garden.'

'Precisely.' John grimaced as he put down his cup. 'Now, then, would you like to go on, or have you had it for this morning?'

We took a different way back to John's house, passing on the way the site of one of the 'tent cities' housing the homeless. 'No tents left. The city keeps coming up with plans for better housing, but it's a very complicated problem. Many of the residents had addiction or mental health issues, and/or were transients, and not easy to house.'

'So,' said Alan as we speeded up and left the compound behind, 'there might have been some motive for the damage to the tents.'

'Yes. The people who find the homeless contemptible and dangerous could well have done it. But the park where it happened was, and is, very well patrolled at night, which is when it happened, and nobody saw anyone or anything.'

'Which might imply that one of the residents was to blame,' said Alan, frowning.

John sighed. 'Of course that was the obvious answer. Except, again – why? Why would they do something to hurt their own?'

'Tempers could run high in a place like that,' I said. 'No, I don't mean to imply that the people are – what did you say? – contemptible and dangerous, but they're living in a miserable situation and being kicked from pillar to post. I can't imagine they're feeling any too kindly toward the world, and those feelings could extend to a fellow-camper who happened to annoy them. As neighbours often do.'

'You're quite right. And the neighbours were questioned. Very, very tactfully, to avoid rousing even more anger and unrest. Everyone in the community, and I mean *everyone*, insisted that it couldn't have been one of them. I believed them. They were incensed over the vandalism, and bitter about the failure to catch the culprit. They would have ratted on the one who did it if they'd known.'

We were silent for the rest of the journey home.

The day had warmed enough that a light salad lunch was just the thing. Any more and I might have succumbed to the afternoon nap that was beckoning seductively. Alan was looking a little less than bright-eyed and bushy-tailed too, but he was polite when John outlined the program for the afternoon.

'This will be a driving tour, because I expect you've had enough walking for the day. There won't be any sinister sites this time. I want you to get a general impression of Victoria's neighbourhoods, from the elegant to the slightly tacky.'

'I doubt I'll remember how to get from place to place,' Alan protested. 'Even with the map, when I could wrest it away from my dear wife this morning, I've become hopelessly confused.'

'Not surprising. The trouble is that this is an island. No matter which direction you look, there's water, and it's disorienting. Add in a number of bridges, and streets that run on the diagonal, and some that change names from time to time, and I don't wonder you're confused.'

'Actually, it sounds just like home,' I said, looking mockingly at Alan. 'You couldn't understand why it took me so long to learn my way around Sherebury, which' – I added for John's benefit – 'is a medieval town with streets that run in every possible direction and change names and end abruptly and street signs that are posted on the corners of buildings, if at all. Throw in a meandering river and lots of hills and a great hulking university built by someone who knew nothing about urban planning. I think I'd better do the navigating when we go out on our own, John. Victoria is much like where I grew up in Indiana, and child's play compared with almost any English town.'

'You're showing off, dear,' said my loving spouse, 'displaying your superior knowledge of North American traffic patterns. Be careful, or I might take you up on your offer. And I haven't forgotten our visit to Indiana some years ago, when you headed down the wrong side of the road a time or two.'

We were not alone. I refrained from sticking my tongue out at him, and we climbed amicably into John's car for our tour.

The only impression I retained at the end of the day was that, indeed, Victoria was a lot like the place where I spent the first sixty or so years of my life. There was a university that reminded me quite a lot of Randolph, back in my hometown. There were several community colleges. The houses were similar, though somewhat more crowded together. John explained that Victoria was growing by leaps and bounds, and we could see large blocks of new condos all over the place. The area was laid out in blocks, for the most part, just like home, though there were a few meandering streets harking back to centuries-old paths.

'The traffic will be much heavier in a couple of weeks,' John told us. 'Canada Day is on July 1. It's a bit like your Fourth of July.'

'It's when Canada was founded, then?'

'Sort of. The three provinces that comprised what is now Canada were united on July 1, 1867, into one Dominion. Of course actual unification took a much longer time, given the various groups with varied agendas.'

'And then there's Québec,' I said, giving it the French pronunciation.

'Indeed. If I remember my history of the States, the Declaration of Independence didn't quite establish your country as a harmonious whole either, did it?'

'No, it was the Constitution that did that. More or less. And then there was the Civil War – oh, for Pete's sake, let's get off history. What happens on Canada Day? Picnics and parades and fireworks, like at home?'

'And concerts. But the famous concert, called Symphony Splash, happens later, on the first Sunday in August. A stage is set up down by the harbour, the Victoria symphony performs, and thousands of people come. It all ends with the "1812 Overture" and fireworks. The point is to celebrate British Columbia Day the next day. And here in Victoria, a number of groups including representatives of the First Nations and the Chinese community are involved. Not just on the actual day, but for months leading up to it.

'And speaking of the Chinese community, here we are at the entrance to the official Chinatown. Very few of the Chinese actually live here now, but some of the shops and restaurants remain as tourist attractions. And there's an intriguing little passageway that we'll explore on foot one day. It's nothing like wide enough for vehicles, barely wide enough for two people to walk side-by-side.'

We wandered. I gave up trying to figure out where we were and just enjoyed looking. Some of the scenery was truly spectacular. There were little parks dotted here and there, most of them with views of one harbour or another. One of them was alive with birds of all sorts, ducks and geese and songbirds.

'Look, Alan!' I pointed excitedly. 'There's a robin! The American kind, not like your little English ones. I didn't know they lived in Canada, too.'

'Very common here,' said John. 'We have quite a varied population of birds, from hummingbirds to eagles.'

'Oh, I love eagles! They're so majestic. And yes, I know they're birds of prey, and fierce, and all that, but they're beautiful.'

My attention was caught by a water bird I didn't know, and I asked John about it.

'Oh, you're lucky!' he said, laughing. 'That's the official bird of Canada – the Loon – though they're very seldom found in the city. Our dollar coins are even called "loonies", for the picture on the back.' He pulled a couple out of his pocket, which reminded me that we needed to stop at an ATM and get some Canadian money.

We moved on to another area, and some of the cityscape, by contrast, was, as John had said, a bit seedy. I was startled to see a couple of shops openly advertising marijuana.

John saw my reaction. 'Yes, pot was legalized for recreational use across Canada not too long ago. It was simply an acknowledgment of what had long been a fact. The pot shops have been here, pretending to dispense the stuff purely for medicinal use. Now the pretence has stopped. Whether it's a good idea or not . . .' He shrugged. 'Time will tell, I suppose. Meanwhile it's made crossing the border a bit trickier, since pot is legal in some states, legal only for medical use in others, and still officially illegal by federal law everywhere in the US.'

Alan nodded. 'And in the UK. The law is widely ignored, of course, which in my view makes it a bad law. Times are changing, and we may soon see cannabis legalized, or at least decriminalized. There's a good deal of opposition to the idea, though.'

'I think part of the rationale here was to concentrate on far more dangerous drugs, like fentanyl, which is now the worst drug problem in Canada. Such a small amount will kill, and it's cheap and therefore readily available.'

'I suppose it's smuggled in by boat,' I said looking out at a body of water (I wasn't sure which) that was alive with sailboats and kayaks and small launches.

'Actually, most of it comes by mail from China; you can buy it on the Internet, advertised as shipped in "detection-proof" packaging. Death by post.'

That was such a distressing thought that we were silent for the rest of the trip.

FOUR

'Now,' said John when we'd sat down in his living room, 'this evening my fiancée is joining us for dinner, and I'd planned to take us to one of my favourite restaurants. Would you prefer seafood or Greek?'

Alan and I consulted with a glance. 'Either,' I said. 'There's no good Greek restaurant in Sherebury, and oddly enough, seafood is scarce in most of England, even though we're so close to the sea. Except for fish and chips, of course.'

John laughed. 'Well, we run more to salmon here. You'll find it on almost every menu, so tonight let's go Greek.' He glanced at his watch. 'And you've plenty of time for a nap, if you like.'

'I didn't want to admit that I'm dragging . . . but thank you! You'll wake us in time?'

I don't know if it was jet lag, still, or just plain age, but I was asleep seconds after I stretched out, and was a bit groggy when Alan nudged me in what seemed like minutes. 'You've been out for nearly two hours, love,' he said, 'and John's fiancée just arrived. You'll want to wash your face and comb your hair.'

That brought me wide awake. 'Oh, good grief, and I need to change clothes.'

'John said not,' Alan soothed. 'The restaurant is very casual. Apparently most of Victoria is casual in the summer.'

'Yes, but I'm meeting this woman for the first time. I don't want her to think I'm a scruffy hick from the backwoods.'

There wasn't much I could do about my hair, which had decided to fly in every direction, but I did a quick face-wash and put on an attractive top, and when I saw John's beloved I was very glad I'd made at least that much effort.

'Dorothy, I'd like you to meet Amy Hartford. Amy, Dorothy Martin. You've met Alan.'

She was lovely, and faultlessly groomed. Her silver hair was smooth in a Dorothy Hamill sort of cut that made me immediately conscious of my cut-it-to-keep-it-out-of-my-face style, if it could be called a style. She wore no make-up except a little lipstick, but neither her skin nor her sparkling blue eyes needed enhancement. She could have been any age, but I was guessing late fifties, if only because I knew she had a grown-up daughter.

Some people, like me, wear casual clothes to protect them from the elements and preserve modesty. Some look like they just came out of an ad for 'casual chic'. This woman's slim jeans and colourful shirt weren't overly new, weren't pretentious, but they made me very aware of my shortcomings.

She held out a hand and smiled. 'May I call you Dorothy? I've heard so many wonderful things about you and your husband, I feel I know you.'

The words were pleasant, but hardly remarkable. Maybe it was the smile, or the warmth. At any rate, I stopped feeling like a poor relation and smiled back.

'Right,' said John briskly. 'Now, what will everyone have to drink? Dorothy, Judith's told me you like bourbon, and Alan, yours is Scotch, yes? Or there's wine, of course, or orange juice.'

We got that settled and sat down with our drinks, and then there was the awkward pause that ensues when people who don't know each other well, or at all, try to find something to talk about. It was Amy who found it.

'Now we have to talk about your move to my daughter's place. John says he's told you about that.'

'Yes, but it seems a terrible imposition,' I said apologetically.

'It's not, so don't worry,' Amy said firmly. 'Sue and I will both feel better about her house if someone's living there. And the car needs to be driven. So it's just a question of your preference. I know you hadn't bargained on taking on that responsibility. But John and I thought it might be easier for you if you had complete freedom to go where you like and do what you want while you're here.'

'We're most grateful,' said Alan, 'but may I ask where the condo is? In what part of town, that is. As we don't know the area at all, I want to make sure we won't get lost.' He grinned at me. 'My wife seems to think I'll be hopeless at driving in North America.'

They both laughed at that. 'It's easy to get lost,' said Amy. 'I've done it myself a time or two. But her place is easy to find. In fact' – she stood and went to the window – 'you can see it

from here. Not Sue's particular unit, but the complex.' She
pointed. 'Easy access, and there's plenty of parking.'

'We'll stop by after dinner,' said John. 'Speaking of which
– is anybody hungry?'

Over dinner we talked about jobs. Almost every conversation
among new acquaintances hits the subject early on. 'What do
you do for a living?' may be a rather crude question, but it's a
good start on learning about a person.

Three of us, of course, were retired. Amy, a bit younger than
John, was still working at her job with the public library. 'Only
part-time now, though. I've tried to retire altogether, but they
won't let me. They've been advertising for a replacement for
ages, but they say they can't find the right person.'

'Are they looking for someone with an advanced degree in
library science?' Alan asked. 'I'd think, with several universities
nearby, that wouldn't be too hard a match.' He forked a chunk
of lamb, so tender it nearly fell apart.

'Oh, they can find a DLS any time they want one, but it's a
little harder to get a good IT person. That's what I do, manage
information technology for the Victoria library system.'

I was impressed. I can use a computer. I look up stuff and
write emails and – true confession time – waste a great deal
of time playing FreeCell. But when something goes wrong, I
head straight to my friend Nigel, who is (a) young, and (b)
the IT coordinator at Sherebury University. He usually shows
me how I could have straightened things out on my own, and
I listen politely, not understanding a word. I am in awe of
people who can make these magical machines turn handsprings.
'Gosh,' I said, sounding like a kid. I felt like one. 'I think
people who can do what you do are amazing. My brain doesn't
work that way.' I chased the last bit of moussaka around my
plate.

'Oh, it's just a matter of training. And experience.'

'But I'm surprised – oh, yes, I'll have some baklava, please, and
decaf – but I'm surprised, Amy, that they can't find someone to
replace you, or at least to fill the position.' Alan cocked an eyebrow.
'Again, the universities must be turning them out by the cartload.'

'The same for me, please. Yes, Alan, they are. The trouble is,
Victoria has become a centre of the technology industry. There

are any number of firms here clamouring for hot new geeks, and of course they can pay far more than a public library. So all the best people go straight to them, and I'm left to struggle along until someone turns up.' She finished her retsina and allowed the waiter to take her plate and glass. 'I have tried – well, as it happens, I have a–an acquaintance in one of the big firms. I thought he might be able to toss a crumb or two our way, but . . .' She shrugged.

John was frowning. Well, not quite that, but he didn't look quite happy, and it took him a moment to notice the waiter at his elbow. 'Ah, yes, why don't you bring us a plate of the pastries? We can choose what we like and take the rest home for a wildly incorrect breakfast. And a pot of decaf, as well.' He rearranged his face into its usual jovial expression, and I wondered if I'd imagined his earlier annoyance, or whatever it was. 'Now, we need to decide what we're going to do tomorrow.'

The conversation was steered firmly away from Amy's work.

We drove past Amy's daughter's condo, which was indeed easy to find, on a main street with an adequate car park. The car we were to be lent, Alan and I were both relieved to discover, was a mid-size sedan, a couple of years old, in a staid dark blue – nothing that looked hard to park, or threatened excessive power. We decided to make the move in a day or two, when John had showed us a few more of Victoria's attractions. When we got back to John's house, Amy gave us the keys to house and car, noted down our phone numbers just in case, and wished us well.

'And what was all that about?' I demanded of Alan when we'd gone up to our room.

He didn't need to ask what I meant. Years of police work have made him an observant man. 'The little awkwardness about the search for Amy's replacement? John didn't like the mention of her IT friend, did he? I wonder why.'

'I think he doesn't like the friend, for some reason. Only Amy called him an "acquaintance", which might mean almost anything.'

Alan yawned. 'We're probably making something of nothing. 'Night, love.'

*   *   *

Once again we woke very early. We were gradually adjusting to the time difference, but we weren't there yet. John had coffee ready, and we ate some of the delectable Greek pastries. 'Why is it that guilty pleasures are so sweet?' I mused, licking honey off my lips, and then ducked at the groans. 'I didn't mean it, I swear. Didn't even hear it coming.'

'Where are you taking us today, John?' asked my husband, polishing off a couple of kourabiethes, the Greek version of Mexican wedding cakes, buttery clouds of powdered sugar that dusted his shirt liberally.

'If you're ready for rather a long jaunt, I thought we might go up north. There's a raptor sanctuary about sixty miles away, and since you said you're fond of eagles, you might enjoy it. They have all sorts – eagles, hawks, falcons – and it's rather fun to watch them fly. You can even hold them, if you like.'

'Um . . . but aren't the talons . . .?'

'They have gauntlets for you to use, and the birds are very well trained. They won't damage you, I promise.'

Well, the idea of holding one of those fierce, proud birds appealed to me, and Alan was agreeable.

'There's actually a reason why I want you to see the birds,' John said as he loaded the dishwasher, 'another disturbance, one Judith doesn't know about, because it happened just recently. I'll tell you about it on the way. Just another apparently pointless nuisance, though it could have been much more serious.'

He chose to take us the long way round, through dense forest land, on narrow winding roads that originally served as logging roads. 'This is mostly second-growth,' he said, 'though there's still some virgin forest left. Logging has been a big industry here for generations, but they've been smart about it. No clear-cutting, and always re-planting.'

'Are they pines?' I asked. I'm fairly ignorant about evergreens, coming from a part of Indiana where there are very few conifers of any kind.

'No, Douglas firs, most of them. They're a dominant species in this part of the country. Which is of course appropriate, in a way.'

Alan frowned. 'Why "of course"?'

'Oh, do you not know about James Douglas?'

We both shook our heads.

'Goodness, he's the founder of Victoria! He was with the Hudson's Bay Company, built Fort Victoria, governed Vancouver Island and later the colony of British Columbia – oh, he's the principal figure in our history. The oldest part of Victoria is called James Bay after him; he had a mansion there. Now the tree was not named after him, but after one David Douglas, a Scottish botanist. But so many place names hark back to old James Douglas, and the trees do proliferate here, so it's a nice coincidence, don't you think?'

We passed some trucks carrying logs – passed very carefully, given the nature of the road – and saw some hillsides that had been stripped bare of trees, but only in small areas.

'Is fire a big problem?' I asked.

'Sadly, yes, and getting worse. Last year was the worst on record. And it wasn't just the fires themselves, but the smoke. Victoria was virtually shut down for days, the air was so bad. All the warnings! What they amounted to was don't be young, or old, or ill, and even if you're none of those things, try not to breathe.' He laughed, but ruefully. 'It wasn't really funny. You honestly couldn't go outside for any length of time. Amy's – that is, someone we know rode his bicycle to work, as he always does. He almost didn't make it.'

There was an odd note in his voice, sounding almost like satisfaction. What had he started to say? Amy's 'acquaintance'?

'Who?' I began, but John was saying, 'We're coming out of the forest now. There's a pleasant little café in this town where we can have a bite of lunch, and then the raptors are very near.'

Well, okay, if he didn't want to talk about that man, he didn't. I looked at Alan and raised my eyebrows, but we didn't pursue it.

FIVE

I t was a nice lunch. Then we pushed on for a few more minutes and arrived at the raptor sanctuary, or The Raptors. I don't know what I expected, but certainly not such a big facility, or such a variety of birds.

The first cage I saw contained a kookaburra, according to the sign. It was not laughing, to my great disappointment, but I couldn't get the silly children's song out of my head for the rest of the day. I learned later that it isn't a raptor, though a predator, and of course is native to Australia, not British Columbia. The Raptors took it in when a facility in Ontario found itself with too many of them, and the sanctuary offered it a home.

We were just in time to watch the flying demonstration. Passing any number of large room-sized cages, we went to an area where bleachers were set up to face a sort of meadow, with trees and bushes and long grass nearby, and a couple of T-shaped contrivances, about six feet tall, made of small tree branches. They looked a little like rustic telephone poles, with no wires.

We sat, along with a small crowd, and prepared to watch.

It was amazing. Various handlers came out with birds perched on their gauntlets (very heavy leather, given the birds' talons). The first one was a stunning bald eagle, and my heart soared with the bird as it launched into majestic flight, mounting high and then hovering over the field and homing in on the food that had been hidden in a bush. It – no, 'he', name of Manwe – came to rest on one of the wooden things, which I now recognized as perches, and I swear he revelled in the applause that greeted his performance, standing proudly, head held high. He was none too eager to return to his cage; a keeper had to signal several times before Manwe condescended to fly to his glove and be carried away.

Okay, I know it's stupid to ascribe human emotions to animals. But I couldn't help it. He *did* look proud, and he had the right. He was a splendid animal.

He was succeeded by any number of other birds, familiar and not. Owls, hawks of various descriptions, a vulture. I'd never thought of them as raptors, but of course they are, and a very necessary part of the ecosystem, nature's garbage collectors.

My favourite, after the eagle, was the smallest bird they showed us, an American kestrel. About the size of a blue jay, it had some of the same colouring, a grey breast that looked blue in the bright sunlight, with dappled brown wings. It was just so cute, especially after the big, fierce birds we'd been seeing. The handler explained that it was often used in falconry, because despite its small size it was an efficient hunter.

'Well!' I said when the demonstration was done. 'That was great! I've never been so close to any birds before. Wild birds, I mean. Though I guess these aren't really wild, are they?'

One of the handlers answered me. 'Not in one sense. They were brought here, some of them, because they were ill or injured, and if in the healing process they became too accustomed to human attention, they could never be released into the wild again. Some of them were hatched here – we do have mated pairs, and nature will take its course. None were captured in the wild and brought here; the organization doesn't believe in that. Their purpose is to preserve species, and to educate the public about them. Many are working birds.'

'Umm . . .?'

'That's one reason for the flying demonstrations,' said John, sounding a bit professorial. 'The staff fly the birds year-round, not just for the public to see. It keeps their skills sharp, keeps them raptors, not just caged pets. And then they're taken out to earn their keep, so to speak. You know how great a danger flocks of birds can be to airplanes, right?'

'They get sucked into the engines, don't they?' Alan commented.

'Yes, and damage the planes in other ways, as well. Gulls, especially, can be a huge problem, dangerous and expensive to deal with. Enter the raptors. They are birds of prey, and their prey is often other birds. Yes, Dorothy, you may wince, but it's the way of nature. Many of the birds here are trained as hunters, and are then taken to airports and landfills, places where gulls have become a major nuisance. They are turned loose to hunt, and hunt they do. The gulls provide dinner for them, and the ones that manage to avoid becoming prey are sometimes smart enough to go elsewhere, at least for a while. The sites pay the centre, the gull problem is dealt with, and the raptors are happy. Isn't that better than shooting the gulls, or poisoning them?'

'I suppose. No, you're right, it is. It's just – I hate to think of these beautiful birds being killers.'

'We're killers too, Dorothy,' said Alan gently. 'At least those of us who eat meat are, but we have the killing done by slaughter-houses, so we never have to see the blood.'

I shuddered. 'I know, I know. I just prefer not to think about it.'

'Think of it this way,' said John. 'We humans can make the choice not to eat meat, if we become disturbed by the idea of killing other animals. The raptors don't have that choice. They are what scientists call "obligate carnivores". Their bodies need meat, and are constructed so as to make them able to get it.' He hesitated a moment. 'I don't know what your religious beliefs may be, and mine are a bit ill-defined, but I do think that God probably knew what he was doing when he created these beautiful birds the way they are.'

Well, that shut me up, because it was unanswerable.

The next treat was getting to know some of the birds up close and personal. One of the handlers brought several birds out for us to see and touch. One little sweetheart was called a spectacled owl, so named because white rings around its eyes make it look very much as if it was wearing glasses. Though a fair-sized bird, it weighed very little, resting on my gloved hand. 'Owls have very fluffy feathers,' the handler explained. 'It's an important part of their hunting armoury, because it means their flight is virtually silent. And of course they hunt mostly at night, so their prey can neither see nor hear them.'

Again I shuddered a bit at the idea, and then told myself I was being an idiot. Everything has to eat. And owls, I thought, ate mostly rodents, and I've never too fond of mice and voles and so on. Which, of course, has nothing to do with the ethical question. Would it be any worse if some owl swooped down some night and gobbled up a kitten? As of course has been known to happen.

And then they handed me that adorable little kestrel, and I dismissed the subject. It was such a pretty little creature, sitting quite calmly on my gauntlet. Its jesses (I think that's the word

– those slender leather straps on its legs) were tied around a ring on the glove, but that didn't seem necessary. The little guy made no attempt to fly away, just sitting there, cocking its head from time to time.

But when the handler loosed the jesses and took the kestrel back, it pecked sharply at her gauntlet with that small but efficient beak. We must have looked askance, because she laughed. 'It's a sign of affection, actually. Kessie likes me the best, and has really chewed up my glove.'

'I'm glad Sam doesn't have a beak,' Alan murmured to me.

Samantha is very fond of Alan, and likes to give him little love-bites from time to time. They don't do any damage, but if she had a mouth like Kessie's it would be a different story.

Our last adventure was a 'Hawk Walk'. One of the handlers (I never did learn their names) took a hawk from its cage and led a small group of us up a wooded path to the top of a gentle hill. Then anyone who wanted was given a glove and instructions about how to stand – straight arm, held out well away from the face. I was perhaps not the only one to find that piece of advice a trifle alarming, but I did as I was told. The hawk, released, flew lazily up to the top of a tall tree and perched there, watching. When I was ready, the handler reached out and put a small piece of meat in the crook of my thumb.

The time could have been measured in seconds, perhaps milliseconds. Before I even knew it was happening, the hawk swooped down, grabbed the food without even lighting on my glove, and took off with it, back to his observation tree.

'Wow!' I wasn't the only one who said it.

Several other people had a go; the show never palled. Our awe at this marvellous bird changed to amusement, though, when he refused to return to the handler's glove, but stayed up in the tree making harsh noises that sounded extremely irritated. 'He wants more snacks,' said the handler with a chuckle. 'He gets plenty of food, but when there are more visitors on the walk, he gets more handouts, so he's annoyed with us at the moment.' She finally persuaded him back to her glove, but he muttered all the way back to his cage.

That brought the official entertainment to an end, and as Alan and I were both tired, and the day had grown warm, we were glad to go back to the car and drink the water that John had thoughtfully brought along in thermoses.

'That,' I said when I had slaked my thirst, 'was amazing. All of it. I've loved bald eagles ever since I started watching live-streaming from a nest in America, and now that I've learned more about other raptors, I'm even more intrigued. I've even adjusted to the idea that they're predators. Well, sort of.'

'You said this morning that you had a reason for bringing us here, didn't you, John?' said Alan.

'Yes, and we're about to see it. It's on the way back home; we'll take the quick way this time. Boring, but much better roads. Does anyone want to stop at the washroom before we hit the highway?'

Well, of course I did. One of the joys of age. And then we turned onto a main highway, went through the little town of Duncan and, after about half an hour of nothing much, turned off onto a gravel road. Not only gravel, but bumpy.

'Looks like we're getting close to what my family used to call the jumping off place,' I said, trying to talk with my mouth almost shut so as not to bite my tongue as the car bounced along.

'You're not far wrong. There's nothing at the end of this road, really, except a small . . . well, farm isn't quite the right word, but it's close. And here we are.'

He pulled the car off to the side of the road, almost in some bushes. 'I'm sorry, Alan, but you'll have to scoot across and get out on Dorothy's side. The road is almost never used, but I had to get as far off it as I could. It would be just my luck to have old Silas come roaring out of his drive, and since he drives like a four-year-old in a bumper car . . .'

'I take your point,' said Alan, working his tall frame across the back seat to my side of the car.

John stopped and held out a hand. 'Now, before we get any closer, I should tell you a few things. First, the man's name is Silas Varner, and although he resembles the famous fictional miser in many ways, he does not take kindly to jokes about his name. He is in fact a curmudgeonly old cuss who hates people on general principles, and even more so of late. So watch what you say and follow my lead. He tolerates me. Most of the time.'

Well, this visit didn't sound to me like the end to a perfect day. Alan looked at me and shrugged. If this was somehow important to John's mission, we'd go along. But reluctantly, at least on my part.

We reached the end of the straggly shrubbery and found ourselves at the foot of a rutted dirt drive leading to—

I stopped and stared. 'Good grief, that looks like a cross between a storage unit and a jail. What is it?'

We were looking at a small building of peculiar design. Built of plywood painted white, it was a little over twice as wide as it was deep, with a small door, padlocked, on the short side. Its roof had a slight pitch, higher in front, lower at the back. There were no windows, only four tightly barred openings on the long side. It rested on a foundation of pavers, and we could just see some kind of chicken-wire enclosure at the back. Odd noises came from it, a sort of cross between a chicken coop and The Raptors.

'That's Silas's mews, his houses for his hawks. Two houses, joined together. He's a falconer.'

'They must be huge birds, if they need birdhouses that size.'

'Not huge. About the size of the hawk that took the food off your glove earlier. But they need room to fly, at least a little. Of course Silas takes them out every day, or nearly. And that's part of . . . ah! Mr Varner, sir.'

The man had appeared with the silence of an owl. There the resemblance ended. He was dressed in patched and filthy overalls and a shirt whose original colour was impossible to discern. His face wore a grey four-day stubble and a fierce scowl. He ignored me and Alan completely and growled at John, 'You here to give me more grief, then?'

'Not at all. Just came by to see how you were getting along.'

'Rotten. No surprise, eh?'

That was the first time I had heard a Canadian use the stereo-typical expression, I reflected. I said nothing, however. I had a feeling Mr Varner was not in the mood for light repartee.

John ignored the comment. He nodded at us. 'I hoped you'd let my friends see your birds. We just got back from a visit to The Raptors, and they've fallen in love with—'

The man spat, narrowly missing my shoe. I thought he looked a little disappointed about his aim.

'In love! Fools! Them birds ain't no house pets, to stick in a cage and croon to. They're predators, got that? They got talons and beaks that're meant to kill, and that's what they do. A hawk ain't never gonna love its owner, y'hear? And a falconer don't go all sentimental over his birds, neither. In love, pah!'

He spat again, and this time his aim was better. I was extremely glad I was wearing tennies rather than sandals.

He moved close to me and shook a dirty, arthritic finger in my face. I took an involuntary step backward. 'And don't you believe a frickin' thing them idiots tell you about hawks! Keepin' 'em in cages, showin' 'em off like they was circus elephants! They oughta be jailed, the lot of 'em, for what they do to them poor birds!'

His breath was no cleaner than the rest of him. I couldn't back away any farther; my back was up against a very prickly bush of some sort.

'And you!' He rounded on John. 'You catch 'em yet?'

John shook his head. 'The police haven't stopped working on it, Mr Varner, but there isn't much to go on.'

'They don't frickin' well care! They think I let 'em loose myself. Look at my mews. Look at the way I take care of my birds. Would I do that to Harry 'n' Ron?'

'I believe you, Silas,' said John quietly. Somehow his use of the man's first name seemed to convince him.

'So you come to see my birds. C'mon, then.' He stomped off toward the door into the mews, and Alan and I followed. I took Alan's arm, not too sure about this little adventure.

SIX

'You stay back, then,' said Silas in the tones of a top sergeant. We obeyed. I admit that I clutched Alan's arm a little more firmly.

Silas opened the door, closed it again, did something we couldn't see, and there, flying out into the fenced enclosure, were two large and magnificent hawks. They landed on sturdy perches and preened their feathers in the sunlight. They were very similar, both about two feet tall, both with brown and tan plumage.

'That un's Harry,' he said, pointing. 'And that's Ron. They're brothers.' He looked at me as if daring me to make some remark.

I said only, 'They're beautiful.'

'They're red-tails, eh? O' course they're beautiful. I feed 'em right, take care of 'em like they was babies. They fly every day when the weather's right. They got no reason to go lookin' for nothin' they ain't got!'

Since I had no idea what he was talking about, I made no response; neither did Alan. John simply nodded.

'Right. You seen what you came to see. I got to get me and my boys ready to fly.'

He retrieved the birds, one at a time, on his glove, disappeared inside with them, and then left the mews and stumped off.

I watched him walk up to a structure that I assumed was a shed, and a dilapidated one at that. Paint flaking off, door hanging awry, a window patched together with what looked like masking tape.

'That's where he lives,' said John quietly as we turned to go back to the car.

I looked back at the neat, freshly painted mews, appalled at the contrast.

'He spends every cent of his pension on his hawks. The neighbours don't appreciate his neglect of his home – one can hardly call it a house – but he doesn't care. He can't be bothered with the house or the grounds. His birds take up all his time.'

I looked around, but could see no houses. 'Neighbours?'

'There's a tiny village beyond that stand of trees.' John pointed. 'Something right out of a picture book. Pretty little houses, well-kept gardens, and one small farm, right on the edge of the village.'

Alan picked up something in his voice that I missed. 'And that's where the trouble happened?'

John looked sharply at him. 'You must have been one super cop in your day. Yes, there was trouble. Serious trouble. Silas's hawks got out. The farmer lost a lot of his chickens.'

'Oh, no!' I realized I was almost shouting. I modified my tone. 'They were killed?'

'Some killed, others hurt so badly they had to be destroyed. What made it even worse was that the chickens were more-or-less pets. Bantams, some of them, that the farmer's kids had raised from eggs.' He hesitated. 'And there was a kitten . . .'

This time I couldn't speak.

'And you don't think Silas had anything to do with it,' said Alan.

'I do not. For a start, Silas has taught me a bit about raptors. The red-tails will almost never go after chickens, for all they're nicknamed chickenhawks. They prefer small rodents. The kitten, now . . . well, that's a possibility. Sorry, Dorothy.

'However, the villagers are not of my opinion. Most of them are transplanted city folks who don't know one bird from another. They think he let them out on purpose, to pay them back for their harassment. And there has been harassment, certainly. Nasty anonymous letters. Threats to sue, claiming his "disgusting property" lowers their property values.'

'Well, the place is fairly sordid, I have to admit.' I made a face. 'Not just the hovel he calls home, but the surroundings. It wouldn't hurt him to get rid of some of those weeds and trim the trees. It's not as if he has a job, and taking care of two birds can't be a full-time occupation.'

'No. But the place isn't as badly kept as you think. He has a very productive vegetable garden behind some shrubbery. Well laid-out, kept clean as a whistle. He just doesn't want anyone to know about it. Maybe he's afraid of thieves, but I think the main reason is to keep his neighbours angry. That keeps them afraid of him, and he revels in that.'

'I can understand why they're afraid!' I said warmly. 'He certainly doesn't have a warm and fuzzy personality. And yet – someone who would name his hawks Harry and Ron – there've got to be some redeeming qualities in a man who's read Harry Potter, unless that's not the reference.'

'It is. He would never admit it, but he has the whole series stuck away in that hovel of his. You wouldn't think to hear him talk that he was even literate, but that one time I went in with him, I saw what I'm almost certain was a diploma, stuffed under a chair cushion. There's a story there somewhere, but if anyone's ever heard it, I haven't.'

'What do you think happened?' asked Alan. 'With the escaped hawks, I mean. There was a padlock on that door.'

'He put that on after it happened. He said the birds came back the next morning. They are, after all, trained to return to him. He was extremely upset, of course, but he says he didn't know what had happened until the police came. Meanwhile, unfortunately, he had calmed the hawks and attached the padlock.'

I groaned. 'So when he claimed someone had set the birds free, the cops pointed to the lock and were sceptical.'

'No, that isn't quite what happened. Silas is a canny fellow. When the police came, wanting to see the birds, saying they'd caused a lot of trouble, Silas pointed to them, now quietly on their roosts. He showed the padlock and said they couldn't possibly have got out, that there were a lot of wild hawks around, and why blame his birds? He got quite combative about it, and of course there was no proof either way. The police had to back down.'

We got in the car, and John drove very carefully out of the shrubbery, turned around, and drove with great care back to the main road.

When we could stop clinging to our seats and conversation was possible, I asked, 'How did you get into it? You're retired.'

'Yes, but the local authorities know me, of course. They seemed to think I could get him to talk to me, I don't know why.'

Alan and I looked at each other. 'I think I know why,' Alan said. 'They knew you'd treat him fairly and with compassion. And he could work that out, too. That said, he still doesn't seem exactly cordial with you.'

'He talks to me. He let me bring you to see him. He even showed you the birds. Trust me, for Silas, that's cordial.'

'So you went to see him,' I persisted, 'and what happened?'

'I had no idea how to approach him. I'd heard all the stories, the slammed doors, the insults, the drawn knife.'

'I'd have thought a good ole over-n-under would be more his style.'

John guffawed. 'And you'd be right, Dorothy, but as it happens he doesn't own a gun. Had one, but when they told him he had to have a licence, he refused to fork over for a licence – with a good deal of well-chosen invective about interfering bureaucracy, I'm told. He did once threaten to set the birds on an especially critical neighbour, but I doubt he'd ever actually do that. Afraid the birds might get hurt! Anyway, I went to see him, and of course the first thing I saw was the lovely mews. They really are models of their kind; I'd done a little research, and I knew. So when he spotted me and came out, breathing fire, I admired them. Sincerely; he'd have spotted flattery in an instant. He was very suspicious. He could tell I was a cop, or had been. There's something about us, I suppose, Alan.'

'So I'm told. Stigmata that never go away.'

'It's the look of authority,' I put in. 'You've lost some of it over the years, but when you start thinking like a cop, it shows again.'

'Well, he kept saying his birds never got out except when he flew them, which was every day, and his neighbours were all lying – er – expletives, and he left them alone and he expected them to do the same, et cetera. And that was it, for the first visit.'

'But you went back.'

'Several times. It wasn't at all easy to convince him I wasn't out to get him. He's not a trusting fellow.'

'Something's made him that way,' I pontificated. 'Something's happened to him to sour him on the world. Nobody's born belligerent.'

'We-ell, maybe. I've known a few . . . well, anyway. I finally made him understand that I was just trying to get at the truth of what happened, and he opened up and admitted that his birds had been out that night. He said he found them in the morning, back on their perches but dishevelled. The doors were open, both of them.'

'Both?' Alan frowned.

'There's an inner door into the cages themselves, a safety feature. That's how the hawks were able to get out – both doors open. There were feathers here and there, not their own.'

'So he must have known.' Alan was leaning forward, intent on the story.

'Of course he knew they'd been out. He can tell a hawk from a handsaw, or hawk feathers from chicken feathers. He swears, though, that somebody else let them out, and put some chicken feathers in their cages, to make trouble for him.'

'He's obsessed with those birds,' said Alan. 'He would lie for them.'

'He would. He has done. But I don't think he's lying about this. You get a sixth sense about that . . .' He glanced back at Alan.

'You do. I was sometimes wrong about that, but not often, not after I'd been on the force for a few years. Body language, among other things. I could spot a liar, though I didn't always know what he was lying *about*.'

John nodded, then slowed down. 'This is one traffic feature you might not know, either of you. At a busy crosswalk, there are traffic lights. They turn from green to a blinking amber, warning you to slow and watch for pedestrians, and then to red, when the walker is ready to cross.'

He drove on down the road, speeding up slightly, though not a lot, as we were now in a small town. 'Do pedestrians normally have the right of way?' asked Alan. I wanted to know, too. I might be doing most of the driving, and truth to tell, I was a bit nervous about it.

'Yes, at an intersection or a crosswalk. Not in the middle of a block. That's jaywalking. They do it, of course. And they step out into an intersection without ever looking.' He shrugged. 'Just like people anywhere. Where was I?'

'Liars,' Alan and I said together.

'Yes. With Silas, it isn't so much body language as his persistence. Every time I see him he wants to talk about the intruder, the one who set his birds loose. He would drop the subject if he were afraid of being caught out in a lie. And then there are the birds. You're right, Alan, his devotion to them amounts to an obsession. He would protect them with his life, quite literally. And letting them fly free that way, with no supervision, is extremely dangerous for them. They could have been shot. They could have caught diseased prey. They could have got tangled up with barbed wire. He would never have risked that, no matter how much he hates his neighbours.'

'So.' I thought about all that. 'So someone else hates him, and his birds, and hoped the raid would land Silas in jail and his birds . . . I suppose they'd be killed?'

'Probably. But you see, I have a different idea. I think the raid was another in the series. Not aimed specifically at Silas, but intended to spread hatred and strife throughout the community.'

'That's sick!'

'Yes. We may well be dealing with a diseased mind.'

'Which can be the hardest sort of villain to catch,' said Alan gloomily. 'Their actions make sense, and form a pattern, but it's a pattern only they can see, and a logic only they can follow.'

'Right.'

And we returned to Victoria in gloomy silence.

SEVEN

We settled down in front of the fire with a drink when we got to John's house, the late afternoon having turned chilly. 'I wonder if it's thinking about rain?' I asked – one of those meaningless comments meant to fill a silence.

'It almost never rains here in the summer,' said John. 'That's one reason I moved here. We're careful to conserve water. It's a mark of honour to have a brown lawn.'

'Oh, yes, I remember Judith saying something about that.'

Silence again.

Alan set his drink down, not quite with a thump. 'John, I think it's time we set out on our own. Unless there's something more you need to tell us about the situation?'

I didn't wait for John's quick denial. 'What I want to know, John, is why you and Amy both shy like startled horses whenever her "acquaintance" in IT is mentioned?'

He sighed. 'I should have known you'd notice. You're both way too sharp. It's nothing, really, just that he happens to be her ex-husband, and they don't have a very good relationship. It was not one of those so-called friendly divorces.'

'Battles over the kids?'

'Not principally. There's only the one daughter. He fought about that, of course, but mostly it was the other great divorce hurdle, money. He has a great deal of it, you see, and he was not over-eager to share. Would either of you like another drink, or shall we have a bite to eat?'

And we're not going to say any more about it. Period. He didn't say it, but he didn't have to. We repaired to the kitchen, had a sketchy meal, and spent the rest of the evening talking about arrangements in the morning.

'There's more,' I said to Alan as I climbed into bed.

'Yes, but we may have to find it out for ourselves. If we want to. It's a bit of a mystery, but it may prove irrelevant.'

'As, according to you, something like ninety per cent of all information you turn up in an investigation proves in the end to be.'

'Maybe not ninety. Maybe ninety-five. Good night, love.' He turned off the light, burrowed into his pillow, and went straight to sleep.

That was a skill he'd learned in his long years as a policeman. Time off for R-and-R could be in short supply in the middle of an investigation. If there was an hour that could be spared for sleep, it had to count.

I'd never been a policeman. Nor a mother, another profession that often curtails rest time. I've never had the gift of instant slumber, even when exhausted. I lay there and worried, eventually dropping into a troubled slumber fraught with disturbing dreams.

I was groggy in the morning, of course, but some good strong coffee and a glance at the morning paper restored a modicum of intelligence. I scanned it for any more peculiar little crimes, but there was nothing except a possible abduction attempt, averted by an intelligent child who refused to get into a car without the family password. Good for her.

Back to the business at hand. 'We need,' I said to John, 'a list of all the incidents, preferably in chronological order.'

He smiled. 'I thought you might.' He handed me a piece of paper. 'I printed this out this morning. I've listed all the details we have, but they're pitifully few, as you see, and there are several approximations. The thefts of the plants, for example. There was really no way to determine exactly when they were taken, only when they were discovered to be missing.'

'Mmm.' I was studying the list. Aconite and oleander missing. Death camas. I looked up. 'Death camas? What on earth does that mean?'

'Oh, Judith didn't tell you about that? Camas is a native plant here, or rather two plants. One is a pretty blue wildflower in the lily family. The other looks very similar, but it blooms a little later, and blooms white. That's about the only way you can tell them apart, though they're a different species. The roots of the blue one are edible, once used by the First Peoples as a staple food. But the roots of the white one, looking just like the roots of the blue one, are deadly poison. Hence death camas.'

I began to see where this was going. 'So someone found some and dug them up.'

'Bingo. The third theft of highly poisonous plants in the space of two or three weeks. And the most difficult. Not from the point of view of security. Butchart is much more careful about that. But few people know where the death camas grows, and fewer still could find it, except when it's blooming.'

'And it wasn't, when it was stolen?'

'No. So someone knew exactly where it was and knew its properties.'

'Three different kinds of highly toxic plants stolen, and then not used. Apparently.' I tried to make some sense of that, failed, and went back to the list. Letter bombs. Various acts of vandalism. Damage to tents occupied by the homeless. And then the release of Silas's hawks. 'They've been escalating, haven't they? From petty theft right up to murder. Oh, all right, murder only of chickens and a kitten, but still deaths. Will the next be an attack on a human?'

'You're assuming,' said Alan in his policeman mode, 'that all the incidents are the work of one person, or a group acting as one person. That's not necessarily the case, you know.'

'I know, but we have to start somewhere.' I was getting a bit testy.

'The local police have considered the matter quite carefully, Alan, and come to the same conclusion, if you can call it that. Maybe it's one person, for some obscure motive. Or maybe these are unrelated episodes. The varying nature of the crimes makes that more likely, along with the apparent absence of motive in several of them. But there is one thing that does tie them together.'

He paused, and Alan nodded. 'They're well done.'

'How can you say that!' I was ready for battle. 'Theft, malicious damage, killing – well done?'

'Well done from the criminal's point of view, love. No one's been able to trace anything. No clues. No leads. Perfect crimes.' Alan glanced at me and changed the subject. 'John, you asked us to come because you thought we could help. Now that we have some idea of what the problem is, tell us what you'd like us to do.'

'Nose around. I can't make it any more specific than that. I've been authorized to give you a small expense account; admission to some of the places you'll need to go isn't cheap.'

Authorized by whom, I wondered, but didn't ask. John might be retired, but his contacts with the Mounties and the local police might allow him a few perks. Or maybe it was coming out of his own pocket. We'd worry about that later.

'I want you to talk to people, visit sites of the incidents. I want you to take a couple of those walking tours of Victoria that I mentioned and ask all the questions you think a pair of green tourists might come up with.'

I nodded. 'Straight off the turnip truck. I can do that. Alan might have a little more trouble. He looks and sounds so bloomin' intelligent and well educated.'

''Oo, me? Yer've got the wrong bloke, mate!'

His Cockney was pretty good, considering. Much better than mine. But I could do a pretty good down-home Hoosier when I put my mind to it.

John laughed. 'You'll do. I don't need to ask you to check in frequently; I know you'll tell me if – when – you learn something interesting. Now, here's a bit of cash to go on with until you can get to an ATM. Keep an accounting log for me, please. Disguise the case of champagne as something else.'

'A kilo or so of cannabis?'

'Ha, ha. Now, if you're packed up, let's get you over to Sue's place. I'll show you on the map where the walking tours start, and then you're on your own.'

'I thought you were coming with us.'

'No, I decided I want you to form your own impressions without my explanations. You can't possibly get lost. Your guide will see to that. And you'll have a great time!'

EIGHT

We hadn't thought to ask John about parking in downtown Victoria. It was easy enough to find the Visitor Centre where the walking tours began; John had pointed it out to us on that quick drive through Victoria. Parking the car was another matter. I finally had to ask a passer-by, who directed me to a lot. By the time I'd handled that hassle, we were almost late for the start of the afternoon tour.

Our guide was an interesting man who gave us snippets of Victoria history, as it related to various buildings and sculptures downtown. We saw Victoria herself, of course, in front of the Legislature buildings, looking a good deal more regal than she does in front of Buckingham Palace, but wearing that same silly little crown. We saw the fabled Empress Hotel. We saw the Inner Harbour, where the ferries from Seattle and Vancouver docked, as well as the seaplanes. Looking southwest, several blocks away, we saw the other side of the peninsula, where gigantic cruise ships docked, and learned that they provided a good deal of boost to Victoria's economy.

'Are the tourists mostly Americans?' I asked in the most American accent I could muster.

'All sorts. American, Japanese – lots of Asians, in fact.'

'I guess you have to watch out for smuggling. I mean, all those people from all over the place.'

He looked at me sharply. 'We have very efficient customs enforcement, madam.' Turning to the rest of the walkers, 'Now up ahead you'll see . . .'

'Snubbed,' murmured Alan.

'Sounded defensive, didn't he? A thought to tuck away.'

We walked. And walked. Uphill and down. There were steps. I learned a good deal about Victoria, painted in the rosy colours one would expect from a tour guide. There was little opportunity to ask any more questions; the guide had decided I was a trouble-maker, and avoided me.

Then we came to a narrow passageway called Fan Tan Alley and struck a vein of history that was of great interest to us. 'This,' said our guide, 'used to be a notorious part of Victoria, famous, or infamous, for gambling and opium dens. Under British rule, the use of opium was legal, perhaps because there was a good deal of profit in importing it from China. But gambling was not. No easy way to tax that, you see. So there were, and presumably still are, passages on the top storey, or the roof, from one shop to another. Gamblers who thought a raid was coming could move quickly to an opium den and be found getting peacefully happy when the government agents arrived. Or they could go down back stairs to some of the alleys that open off this one. There was a virtual labyrinth of them.'

Since we were on the subject, I thought I could venture a question. 'Are they still there? Those little alleys?'

'Yes. There's an entrance to one of them.' He pointed out a wrought-iron gate, securely padlocked. 'Closed off now, as you see,' he added sternly. He still didn't like me. 'This used to be the heart of Chinatown, which was large and prosperous many years ago.' He turned his back on me and went on to discuss the rise and fall of Victoria's Chinatown.

So he didn't want to talk about the 'labyrinth'. Fine. Or else he just didn't want to talk about it to me. Was it suspicion that I might be planning some nefarious deeds? Or, just possibly, that he knew of some that had already taken place, involving smuggling and/or recourse to Fan Tan Alley and its byways?

The Alley was now obviously geared toward tourism. Shops sold all manner of souvenirs, from the beautiful and expensive to the truly tacky. Even so, even with the chatter of our tour group and the bright (tiny) shop windows, the place felt vaguely menacing. Partly it was the constricted size. The alley is said to be the narrowest street in Canada, and though 'street' was a debatable term, it was certainly narrow. There were places where two could not walk abreast, and the walls seemed to press in. In spots there wasn't a great deal of light. I began to be a little short of breath, and Alan, who understands about my claustrophobia, murmured, 'All right, love?'

I moved on to where he could walk beside me, clutched his arm, and tried to smile. 'I will be, as soon as we get out of here.'

He pointed ahead to where we could see the end of the alley. 'Courage, dear heart.'

That's one reason I love this man so much. He never makes fun of what both of us know to be an irrational fear.

And then we were out of the horrid place and into Chinatown proper, what was left of it. The guide explained that although there were still many families of Chinese descent in Victoria, they had moved out of Chinatown years ago and become assimilated into the general population, so although there were still a few restaurants and shops in the area, the large factories and ware-houses that used to exist there were now merely façades, with condos behind them. He pointed out one with a large sign that read KWONG ON TAI CO.

'Sad,' I commented to Alan. 'A thriving business once, now nothing but a wall and a sign.'

'You don't know that, Dorothy. Perhaps they moved elsewhere, to a modern facility. And isn't it a good thing that the Chinese are no longer confined to their ghetto, but are living and doing well all over the city?'

'Yes, of course it is. But all the same, it's a shame when people lose their cultural identity. I think of the Poles who moved to the US near the end of the nineteenth century. Despised for decades, they lived in their own enclaves and pursued their own interests. But in the end, they had either to assimilate or live in poverty. So now, in many cities, very few of them can even speak Polish. Their churches are no longer exclusively theirs, their social clubs have died. I wish we could have both: immigrants fitting in to their new culture without losing their birthright.'

'That can happen only when the people in the host country lose their fear of the newcomers, the "others". We're not there yet, Dorothy.'

The rest of the tour group had moved on without our noticing. They were halfway down the street, and I wasn't minded to run and catch up. 'I'm tired, Alan, and hot and thirsty. And I need to find a loo.'

'A pub would deal with all those necessities. Do they have pubs in Canada?'

'You're asking me? They don't exist in America, even though some bars call themselves that.' I looked around, as Alan did the same. We had moved away from the touristy Chinatown proper, and there seemed to be no establishments purveying food and/or drink, Chinese or otherwise. There weren't quite as many people around, either. In fact, the neighbourhood seemed to have gone from glitzy to glum in the space of half a block.

I peered into the window of a shop that had no sign, on the off-chance that it could be a café of some sort, but the interior was dark. 'No luck.' I turned back. 'Alan, let's— Alan?'

He'd been right behind me. Now he wasn't. Had he turned down one of the narrow passageways between buildings, in search of a pub? Surely not. They weren't as narrow as Fan Tan Alley, but they were dark and uninviting. Where on earth?

'Madam?'

A man came up to me, a respectable sort, fortyish at a guess. 'Is your name Dorothy?'

'Yes, but—'

'Your husband is asking for you. He's had some sort of stroke, or maybe a heart attack. Anyway, he collapsed in a doorway just a few minutes ago, and he wants you. Let me take you to him.'

The man held out an arm. Nervous and frightened, I almost took it. But then some warning signal went off in my muddled brain. I remembered that intelligent child. 'Wait. What's the code? Give me the code.'

'I beg your pardon?'

'We have a code. I'm not going anywhere until you tell me what it is.'

'I . . . he's drifting in and out of consciousness. He couldn't—'

'You said he was asking for me. He's conscious. Give me the code.' I pulled a whistle out of my purse. Not quite as shrill and demanding as an English police whistle, it would nevertheless attract attention. I put it to my lips.

'I . . . must have made some mistake. You're not the right woman. Sorry to have bothered you.'

He was gone, vanishing down one of the passageways as I blew the whistle with all my might.

People, suddenly. Passers-by, asking if I was all right, if they could help. A very welcome policeman.

Alan.

I pushed everyone else away and flung myself into his arms. 'You're all right! Nothing happened to you! I was so scared, but—'

'He said they'd taken you away! It took me far too long to get away from—'

We were both talking at once and not making a lot of sense. The policeman shooed away the bystanders and said, 'Let's go somewhere quiet, where we can talk properly.' He showed his badge. 'My car is just here. Ma'am, let me help you.'

I needed the help; I was suddenly unsteady. The adrenaline had left me and my bones seemed to be made of Jell-O.

Alan cleared his throat and said, 'Could you take us to a coffee shop or the like? I think my wife needs a stimulant.'

'And a washroom,' I croaked.

The man obligingly took us around a corner to a bright, inviting café, and when I had used the facilities, and we had exchanged introductions, we sat in a corner booth and told him the whole story, Alan speaking first.

'We were both looking around for a pub or the like, when I got separated from Dorothy. I thought it a bit odd, since we had left a much more crowded area, but I didn't worry until I found myself being pushed, as if by accident, into one of those rather nasty alleys.'

'You didn't cry out?'

Alan looked a little embarrassed. 'I suppose I should have done, but I had no sense of being in danger, only irritation at what I assumed was someone's appalling manners. I protested, of course. And then I felt what I took to be a gun in my back, and stopped making any noise at all.'

'Very wise.'

'My chief concern then was for Dorothy. The thug who had hold of me started talking then, saying that his accomplice had taken her away, and they were going to hold her until I ransomed her.'

I interrupted 'Ransom? What made them – him – whoever, think you could pay ransom? We're not rich. We live thousands of miles away; nobody here knows us, even.'

'We'll sort all that out, ma'am. Right now I'd like to hear the rest of the story.'

I subsided.

'That, though, was exactly what I wondered,' said Alan. 'If this was just a straightforward mugging, it was taking a very odd turn.'

The sergeant – Moore, that was his name – gave Alan a searching look. 'You're familiar with what you call a "straightforward mugging" then, sir?'

Alan sighed. 'Sergeant, I was a policeman in England for a very long time. I retired as Chief Constable of Belleshire some years ago, but there are some things one doesn't forget.'

'I see.' Clearly there were things the sergeant didn't see, but like him, I wanted to hear the rest of the story.

'So. I waited for the bloke to tell me what sort of ransom, meanwhile working out what I could safely do to get free. And then I heard Dorothy's whistle.'

'Quite distinctive,' commented the sergeant, with a straight face.

'Yes. It distracted my captor enough that I could pull myself free and twist his arm back. He dropped his "weapon", which turned out to be only a piece of wood, and I ran. And ran into Dorothy's situation.'

'Yes. Now your story, if you please, ma'am.'

'As Alan said, we were looking for a pub, when I realized Alan wasn't with me. I thought he'd just got lost in the crowd. Only there wasn't really much of a crowd. That was when this man came up to me with a tale about Alan being ill and asking for me.'

'He used his name?'

I thought for a minute. 'No. He just said "your husband". But he called me Dorothy.' I paused. The sergeant nodded for me to continue.

'So I was scared, of course, and I almost went with him. But then I remembered something, and I asked him for the code.'

Both men looked puzzled.

'That little girl who almost got taken by some stranger. In the paper this morning?'

Dawning comprehension.

'So I told him I wouldn't go with him without the code, and when he started to back off, I blew my whistle. And you know the rest.'

'Dorothy, we don't have a code.'

'I know that, dear heart. But he didn't.'

The sergeant closed his notebook. 'Well, both of you acted very sensibly. As you say, Chief Constable, this doesn't look like a simple street crime, which makes it somewhat puzzling.'

'It's just plain Mr Nesbitt these days, Sergeant. I'm long retired. And there's something you should probably know.' He looked around. The café was filling up, creating noise and giving us reasonable privacy, but he lowered his voice. 'We are not here entirely as tourists. You know we live in England, though Dorothy is from the United States originally.'

'Ah, that explains it.'

He was referring, I knew, to the trace of American in my accent. I've given up trying to eradicate it, but I was a bit surprised that a Canadian would catch it.

'Well, if that's all—'

'No. The fact is, sir, that we're here to investigate a problem here on the island. One of your retired Mounties, John McKenzie, has asked our help in untangling the web of small crimes that began with the theft of plants and has escalated to the release of hawks up near Duncan.'

'Ah.' The sergeant gave both of us a sharp look. 'The Victoria police, along with other forces in the area, are of course aware of Mr McKenzie's efforts. Like you, sir, he prefers not to use his rank, now that he is retired. But I'm afraid I don't quite understand how you and your wife became involved in – er – investigating our little problem.'

We both sighed. This looked like being a long story. I nodded to Alan, who can exercise tact much better than I.

In a few carefully-chosen words he explained that the two of us had become concerned in several investigations in England. 'My wife, you see, brings valuable insights from her non-English background, as well as a knack for asking the right questions. People find her easy to talk to. And as we are good friends of Mr McKenzie's niece Lady Montcalm, are in fact godparents to her son, she thought we might be able to help in some small way here. I am of course familiar with the problems of police forces everywhere: understaffing, overwork. Mr McKenzie asked us to come, and here we are, hoping to help in any small way we can.'

Bravo, Alan. The snob appeal of a titled friend. Even in democratically-ruled Canada, her history and Commonwealth status mean that titles still carry some weight. Add in the mention of his exalted one-time rank, sympathy for local difficulties, and a humble offer of help, and he couldn't have done better.

It worked, too. Sergeant Moore thawed considerably. 'Ah, well, we can use all the help we can get. As you say, sir, we are considerably overworked. Victoria is a law-abiding place for the most part, but I'm sure Mr McKenzie has told you about some of the tensions between various elements of the community. But now, much as I hate to say it, it looks very possible that you and your wife were specifically targeted in the attack just now. It could just be that it has to do with your "investigation".'

I could clearly hear the quotation marks, and I resented them, but a look from Alan kept me quiet.

The sergeant opened his mouth to continue.

'That had occurred to us, of course,' Alan said, smoothly overriding him, 'and although we haven't had time to consult with each other, I know I can assure you that we intend to pursue our efforts even more vigorously. We'll take all due precautions, of course. We have no intention of creating even more work for you by getting killed.'

Sergeant Moore was no fool. He wasn't keen on the idea, but he had no way to stop us, and he could see that Alan intended to carry on, no matter what. 'Neither do I want to see you killed. It would create endless paperwork, what with you being tourists, and all.' He allowed a tiny smile to show us he was joking. Sort of. 'Meanwhile, the biggest help you could give right now would be a description of your assailants.'

Alan, who was trained to be observant, could give fairly complete details. I, who was not, could speak only in useless generalities. Male, white, maybe fortyish, well-dressed, no particular accent. 'I'm sorry. I was thinking about Alan and didn't notice much.'

'Quite understandable.' His tone left me in no doubt about his opinion of me. Fine investigator she'd make! He might as well have spoken it aloud. I gave him my sweetest smile, thinking of what I'd like to say to him.

He stood. 'Right. I'll be on my way. You'll let me know of anything you find out? And I'll do the same.' He sketched a salute and went on his way.

'Save it, Dorothy. We'll find a pub and you can explode there. And you know, it might be a good idea to dream up a recognition code, don't you think?'

NINE

We found a pleasant watering place not too far away, sort of a cross between a pub and an American bar. No dark oak stained by centuries of smoke, but proper oak tables, a dart board, and a friendly bartender who recommended the local cider for me. 'You'll have had English cider,' he said, apparently picking up on that aspect of my odd accent, 'but this is different. Different apples, for one thing, and nothing like as strong. And we serve it over ice. Most ladies like it – very refreshing.'

The day had grown very warm; ice sounded good. 'I'll try anything once.' Alan opted for a straightforward pint. We took our drinks to a nice quiet table in a corner.

'It wobbles,' I commented. 'I feel right at home.'

Alan stacked a couple of beer mats under the short leg and took a healthy swig of his beer. I tasted my cider more cautiously, and was very pleasantly surprised. 'It's just a bit sweet and apple-y, and very light. He's right. Refreshing is the word. Alan, what do we do now?'

'We finish our drinks and go home,' he said pleasantly. 'We've a lot to talk about, and I've had enough of sensitive discussions in public places.'

'The café—' I began.

'That was a calculated risk. We couldn't be overheard, not where we were and with the ambient noise, and if a villain saw us talking with the police, it would be assumed we were telling him about our nasty little narrow escape. In fact, I rather hope some criminal type did see us. They'd know then to lie low for a bit, and it's unlikely they'd try that particular little trick again.'

He'd said that in a voice so low I could barely hear him. No one else could have, I was sure of that. And he'd turned his head away from the rest of the room. He was taking no chances at all.

That might have frightened me as an acknowledgment that he believed we were in serious peril. In fact, it reassured me. Alan was in command of the situation, and I had utter confidence in him. I smiled, toasted him silently, and drank my cider before we headed 'home'.

We stopped at a supermarket on the way and purchased some staples, but I had qualms. The condo didn't feel like home. It was too neat, too clean, too unlived-in. I would have welcomed a nice cat or two, or a little clutter, or something that made it feel less like a set for a *House Beautiful* photo shoot. 'I'm afraid I'll drop crumbs, or spill something. I don't know if I can bear to cook in this immaculate kitchen. On an electric stove.'

'It's that or restaurant meals, love. Or take-away. I do draw the line at frozen meals.'

'Some of them are not too bad, you know. Sainsbury's does some good ones you've eaten before, and liked them. But everything's different here. More like America in some ways.'

'It is America, dear heart. The North American continent isn't occupied exclusively by your homeland.'

'If you love me, Alan, don't lecture. I haven't had a very pleasant day.'

'Nor have I. When I thought I might have lost you . . .' His voice trailed off. He cleared his throat. 'What have you planned for supper?'

'I bought some salmon that looks lovely. I can broil that and make a salad.'

'There's a grill out on the deck.'

'Alan Nesbitt, if you think I'm going to be responsible for cleaning someone else's grill! The oven broiler will be fine, and I can bake a couple of potatoes. That way I don't have to deal with the surface burners immediately. I'll put the potatoes in as soon as we get this stuff put away.'

'Which we will do in a few minutes. Right now I want you to sit down and take several deep breaths while I make you a cup of tea. No arguments!'

I wasn't actually minded to argue. The trauma of the afternoon had left me more shaken than I had realized. I hadn't had time, when it happened, to think about anything except Alan, and how to get away from the threat. Now I felt wrung out. I was happy to sit and let Alan pamper me, all the while thinking of how life without him . . . no, I wouldn't think about that.

Alan makes excellent tea. Having lived as a widower for some years, he's quite competent in a kitchen, and had found tea, pot, cups and accompaniments without fuss. There were also a few pieces of shortbread on a plate.

'How did you manage that? I didn't think I bought any biscuits.'

'You didn't. An oversight which we will remedy soon. I found a new packet of Walker's in the freezer and nuked it for a few seconds. I suppose Sue had just bought it when she went away, and didn't want ants to get into it. We can replace it for her.'

'Mm.' I nodded with my mouth full.

We sipped our tea in companionable silence, and when I'd finished I put my cup down, blessing its restorative qualities, and said, 'We were awfully lucky, Alan.'

'Luckier than we deserved, as stupid as we'd been.'

'We didn't really take it seriously, did we? Or I didn't. Chattering away in public!'

'That's putting it a bit strongly, love. We didn't exactly "chatter" about anything sensitive. But plainly we said enough to raise an alarm in some quarter or other. And paid the price.'

'It could have been a much higher price.' I tried to keep my voice steady, and almost succeeded. I was glad I wasn't holding a teacup, though. My hands were less controlled.

'Yes.' Just the single word, but it said volumes.

'We have to tell John about this,' I said, attempting to return to the mundane. 'I hope he doesn't decide we need to take our marbles and go home.'

'I have a feeling he probably already knows. There are no flies on Sergeant Moore. He may not think we're of the slightest use, but he won't neglect— Ah.' Alan's mobile warbled. 'This will be John now.'

But it wasn't. Alan's face showed more and more anger as he listened in silence to the voice on the other end. Still without saying a word, he clicked off, immediately going back to check the number. 'Blocked,' he said. 'No surprise.'

'A threat? What did he say?'

'Or she. The voice was filtered electronically. Could have been either man or woman. It was just a standard stop-it-or-else threat. The "or else" was spelled out rather dramatically. And foolishly.

I won't give you the details, but many of our promised fates are quite literally impossible to accomplish.'

I made a face. 'Alan, does it strike you that there's something very amateurish about today's efforts? An attack meant to scare us off, and now a phone call straight out of a bad thriller? Somehow it doesn't seem to fit in with the other incidents, which were disturbing, but subtle. Well, except for poor Silas's hawks, but even that was well-managed.'

'I agree. You know we speculated that more than one person or group might be involved in the disturbances. This last—' The phone warbled again. This time Alan looked at the display before answering. 'Hello, John. I had a feeling we might be hearing from you soon. No, I . . . but . . . no!' He listened for a little. Even from several feet away, I could hear the agitation in John's voice. 'Look, I think this may be much less serious than you think. I can't explain over the phone. Why don't you come over here and we can talk. Dorothy's about ready to start preparing a meal, and— No, of course not! We'll expect you in a few minutes.'

He clicked off. 'You'd better put three potatoes in the oven.'

'I heard. What's up? John sounded really upset.'

'There's been a development. I'll let him tell you about it. I don't think it's as serious as he believes, but it's impossible to be sure. If you don't mind being left alone for a few minutes, I'm going back to the supermarket for some bar supplies. Lock the door after me.'

I locked it and put the chain on, and then started the oven and scrubbed three big potatoes. They wouldn't, of course, be Idahos, but they looked enough like baking potatoes that I hoped they'd work. I was getting out salad makings when the knock came.

I dropped the cucumber. Taking a deep breath, I picked it up, dusted it off, and went to the door, wishing there were a peephole. 'Yes?' I willed my voice not to quaver.

'Dorothy? It's John. Are you all right?'

So much for trying to sound normal. 'Yes, John, but it's been a trying day. You'll think this is foolish, but what's the name of your niece in Suffolk?'

'Judith. Lady Montcalm. But what—?'

I opened the door. 'Just taking precautions. Alan had to go out for a moment. Do come in and sit down. When Alan gets back he'll pour you a drink; there wasn't anything in the house.'

'Oh. No. I should have brought – but I didn't think – did Alan tell you?'

'No, he wanted you to give me the details. And here he is.'

It didn't take long for Alan to find glasses and pour us each a libation. We moved to the kitchen where I could get on with dinner preparations while John told his story.

TEN

'I've been thinking about what you said,' John said to Alan, taking a sip of his drink. 'I overreacted, just like the grandparents who get scam calls about a kid in trouble. After I called you, I called Amy. She was at work and couldn't talk long, but she's fine. At least for now.'

'Clue me in, John. You told Alan, but he didn't say a word to me.' I started slicing the cucumber.

'I got a call. Don't know who the caller was. He said—'

'Wait.' Alan held up a hand. 'It was a man calling?'

'I couldn't actually tell. The voice was distorted. Could have been either.'

'Ah. Go on.'

'He – it – said Amy was in danger, that she would be abducted and–and tortured . . .' He stopped to drink a little more of his whisky. 'He spelled out details. I won't go into that. Then he said I could prevent it if I stopped trying to . . . well, it was pretty crude, but what it amounted to was, I was to keep my nose out of the investigation into the incidents we've been looking into.'

'Yes.' Alan put his glass down. 'I thought it would be something like that. I got a call almost exactly like yours, and just a few minutes before yours. Almost identical. Altered voice, filthy language, strong intimidation. I take it you haven't heard about our little adventure today?'

'No. What happened?'

'Alan, get out some of that brie we just bought. Dinner will be a while. Meanwhile, John . . .' I summarized our experiences, while still slicing the cucumber. 'It was extremely frightening at the time, but looking back on it, Alan and I both decided it was pretty feeble. Well-meaning – or rather, ill-meaning amateurs trying to scare us.'

'Which they did, I have to say.' Alan put down a plate of cheese and crackers. 'Thank God Dorothy kept her head.'

'And so did you, my love. Even though you thought he was holding a gun on you. But you see what we mean, John. If these had been professional crooks, it would have been a real gun. They would have just bundled both of us away and either killed us, or held us for ransom.'

'Or both.' John helped himself to a chunk of brie. 'Yes, I do see. Intimidation, rather than any real attempt at harm. And quite a different approach from the incidents we're looking at.'

'Exactly.' Alan slapped his hand on the table. 'But obviously connected with them. Witness the threats. Now. Given what we know now, and what we can infer, what conclusions can we draw?'

'Two groups working toward the same ends. One competent, one not. The incompetents ought to be easy to apprehend. I take it the police have descriptions of your thugs?'

'Alan was able to give a pretty good one.' I put the salad bowl on the table and opened the oven to check on the potatoes. 'I wasn't much help. I was too scared. Move, dear, and let me get these potatoes out and the salmon in to broil. And we're going to talk about something else while we eat. Sue has a lovely place here, John. We're going to be very comfortable.'

And not another word of disaster talk did I allow until we had nearly finished. I apologized for the lack of dessert.

'Dorothy, we're stuffed! That was a lovely meal.'

'Thank you, John, but my Hoosier grandmother would be appalled that there was no pie. More wine, anybody?'

Next morning dawned bright and a bit chilly. As usual. 'I think,' I said to Alan over coffee and toast, 'that weather wouldn't work well as a conversational gambit here. "Oh, what a beautiful day" would wear a bit thin after a month of them. What are we going to do today?'

'Hmm. John's suggestion of talking to people didn't work out too well, did it?'

'Not here in Victoria. Alan, I confess to feeling more than a little intimidated.'

'That, of course, is exactly what they were trying to accomplish. Whoever "they" are.'

'Well, it worked. You know, we're operating under a handicap here. Not only do we have no official standing, we don't know anybody. At home you still have some clout because of your position, even though you're retired. And for a while I could go around asking questions because I was an American, not expected to know anything or pose any threat.'

'No longer true, of course.'

'No, now everybody in Sherebury knows I'm your wife, and pathologically nosy, but they also know we've solved a few problems for people. So I can still talk to people, and of course, so can you.'

'Hmm. So how can we turn those handicaps around and use them?'

'I see: the lemonade approach. Bah humbug. Well, I'm not sure there's anything we can do with these particular lemons. Let's see. We don't know anybody.'

'Which also means nobody knows us. We were spotted yesterday because we made ourselves conspicuous with our questions. And because a pair of goons were out on patrol.'

'Well, we need to ask questions. And those goons now know who we are.'

'I may be wrong, Dorothy.'

'Surely not!'

'Sarcasm is the tool of the devil, as you so frequently remind me. In this case, what I'm about to say is pure speculation and may well be mistaken, or perhaps wishful thinking. But I believe that yesterday's goons were operating without the knowledge of their principal.'

'Who is presumably the author of the – we can't keep calling them "incidents". Too trivial.'

'How about "nastiness"?'

'The recent nastiness. Yes, I like that. Is there more coffee?' I held out my cup.

Alan filled it and went on with his thought. 'We've decided that the attacks on us were almost certainly related to the nastiness, but perpetrated by a different person. The original villain is careful and clever. Does it seem at all likely that he would have authorized something so incompetent, unnecessary, and unproductive as the attacks on us?'

'Well, if you put it that way, no. All that was accomplished was to frighten us—'

'A little.'

'Okay, a little. And to identify us. But on the flip side, we can also identify them. The principal, as you call him, has never been seen.'

'Right. So the rest of my speculation states that at this point, said principal – shall we give him a name?'

'Beelzebub.'

'Apt, but cumbersome.'

'Then how about Bub, for short? I don't know if it's ever used in England, but in America, or at least in American fiction, the police would walk up to someone suspicious and address him as "Bub". As in, "Okay, Bub, what do you think you're doing?" Or somewhat saltier words to that effect.'

'I like it. Bub it is. Very well, then, I think that Bub is now very angry with his goons, and will keep them out of circulation. Probably out of the province.'

'Out of the country, even? Seattle's only a few miles away.'

'You're not thinking, Dorothy. Finish that coffee. Anyone leaving the country has to show a passport. If the police are taking this seriously, they will have alerted the border people.' He held up a hand as I opened my mouth. 'And even if they're not, as we suspect, Bub can't be sure of that, and he's always careful. In any case, I doubt we'll ever see or hear of those particular villains again, and I'm pretty sure we're safe as long as we don't go and do something stupid.'

I finished my coffee as ordered, and thought about that. 'Okay, I'll buy it. Provisionally. So, as I said way back when, what do you think we should do today?'

'If you're agreeable, I think we start acting like the tourists that, in fact, we are, and go to some of the places where the nastiness was perpetrated. Starting at the beginning, at Butchart Gardens. And we talk. I suggest going back to one of Hercule Poirot's first tenets, that if people talk long enough, they'll reveal more than they intended to.'

I thought about that for a moment. 'He was talking about criminals. That was so often the way he caught them.'

'True, but it applies to anyone. People like to talk. Let's talk to anyone we can at Butchart, let them start telling stories, and see if any gold appears among the dross.'

We tossed for the driver's seat, and I lost. Or won, depending on how you think of it. At any rate, I was at the wheel when we headed into downtown Victoria to find an ATM, and then on out to Butchart on the route mandated by the lady in the dashboard. Somewhat to my own amazement, I got us there without a hitch.

It was still early enough that there was plenty of room in the parking lot. I said something to the man at the ticket office. 'It's early in the day, and early in the season. It'll be picking up every day now through the end of September or so. Here are your maps. Enjoy the gardens.'

'What's that?' I said as Alan put away his change. 'It looks like plastic.'

'It is. The banknotes here aren't engraved on paper. But some of them do, you will observe, include the proper picture.' He pointed to the portrait of Queen Elizabeth on the twenty-dollar bill, and grinned.

'God save the Queen. Even in a place where she doesn't reign. Okay, where are we going first?'

Alan thought a moment. 'Any place where there are gardeners at work. They're the ones we need to talk to first, don't you think?'

'As long as they're not too busy, yes, I think so. They wouldn't appreciate being held up in their work.'

'My dear, if they're like any other gardeners on the planet, they'll welcome a break.'

We came across a whole crew of them almost immediately, working in the huge Sunken Garden, the first garden we saw on the tour. They were digging up tulips and planting snapdragons and marigolds and other summer annuals.

'What a job!' I said to one of them. 'I don't do that sort of thing anymore, but I used to, years ago when I lived in Indiana.'

'A big job, as you say. Do you visit often? You said you were from the States, but don't I hear an English accent?'

'I've lived in England for quite a while now. Over there they think I still talk like a Yank. On this side of the pond people think I'm a Brit. But no, this is only our second visit to the Gardens. My husband really is a Brit, and neither of us has ever been to this part of Canada before.'

'You must come back in full summer! You'll never see the same garden twice. Not just the seasonal changes, I don't mean, but plants are constantly being replaced, new ones introduced – it's a work in progress.'

'All gardens are, though, aren't they? Plants get aggressive and take the place, or else for some inexplicable reason they die. Nothing is static in a garden.'

He shook his head in rueful agreement. 'And of course in a public place like this, occasionally something gets stolen.'

'Oh, dear! That's really terrible! I'd think people would respect the fact that all this beauty is here for everyone. And surely there are guards?' I made it a question.

'They can't be everywhere at once. In fact, someone stole some of our aconites last fall. An odd choice, one would think. They're quite pretty when they're in bloom, aconites, but this was in late October when they were going dormant, nothing much to see. And of course you can buy them at any nursery; they're not rare or anything. Peculiar.'

Something told me not to admit that I knew a fair amount about aconite, including some of its gruesome common names, and its highly toxic qualities. I agreed that the theft was peculiar and changed the subject.

'I suppose you get visitors from all over Canada and the States,' I commented, hoping I sounded ignorant and naïve.

'From all over the world, actually. It's amazing, really, but Japanese come here by the thousands to see our Japanese garden.'

'One would suppose,' put in Alan, who had been listening silently, 'that they had enough in their own country not to need to travel so far.'

'You'd think so, wouldn't you? But there are some special things about this one. I'm not sure what; that's not my field. You could ask at the Visitor Centre. They know everything!'

'Are you a botanist, then? You speak of "my field".' We were straying very far from any possible connection with the nastiness, but I was curious about this young man, who seemed both bright and capable, and surely capable of holding down a better job.

'Yeah, sort of. This is just a part-time job. I'm studying biology at UVic.' Seeing my blank look, he added, 'University of Victoria. You might not know, but it's one of the finest universities in

Canada, and in some disciplines, in the world. I'm just beginning my second year, so I haven't decided on a specialty yet, but I'm thinking of getting into earth sciences. The trouble is, there are so many great programs! They do a lot of really important research, and there's never any problem getting funding for projects; they have an awesome endowment. See, there are a lot of fat cats in BC, 'specially in Victoria, because of the tech boom. And they love to go throwing their money around and looking like Santa Claus. It's okay with me. They get the laurel wreaths, we get the benefit. Everybody's happy.'

He bent back to his work. 'And speaking of happy, my boss won't be if I don't get this done.'

'Oh, sorry to keep you away from it. But it was lovely to talk to you, and we both wish you luck with your future.'

'So did we learn anything useful?' I asked Alan when we were out of earshot.

'One thing, perhaps. He wasn't hesitant to talk about the theft of the aconites. That means there's been no attempt to hush it up.'

'Hmm. And that tells us . . .?'

'Don't know. Just something to be tucked away. Shall we talk to another gardener, or someone at the Visitor Centre, or one of the tourists, or—'

'I vote for somewhere we can sit down. The coffee shop? We can talk there.'

We had barely sat down with our coffee when Alan's phone rang. He listened for a moment, his expression growing more and more dismayed, and said, 'We'll be there.'

He stood and put some money on the table. 'We have to go, Dorothy. As fast as we can.'

ELEVEN

'What did he say?' I waited until we were well away from people. It was obvious that something dire had happened.

'There's been a death. John didn't say much more than that, except it's possible that the falconer's birds were involved.'

'Oh, no! So are we going up there?'

'Not yet. John is meeting us at the condo. He'll take us up; he didn't think we could find the way.'

'I don't either.'

We were silent the rest of the way back home. I needed to concentrate on driving; Alan was brooding.

John was waiting when we got there. I made us all coffee – instant was good enough in this crisis – and sat down to listen.

'First things first,' John said, sounding very tired. 'A young woman was found this morning not far from Silas Varner's place. She was horribly wounded: deep cuts all over her face and upper body. I have no intention of giving you the details. They're sickening, and you don't need to know. The cause of death is presumed to be loss of blood.'

'Presumed?' That was Alan.

'Until the autopsy. But it's fairly obvious.'

'You saw the body.'

'God, yes!' He shuddered and gulped down his coffee. 'I'll see it for the rest of my life.'

'How did you get involved, John?' I asked. 'This would have been a case for the . . . what, the RCMP who were first at the scene?'

'Right. They're the first line of defence in most of the rural areas of BC.'

'You said the body was found near Varner's place. Was he the one who called?'

John grimaced. 'I doubt the old sinner owns a phone. No, that's one of the very interesting things. The call was anonymous.'

'And it couldn't be traced?' Alan was operating in full policeman mode.

'The number was blocked.'

'Just like the phone that made the threatening calls yesterday.'

'Yes.'

The two men looked at each other.

I repeated my question. 'Is that why the Mounties called you in? The slight similarity?'

'No, the officer first on the scene didn't know about that until I told him. He happens to be a friend who knows about my interest in the whole mess, and he knew I'd want to get into the act. Not officially, of course.'

'And the victim? Who is she?' Alan the policeman again.

John pulled out his notebook. 'We don't have a name yet. Height approximately 175 centimetres, weight around 63 kilos.'

I got out my phone and began searching for a metric conversion chart.

John went on. 'Black hair, medium brown skin. Well-nourished, well-groomed. We think she's a First Nations woman, most probably Cowichan, the dominant tribe where she was found. The features' – he stopped, swallowed, and continued – 'were too badly damaged to be of help in identification, but the skin colour is right, and the clothing. She wore conventional slacks, brown wool, and a white cotton shirt, but her jacket was distinctive, a Cowichan knit without doubt. The wool and the pattern are both unique: raw wool, hand-spun, hand-knitted.'

'Shoes? Or boots?' Alan was going down his mental list.

'Flat-heeled brown leather shoes, expensive, almost new, well-polished. No jewellery. No watch.'

'Was her phone damaged, or could they get some information from it?'

'No phone.'

'Now that really is peculiar!' I had listened closely, and this detail didn't fit. 'Almost everyone carries a mobile these days. And she sounds like a professional woman, or at least one with a decent income and a lifestyle that made her concerned about her appearance and able to keep it up. And yet she had neither watch nor phone. Purse?'

'No. No wallet, no keys – nothing at all in her pockets except a tissue. Clean.'

'Someone didn't want her identified,' said Alan.

'At least not instantly. If she'd had any dental work done, that might do it. If we can find the right dentist. And you can guess that if she turns out to be a native woman, there'll be hell to pay. Relations with the Anglos are always on the touchy side, and if it turns out that Silas's birds killed her . . .' He shook his head.

'There's some doubt about it, then? I hope so. I hate to think of that poor old man losing his hawks, his only friends.'

'I'm not sure I'd agree with that description of him. He's a cross old codger, and wouldn't thank you for calling him a poor old man. But you're right about his only friends. If they take them away and kill them, I don't know whether he'll just pine away, or work himself up into a rage and die of a stroke. I do know he won't be able to go on living here. The Cowichan won't have it.'

Alan and I were both silent for a moment. Then I asked, 'Have you talked to him? Mr Varner?'

'No one's talked to him, not yet. He won't answer the door.'

'That must mean he knows what's happened. Which might mean—'

'It might mean anything,' John responded crossly. 'With him, anything. Got up on the wrong side of the bed, woke up with a hangover – though I've never known him to drink much – madder at the world than usual, anything. He could even be out flying his birds. Until we have the results of the autopsy, we can't get a search warrant.'

'So. You're waiting for that, and for identification of the body. But will the neighbours and the tribal authorities wait?' Alan's face was grim.

'That's why the RCMP have posted a guard on Silas's property. We can't have a lynching, and honestly, he's stirred up feelings so much, it might come to that.'

'Is there any doubt that this was a raptor attack?'

John paused. 'This is confidential information, but actually there is considerable doubt. Something about the pattern of the wounds is apparently not at all typical. That's why we – they – are pushing the autopsy through.'

'And how can we help?' I asked, after a long pause.

'Would you be willing to do a little shopping?'

I waited.

'Duncan is a small town, but it's a great place to shop. You can buy Cowichan items almost anywhere, especially the sweaters.

I'd like you to go into some of the shops, get to talking about the Cowichan garments and the tribal background, and see what you can pick up. Anything could be important, even the emotional temperature of the conversation.'

'That sounds like something I could do. And Alan?'

'Nose around town. Listen. Observe. If possible, don't look like a policeman.'

That brought a welcome laugh. 'I'll do my best. But I've put a lot of practice into the intimidating look. It isn't easy to let it go.'

'I'll need detailed directions for how to get there,' I said. 'I'm still the designated driver until Alan gets used to driving on the right.'

'It's not hard. Basically you just follow Highway 1, but I'll show you on the map, and then you can rely on Sadie.'

'Sadie being, I take it, the lady in the dashboard.'

'Right. I named her after a dictatorial aunt of mine, years back. Pleasant, but insistent on having her own way. Now look, here's where you want to go.'

I got mildly lost only once, and of course Sadie reproved me (courteously, but firmly) and got me back on the right track. We reached Duncan in time for lunch, found a little café serving great soup and sandwiches, and then set out on our appointed tasks.

The first shop I walked into had some beautiful sweaters on display, and an elderly woman sitting in the corner knitting. Her face was deeply lined, but her eyes were bright and her gnarled hands moved steadily, apparently without pain.

'Goodness, have you made all these? They're gorgeous.'

'My family and I, yes. They are traditional Cowichan sweaters. Very warm, waterproof. They will last for many years.'

'I saw on a map that this is the Cowichan Valley. You've lived here always, then?'

'Always. We were here long before the white people came, thousands of years before.'

'Did they – the white people, I mean – did they treat your people badly? I ask,' I added when her face took on a shuttered look, 'because I'm from the United States originally, and the white settlers there treated the native people very badly indeed, for a very long time.'

'We do not often talk about that,' the woman said, her hands and needles never ceasing their constant motion. 'Yes, it was bad for our people. There were diseases. Then the settlers took our lands, promising to pay for them. They never did.'

I shook my head. 'My race has much to answer for, all over the world.'

'It has been the same everywhere, yes. The white people come and the First Nations are wiped out.'

'The Cowichan have not been wiped out.' I pointed to the piles of sweaters, scarves, hats.

'Nearly. The diseases took nine out of ten of us. Then the white people made laws, forbidding us to practise our own ceremonies, taking our government away from us. They sent our children away to their schools, teaching them English, trying to wipe away their memories of the old ways.'

'But some of the old ways have survived.' Again I looked at the beautiful work of her hands. 'You still know how to make these wonderful designs.'

She nodded. 'And how to clean the wool, and spin the yarn. And I have passed this knowledge down to my children, and grandchildren. Things have become better for our tribe in the past few years. The government has allowed us to return to some of our ancient culture, and there are talks about returning some of our lands, and paying for some of what they keep.'

'I'm glad to hear that! But this is all really interesting. I hope I'm not taking up too much of your time, but I've never been to this part of Canada before, and I knew nothing about the First Peoples here. Do your kids – I mean not just yours, but the tribe's – do they go to white schools, or your own?'

'Our own. They are not large, but they are best for our children. There they learn what they need to succeed in the modern world, but they also learn their own language and traditions. In the same school, they learn tribal dances and computer skills!'

She laughed at that, and I laughed with her.

'So they're prepared for jobs almost anywhere, then.'

'Oh, yes, and for university, as well. We are not rich, we Cowichan, but there are scholarships for students who can profit from university education. There is one young woman who graduated from UVic with an honours degree, and went on to a very good job working with computers. Me, I don't understand what she does, but she earns lots of money and sends much of it home to her family. We are very proud of her.'

'You must be.' I was getting a sinking feeling about this and didn't want to continue the conversation, but I felt I must. 'She doesn't still live with the tribe, then?'

'No, she moved to Victoria to be nearer her job, but she comes back when she can. She has changed; she is thin like a white woman, but she still loves the place where she was a child, loves to walk the woods. She is a true Cowichan.'

A few customers came into the shop, giving me a good excuse to stop. There was a clerk to help people with purchases, but these folks looked eager to talk to the matriarch. I bowed. (Somehow a handshake seemed inappropriate, even if both her hands had not been occupied.) 'I've very much enjoyed talking with you, but I must let you get on with your work. I'm going to try to find a sweater that fits me.'

I came out of the shop a good deal poorer than when I went in, and not sure what Alan was going to say to me, but I was happy with my purchase, a heavy sweater-jacket knitted in cream and black and grey, with stylized eagles on front and back. I wondered how many centuries back the eagle design went.

I went on thinking about knitting to avoid thinking about the young woman who had gone to university and done so well, the one the tribe was so proud of, the one who had become thin. There was no reason to identify her with . . . with anyone I knew about. If something had happened to her, the tribe would surely know.

Not until the victim has been identified, said a nasty little voice in my head. And how were the police going to do that?

Dental records. DNA. Even her jacket, perhaps. It was hand-knit, and the knitter might be able to identify it.

The knitter might even have been the woman herself. Somehow that was a particularly nasty thought. Brought up in a close community, taught as a child an art sacred to her tribe, learning to do it well, making herself a beautiful jacket that proclaimed her origins even as she achieved success in the white people's world . . .

Stop it! Anyone can have a Cowichan jacket. You have one yourself, Dorothy Martin. Stop spinning horror stories that have no basis in fact.

None whatever.

I found the car, put my heavy parcel in the trunk, and searched for the next shop. There were a lot to choose from, but only a few specializing in First Nations art and artefacts. One art gallery had delectable boxes and baskets, jewellery, even totem poles, all made by native artists including the Cowichan. I talked to a few of the artists, and learned a good deal about the noble history of arts among the native peoples, but nothing of special relevance to my search.

Then, as a last resort, I entered a sports shop, not exactly my native habitat, to inquire about falconry supplies.

'We don't sell them,' the clerk said, looking at me rather oddly. 'Not thinking of taking it up yourself, are you?'

'Goodness, no. I'm actually a bit afraid of birds of prey, though I admire them, especially eagles. No, I have a friend in Indiana who would like to learn more about it, and I thought I might make him a present of some small supplies, like jesses and hoods – if I have the words right.'

'You're from the States? You sound English.'

I was getting a little tired of this particular question, but I explained briefly and went on, 'I don't suppose you know anyone who could give me any pointers I could pass on to my friend?'

He frowned. 'There's one guy – but no, you wouldn't want to talk to him. He doesn't like women. Doesn't like much of anybody, for that matter. They say he knows his birds, and treats them well, but he's a real nuisance to his neighbours. His place is a disgrace, except for the mews – that's what they call the sheds where the hawks live. They're supposed to be secure, but somehow his birds got out one night, not too long ago, and they killed some chickens. Not a popular fellow. No, if you want to know about falconry, your best bet is the raptor sanctuary just up the road.'

He gave me directions, and I thanked him without mentioning that I'd already been there, and left the store.

Plainly he knew nothing about the latest trouble involving Silas and his birds. The word hadn't spread yet. Nowhere in town did I sense any of the unease there surely would have been if rumours about a gruesome death were circulating.

I went to look for Alan.

TWELVE

I found him in the car, in the driver's seat. 'I was ready to come in search of you.'

'And I was looking for you.'

We sat in the car for a little while, wanting to compare notes where we couldn't be overheard.

'The only thing I learned for sure,' I said, 'was negative. Nobody's talking about any recent tragedy, or gossiping about Silas or his birds.'

'No. Of course the body was discovered in quite a remote area, and so far as I know has not yet been identified.'

I took a deep breath. 'I may have a clue to her identity. I hope I'm wrong.' I told him about the brilliant young Cowichan woman. 'It's probably nothing. I hope it's nothing.'

'I'll call John,' he said briefly, and pulled out his phone. He passed along what I had told him, waited for a response, and then said a few yesses and nos and ended the call.

'And?'

'There's some dental work. They're trying to find a likely dentist. They were concentrating on this area, Duncan and environs, but now they'll broaden it out to Victoria. If the woman lived and worked there, she probably would have seen a dentist there.'

'Which will take much longer. Couldn't they check the IT firms for a missing employee?'

'They'll do that, of course.'

'Of course.' I was suddenly very tired. 'And there's nothing we can do to help with any of it.'

Alan gave me a long look and then started the car, but drove only a couple of blocks and then parked in front of the café where we'd had our lunch. 'Let's talk about it over a cup of coffee.'

I didn't want coffee, but I wasn't in a mood to argue. I followed him, feeling old.

Without consulting me, he ordered coffee and a piece of pie, and didn't say another word until I had polished off the pie and

a second cup of coffee. Then he gave me an appraising look.
'Low blood sugar, that's what was the matter with you.'

'You always think food and/or drink will cure everything.'

'And how often am I right?'

'Most of the time. Which is what's so maddening! Okay, I do
feel better. But do you honestly think we're doing anything useful
here? It's costing Edwin and Judith a bundle, and we've done so
little.'

'Yes, I think we're doing what we came here to do. And I
think we need to keep on doing it. And let's continue this discussion in a less public place. Care for a walk?'

We walked away from the centre of town and found a convenient park bench.

'Part of your problem,' Alan said, continuing where he left
off, 'is that you don't like where all this is leading, but think of
it this way. If your speculation about the victim's identity is
correct, and our idea that this was a deliberate murder is also
correct, don't you want to help find the person who took a young,
intelligent woman's life?'

'Yes, of course I do. If I can. And find out who's at the bottom
of all the rest of the nastiness, too. If it's the same person. This
last seems not quite in character with the other events.'

'I agree. The others seemed to be designed simply to spread
unrest. They were "safe" crimes, if you will. Annoying, irritating,
certainly not good for the community, but not important enough
to warrant a full-scale investigation. If this does turn out to be
murder, the villain is now in a much different position.'

'From yesterday, really. Those attacks on us. Stupid, unproductive, and risky for the guiding hand, whoever that may be.'

'Yes.' Alan ran a hand down the back of his head, a gesture
I knew meant he was thinking hard. 'Is it possible that Bub set
his goons on this woman as a punishment for their stupidity? Or
not exactly that.' He tented his fingers in lecture mode. 'We agree
he – or she, but one pronoun is easier – he didn't intend us to
be attacked, and he was almost certainly furious at his henchmen.
If he sent them out, then, to do something to further discredit
Silas, and if they encountered this woman walking alone, and
they had the means to harm her in a way that would simulate a
raptor attack, might they not be stupid enough to do it? Not

intending to kill, perhaps, only to hurt her badly enough that Silas would be . . . well, seriously inconvenienced, at best.'

'Alan, that makes sense! Bub would keep his hands clean, apparently, and if his goons got caught, well, it was only what they deserved after being so foolish about us. And then things went wrong again, and the woman died. So now Bub is doubly incensed. But Alan, why would anyone be so determined to get Silas in serious trouble? I mean, the release of his birds does fit in with what we think is the underlying purpose of the nastiness. But this latest horror seems directly aimed at that poor old man.'

'We're speculating ahead of our data, as Sherlock Holmes warned Watson never to do. I say again, we don't know that the victim was attacked by birds.'

'But we know, at least John knows, what it looked like,' I insisted, 'and when that gets out to the general public, Silas is in for it.'

'John said the RCMP posted a guard.'

'Right, and that will probably keep a mob from attacking him physically. But it won't stop the neighbours going to court and forcing the destruction of the hawks. And that means the destruction of Silas. He lives for those birds.'

Alan lifted his hands in the classic gesture of resignation and stood. 'We'd better go back to the car and call John for further orders. I think we've accomplished just about all we can here.'

Which is next to nothing, I thought. But I didn't say it out loud.

Alan placed the call, but it went to voice mail. 'So what now?' I asked, starting the car.

'Back home, I think. No, not to England. We could use a little time for reflection, don't you agree? We've been running as fast as we could, but rather like Alice.'

'Indeed. Not only staying in the same place, but sometimes going backwards. Oh, shut up!' This last was to Sadie, who was insisting that I turn into what was apparently a driveway.

She was right, of course, and I retraced my steps harbouring no good thoughts about electronic devices that were smarter than I.

I had just made it back to the condo, with Sadie's annoying help, when my phone rang. It was in my purse, so Alan obligingly pulled it out and answered it while I parked the car.

'No, you didn't get the number wrong. Dorothy was busy driving, but here she is.' He handed the phone to me. 'Amy.'

'Oh, I suppose she wants to know how things are going with the car and the house.' I answered as we walked inside. 'Hello?'

'Hello, Dorothy. No, that's not why I called, but how *are* things going, while we're on the subject?'

'The car's working out fine, though Sadie may drive me crazy! But she gets us where we're going, which is the main thing.'

'And the house? Any problems?'

'Not so far, except I'm not used to an electric stove, and Sue's such an amazing housekeeper that I live in terror of spilling something.'

'Good.'

She hadn't really been interested in the house or the car, had she? I waited for her to tell me why she called.

'Look, Dorothy.' She had lowered her voice. 'Can Alan hear what I'm saying?'

'No.' He had left the room, probably headed for the bathroom. We'd had quite a lot of coffee, and I needed to run that errand, myself. 'What's up?'

'I need to talk to you. Just you. Can you come to the library this afternoon? I'm at the Central Branch, right downtown, and there's a little room where we'd be quite private.'

'Sure. What should I tell Alan?' He was still out of earshot. I hoped.

'Just say it's a secret. Can you imply that I'm cooking up a surprise for John? Without actually saying so?'

Alan was back in the room. 'Sure, I can manage that,' I said into the phone.

'Good. In an hour or so, then?'

'Right.'

'What can you manage?' Alan nodded at the phone.

'Getting over to the library to see Amy. She wants to talk to me about . . . something.' I grinned and let my voice sound conspiratorial.

'You're up to something.'

'Of course. Right now I'm up to making sandwiches. I'm not hungry for much, after that pie, and Amy wants me there in an hour.'

'Just you, not both of us?'

'Just me. Ask me no questions and I'll tell you no lies. Ham or cheese, or both?'

It took me a moment to look up the library on my phone and find the address. Then I had Alan program it into the GPS, and I was off.

I'd tried to hide my anxiety in front of Alan, but I was sure he'd picked up on it. His natural talent for keen observation was honed by his police training, and we'd been married long enough to be pretty well attuned to each other.

On the whole I was happy to think he might smell a rat. If there should be trouble ahead, he'd be quicker to come to my rescue if he were already uneasy.

And why should I be thinking in those terms? There had been nothing in Amy's phone call to prompt such a response. Nothing, at least, except a certain tension I thought I detected in Amy's voice.

Balderdash! You don't know the woman at all, really. How can you tell her mood? And on the phone, yet!

And then, said that insidious inner voice that so annoys me, there's always the fact of the nastiness, up to and including murder, that seems to be surrounding us like a cloud. Of course that wouldn't make you nervous, would it?

'Shut up!'

This time it wasn't directed at Sadie, but she responded anyway, with a chilly little 'Excuse me. I didn't quite catch that.'

It's fortunate that God apparently ignores instructions issued in a fit of temper, or the entire electronics industry would at that point have fallen into the nether pit.

There was a handy parking garage very near the library. I hoped I had the right money to get myself out, but Amy could doubtless help if I didn't. I had to ask how to get out of the garage and up to the library, and found Amy waiting for me just inside the doors.

'There's a study room no one's using; we can be quite private there.'

She led the way. We closed the door and sat down, and I waited for her to begin.

'I suspect you think I'm being very melodramatic about all this,' she said with an attempt at a laugh. It wasn't very successful.

'I did wonder if something had happened. You sounded a bit strained.'

'Yes, well.' She looked down at her lap, then up at me again. 'I don't know how much John has told you about my former husband.'

Whatever I was expecting, it wasn't that. 'Very little, except that he was quite wealthy, working in the tech field, and that your divorce was not . . . um . . . amicable.'

Her smile was bitter. 'You could put it that way. Paul fought me every step of the way over the settlement. He could afford to hire a really good lawyer. I could not. He has millions in assets, perhaps billions by now. I had only my income. It is not inexpensive to live in Victoria.'

'Why, if you don't mind my asking, was he so difficult about the money? Unless you were asking for some exorbitant amount, it would surely have seemed insignificant to him.'

'It had nothing to do with the money. He had to win. He always has to win every battle. And this one was especially important, because it had to do with my rejection of him. That was simply not acceptable. He is the most egocentric person I have ever met.'

I guess she read my next question in my all-too-mobile face, because she shrugged and smiled that non-smile again. 'So why did I marry him? He can be very charming. I was flattered that he paid attention to me, because he was An Older Man, and he was so important. He is, you know. He throws his money around, supporting this, endowing that. Every good cause in the area looks to him as Santa Claus.'

'All right. I understand. What I don't understand is why you're telling me all this. I'm virtually a stranger.'

'But you've befriended John and me. You're living in my daughter's house and driving her car. You are connected with me, however tangentially. And that could make you a target of Paul's attention.'

I frowned. 'How would he know?'

'Oh, my dear! Nothing goes on in this town that he doesn't know. He has methodically cultivated contacts everywhere, and people tell him things. He's getting into politics, so he has a finger on the pulse of the community. John has been fairly visible in his investigation of the odd things that have been going on, so Paul certainly knows about that. I just . . . I'm uneasy. Paul is a vengeful person. Anyone who offends him is anathema, forever. I offended him. In fact, I defeated him, in the matter of the settlement, and also in the custody battle for our daughter. That was many years ago, but it still means that I am cast into the outer darkness, along with all my friends and acquaintances. And now that includes you and your husband.'

'And you didn't want Alan to hear all this. Why?'

'You're a woman. You would understand the way I feel. Alan might have brushed it off as the ramblings of an unbalanced woman.'

I shook my head. 'You don't know him, but I assure you he would not brush you off. Would John?'

'Well, no, but—'

'John is an experienced policeman. So is Alan. They've both seen just about every variety of human behaviour, much of it unpleasant. A senior policeman is as impossible to shock as a priest. They've heard it all. I can't speak for John, but Alan is almost infallible when it comes to judging character. May I tell him about our conversation? I seldom keep anything from him.'

'Oh, I never meant to ask you to hide it from him! I just thought it would sound more reasonable coming from you. Uh-oh!'

She was looking toward the room's glass door. I turned and saw a man walking toward the front lobby. I couldn't see his face, but he walked, strode, with the air of one who owns the world, exuding confidence.

'Paul?' It wasn't really a question.

She nodded. 'I hope he hasn't seen us.'

'Would it matter? If he already knows we're friends?'

'He'd know we weren't just chatting. For that you would have come to my office.'

'Ah. Point taken.' I stood. 'Well, my dear, it's time I got back to my husband and our mission. Take heart of grace, as some Gilbert and Sullivan heroine said. We'll be in touch.'

The man was still in the lobby, schmoozing with a couple of

women at the front desk. I remembered the line about the best defence being a good offense, and walked up to him. 'I'm sorry, I don't mean to interrupt, but I've just been talking with I believe your former wife? We haven't met, but you are Paul Hartford, are you not?'

I was nearly undone when he turned to face me. He was, without doubt, the handsomest man I'd ever seen off the screen. And he would outdo most of Hollywood, at that. Bronzed face, piercing blue eyes, hair just touched with grey at the temples, a dazzling smile.

Tanning bed, I told myself, firmly building up resistance. Contact lenses. Touch up job on the hair. Dental implants.

Those blue eyes did a quick scan. I had the uneasy feeling that my appearance was now filed in his brain, under Antagonist. 'And you . . . you must be Amy's new friend from the States.' Charming voice, too.

'Via England, but yes. Dorothy Martin.' I put out my hand, and he took it in a warm, firm grasp. Not a knuckle-crusher, not limp. Perfect. Practiced.

I seldom dislike anyone at sight. I wondered if my reaction would have been the same if Amy hadn't warned me, and decided that it probably would. I mistrust charm, and this man laid it on with a trowel.

'But this is delightful!' The smile, incredibly, brightened by a few megawatts. 'I have been longing to meet you and your husband.'

That was a mistake. A minor one, but it pleased me that the man showed some signs of human frailty. 'Oh? How is it you knew about us? Neither of us knows much of anybody in the world of computer technology, certainly not in this part of the world. Amy did say that's where you work?'

His smile dimmed again. 'Yes, in a manner of speaking. I own a concern that's working in AI. Artificial Intelligence,' he added, patronizingly.

'Yes, I am familiar with the term.'

'As for how I learned of your visit, I really can't recall. Victoria is not a big city. One hears things.'

'I'm sure. Rather like my city in England. Except there, of

course, everything revolves around two centres of information, the Cathedral and the university. Human Intelligence, genuine intelligence, I suppose one could say.'

His eyes shifted from my face to something behind me. 'Ah, James! If you'll excuse me, Mrs Martin, I must just—'

I smiled and turned away. Plainly someone more important had turned up, and I could make my escape.

THIRTEEN

'Really, I don't know where I came up with such an acid tongue,' I said to Alan as we sat around the kitchen table sipping tea and I finished describing my encounter with Hartford. I had not minced words. 'Something about that man brought out the worst in me.'

'You've never liked obviously charming men. Except for me, of course.' He raised his teacup in a salute.

'You're not charming. Not in that sense. You're real. You've always cared more about other people than about yourself, and you don't waste time planning how to impress them. Which means that, in the end, you do impress them.'

He was embarrassed, as Englishmen usually are by a compliment. He grunted something and finished his tea before he spoke again. 'At any rate, I hope Mr Hartford wasn't offended. If Amy is right about him, he might be a bad enemy.'

'But he's already our enemy, if Amy's right. She may not be. A woman is seldom completely impartial about a man who has treated her badly. No, what worries me is that I might have made him reassess me as an adversary.'

Alan cocked an eyebrow.

'I mean, if he thought I was a doddering old lady from Hicksville USA, he doesn't think so anymore. I think I may have been too smart-alecky for my own good, but he riled me. *So* condescending.'

'But smart enough to catch your innuendos?'

'Oh, he caught them, all right. And resented them, and I'm sure filed them away for future action.'

Alan tossed it away. 'Never mind. One testy bloke isn't our problem right now. I'm going to try again to call John and find out if there's any news.'

This time John was available. Alan put him on the speaker so I could hear, too.

'I'm afraid there's not a whole lot of progress to report. Of course I'm not official anymore, so I can't demand information, but the Mountie in charge of the investigation is being kind. And

I truly hate to say this, but the victim has been positively identified as the woman you mentioned. Her name – her English
name – was Elizabeth George.'

I had to swallow hard before I could ask, 'And her people
have been informed?'

'Yes. Once the coroner had a probable ID from her dental work,
he called her parents. Her father came in and identified the body.'

'That must be the hardest thing any parent would ever have
to do. Your kids aren't supposed to die before you do. And they
were so proud of her . . .' I couldn't go on.

'How are the family taking it?'

'It's hard to tell. The Cowichans don't readily let their emotions
show, especially in front of white people. They are a proud people,
and they have suffered endless persecution from the invaders.
They have learned to endure.'

Alan had to swallow a couple of times himself. 'And has the
coroner determined the cause of her wounds?'

'Not with any certainty, except that he has ruled out any kind
of avian attack. They didn't tell me everything that was said, but
apparently the placement and nature of the gashes left the coroner
quite certain. Also – Dorothy, you won't like this, either – he found
a head wound consistent with a blow from something hard and
round. Probably a rock. It could not have been caused by her fall.'

'Then . . . it was murder.'

'Dorothy, love, you know medical examiners don't draw that sort
of conclusion. They observe and report what they see. The police
then make inferences from what the medical evidence tells them.'

'Right.' I was annoyed by what I considered nit-picking. Which
was probably why Alan said it. Like most men, he becomes
extremely uncomfortable in the presence of a crying woman, and
he especially hates to see *me* cry. He's discovered that anger will
almost always drive away my tears. 'Blast it, I know that. But
I'm not with the police, so I'm allowed to make inferences and
draw conclusions all I want, and I say that poor woman was
murdered. And I hope a particularly hot fire is being prepared
in hell for whoever did it!'

'Doubtless it is. And doubtless Lucifer, or whoever is in charge
in that realm, knows who's going to end up in that fire. It would
be helpful if we had any ideas ourselves.'

I don't know what triggered it, but an idea began to take shape in my brain. No, idea was too strong a word. A vague notion, a link. 'John, now that they know who the woman was, do they know who she worked for?'

'Dorothy, it took me a couple of hours to think of that question, and you come up with it first crack out of the box! Yes. She worked for AIntell. Paul Hartford's firm.'

'There could be no connection at all.' Alan's voice sounded weary. He'd said the same thing, in various words, several times already.

We were gathered on John's patio, tall cool drinks in front of us, watching the evening turn from pearl to amethyst and hashing over everything we knew and surmised about the death of pretty, bright, ambitious, young Elizabeth George. I'd stopped saying 'What a waste!' every five minutes. I couldn't stop thinking it.

'Very well, we know that Paul Hartford is not a pleasant person,' Alan went on. 'In fact, he is a distinctly unpleasant man under that veneer of charm.'

'Which hoodwinks most people,' said John grimly. 'Especially women.'

'Yes. And we know that Miss George worked for him. That doesn't prove they knew each other. How many employees does Hartford have, John?'

'Maybe three hundred. It's a fairly large outfit, as tech companies go.'

'So he wouldn't necessarily have known the woman, unless she was in the higher echelons.' Alan ran a hand down the back of his head, always a sign of frustration.

'No. And that's where you two might help. Someone needs to do some digging, find out more about Miss George and her position in the company, and any possible ties to Hartford. The RCMP have their hands full. Not only are they short-staffed, but last night a large shipment of drugs was seized, coming in by ferry from the mainland. Every possible resource is working on that case. Do you think you could nose around AIntell, talk to people, see what you can find out? I can't, of course. Hartford hates me with a passion, and I confess I'm not too fond of him, either. He'd have me thrown out of the building before I put a second foot through the door.'

'But he knows us, too,' I objected. 'At least he knows me. He memorized my face in about a second. He'd know me again, for sure. And he knows Alan is here with me, and he'd smell a very large rat if we came to his office.'

'I'm not sure that matters, Dorothy,' said Alan thoughtfully. 'He already knows we're a nuisance. We're connected with John and Amy; therefore we're on The Other Side. If he has nothing to hide, he might be pleased that we took the trouble to come and admire his business. We might be so impressed that we'd change our minds and join the ranks of his sycophants. If on the other hand he is in fact up to something nefarious, he would be certain that his minions would deal with the problem. If I'm reading his character properly, he thinks he's invincible.'

'You're absolutely right about that,' said John. 'All the same, you could be walking into danger. I shouldn't have asked. Forget it. We'll find another way.'

'No.' I spoke more sharply than I had intended. I modified my tone. 'John, we came here to help. This is the first venue where we might really be of use. The company headquarters is located actually in Victoria?'

'Yes, near the university. UVic, that is. But—'

'No buts.' This time it was Alan speaking decisively. 'Dorothy is quite right. This is a very civilized city in a civilized country. I find it hard to believe that we could come to any real harm among the cubicles. We'll start first thing tomorrow. Oh, confound it, that's Saturday. Will they be open?'

'There won't be a full staff, but the offices will be open for business.'

We went home soon after that, decided we weren't in need of a meal, and went gloomily to bed.

When morning came, I was somewhat less enthusiastic about our mission. I couldn't help remembering those cold blue eyes. 'He's a ruthless man, Alan. I don't look forward to this.'

'Chin up, old girl. This is an opportunity for you to use two of your famous gifts. Where are my shirts?'

'The same place they were yesterday, in the closet. What gifts?'

'Ah, found them. First, your renowned ability to strike up a conversation with strangers and turn them into instant friends.'

'Mmm. But I don't know a thing about the more esoteric limits of technology.'

'And you can use that. Claim you're uninformed but enthusiastic, and ask for enlightenment. And that brings me to your other unparalleled talent, that of thinking up believable lies.'

That made me laugh, as Alan probably intended. 'I admit I've never minded lying in a good cause. Now let's see. Why are we going to visit this place, we who know nothing about AI and care less?' I thought for a moment. 'Oh, that's it! We're feeling left out of things. The world is passing us by. We want . . . no, we need to be up to speed on the world of technology. Because . . . um. Because your grandchildren know so much more than we do, and it's humiliating. And because we want to take back some advanced ideas, back to England, to . . . to help the Cathedral with some data-management problems. How's that?'

'I'm not sure AI is used in data management.'

'Then that makes our claim of ignorance that much more believable. Though in my case, at least, that part of it is Gospel truth. And throwing in the Cathedral makes us sound so ultra-respectable.'

'Dorothy, I do love you! The picture you invoke, tossing the Cathedral about . . . and before we've even had our coffee. Let's remedy that omission and get cracking.'

The AIntell building was impressive, at least from the outside. Four storeys high, white stone, with large blue glass windows that made the whole thing look a little like a striped toy. 'Cold,' I remarked to Alan.

'You're projecting your feelings.'

'My feet are certainly cold,' I admitted.

Alan opened the door for me and gestured me in. 'Lights, camera, action,' he murmured.

'I'm not ready for my close-up yet, Mr DeMille.'

Alan gave me a gentle push, and I found myself standing in front of a security desk manned by an unsmiling guard.

'Your name, please?'

I wasn't prepared for that, and stammered for a moment, wildly trying to come up with an alias. But what if he asked for identification? I turned the stammer into a cough and gave him my real name.

He looked at the computer screen. 'I'm not finding your name, Ms Martin. Did you have an appointment?'

Worse and worse. Why had it never occurred to me that such a business would have elaborate security protocols? 'Oh, dear,' I said, affecting as English an accent as I could manage. 'I'm frightfully sorry. We didn't realize we'd need an appointment. Actually I'm just here to learn a little about Artificial Intelligence – is that the right term? My church back in England, Sherebury Cathedral – perhaps you've heard of it?'

'No, ma'am.'

'Oh, well, anyway, they're working out new systems of data management, and though I know almost nothing about computers, I read somewhere that your company is very highly thought of in the tech industry, and I thought I might talk to someone and perhaps take back a business card, or . . . or something.'

The guard just looked at me.

'And I brought my husband – this is my husband Alan – I brought him along for moral support.' I giggled. 'I suppose you can tell I'm scared to death. I'm really out of my depth here.' And that, as an old aunt of mine used to say, was more truth than poetry. I was trying hard not to shake.

'I see.' The guard looked us over. 'This is not our usual procedure, but we do occasionally give guests a tour of the facilities. If you'll give me your bag to search, ma'am, and if you will both step through the metal detector, I'll call someone to take you through.'

'Oh, that's so kind of you! And will our guide be someone who can answer my questions? They may be very stupid ones, I'm afraid.'

'Don't worry. I'm sure she'll be very helpful.'

The guard by now was bored with us, having decided we were stupid and harmless. He was thorough in his examination of my handbag, though, and with my passport right there on top, I was very glad I hadn't lied about my name or residence.

By the time we'd gone through the scanner, a young woman had appeared. 'These are the people who want to learn something about our operation here,' said the guard, only just managing not to sneer.

So far I wasn't overly impressed with Paul Hartford's employees. Helpfulness and courtesy did not appear to be high on the list of company values.

The young woman was something of an improvement. Dangling around her neck was a badge proclaiming her to be Teresa Betz. She was in her late twenties, I estimated. Her face was pleasant, but wore an expression I couldn't quite read. At least she didn't scowl at us.

She managed a smile as she handed us guest badges. 'I'm happy to show you around and answer your questions as best I can, but I'm just a secretary. I don't know a lot about the actual work the techies do.'

'Oh, that's fine.' That's perfect, I wanted to say, since I don't want information about the actual work. 'I'm a computer dunce myself. I just need to learn enough to know whether AIntell can be of help to my church.'

'Where did you say you're from?' she asked as we left the security area and went down a hallway lined on either side with doors.

Oops! I'd let the English accent slip a little. Here where everyone talked almost like the people I grew up with, it was hard not to revert. 'England now, Sherebury, in Belleshire. But I'm from Indiana originally. Have you always lived here?'

'No, I'm from a small town in Manitoba. I came here to work for AIntell, because I couldn't find a good job where I lived, and they pay well here. I don't know, though. Now . . . oh, we're passing the offices of most of the programmers. I can't let you see what they're doing, because some of it's really secret, but you can look in one of the offices.'

'Oh, my. Secret as in government secrets?'

'No, no. Just industrial secrets. AI is a really important, growing field, you know, and there is a lot of competition as to who will solve some of the problems first, that sort of thing.'

She knocked on one of the doors and asked if visitors could come in. The woman at the desk pushed a key that, I assumed, darkened her screen, and nodded.

'There's nothing much to see,' the woman said. 'You've seen one computer station, you've seen them all.'

That was plainly true. Except that her screen was bigger than most I'd seen, her office looked exactly like my little cubbyhole at home, where I wrote letters and looked up stuff and played far too many games of FreeCell. 'It's a lot neater, though,' I commented. 'Most seem to be way more cluttered.'

'That's company policy,' said the woman with a grin, 'and it's a pain in the neck. We have to keep our working materials safely stashed away in the desk except when we actually need to use a piece of information. Wastes a lot of time.'

'Oh, and we're wasting your time now,' I said. 'I did want to ask, though: is there a brochure somewhere that describes the services AIntell offers?' I launched into my cover story, and she reached into a drawer and handed me a glossy booklet.

'Our most recent annual report,' she said.

'Oh, but don't you need it?'

'If you've ever read an annual report, you know the answer to that. Besides, I can get another if I should want one.'

I thanked her and we turned to leave. Just as we headed out the door, I heard her say, quietly, 'Are you all right, Teresa?'

I didn't hear her answer, but when she herded Alan and me out the door, I saw tears welling in her eyes.

'Teresa, I don't mean to pry, but I can see that something's wrong. Is there any way I can help?'

'I'm sorry. I didn't mean to . . . it's just that someone close to me – my best friend, actually – she died yesterday, and now—' Her grief choked her.

'My dear, I'm so sorry. Would you like to forget about our tour? I think you may need some time to pull yourself together.'

'No, it's all right.' She sniffled; I handed her a tissue. 'But maybe we could go get a cup of coffee or something? The canteen's not too bad, and it'll be nearly empty this early. Mostly people don't take a break till around ten thirty or eleven.'

I shot a guilty look at Alan. I felt like a monster, encouraging this poor child to talk. I had very strong suspicions that the person she was mourning was the murder victim, and Teresa ought to be home letting the tears flow. I quirked an eyebrow at Alan. Should I go on with this?

He made the tiniest of nods. Well, then, we'd be monsters together. How sweet.

The canteen, as predicted, was deserted. Everything was self-serve, so Alan fetched us three cups of coffee and three doughnuts that had seen fresher days. They would suffice for dunking, though, and Teresa needed the sugar, though we certainly didn't.

'Would it help to talk about it, Teresa?' asked Alan gently. 'I have daughters, myself, and sometimes crying on my shoulder used to make them feel a little better.'

She tried to smile. 'You're very kind. I don't usually get so soppy. It's just that . . . well, I didn't find it really easy to make friends here. I'm a Métis, you see. If you know what that means.'

'You have a heritage that includes First Nations people. Am I right?'

'Yes. My grandfather, my mother's father, was a Cree. Manitoba has a lot of indigenous people, even still. My grand-father was a wonderful man, strong but gentle. Back when he was young, the Cree were–were sometimes not treated very well. There was a good deal of bitterness, on both sides, when he fell in love with and married my grandmother. Things are better now, but . . . anyway, I thought when I moved here, I could make my own way, but there are still barriers. Subtle, but real. So until I met Elizabeth, I was pretty lonely. She understood. She was brilliant and funny and beautiful, and she was a full-blooded Cowichan, so she knew—'

I handed Teresa another tissue. I could hardly speak myself.

Alan went on, gently but without overt sympathy. He knew from years of talking to the families of crime victims that too much sympathy could hurt as much as too little. 'Your friend was a co-worker, then?'

'Yes, didn't I say? Not a co-worker, exactly. She was way up in the company, a senior programmer, reporting to Mr Hartford himself, and I'm just a peon. That's one reason it was so great that she was nice to me.' Teresa blew her nose and tried to smile. 'I don't know what made me tell you all that. I'm so sorry. We'd better get on with our tour, or someone will catch me loafing.'

FOURTEEN

I thought there was now very little reason for us to continue, and I was more and more uneasy about running into Paul Hartford, but Alan signalled silently that it was best we see it through. So we followed Teresa from the canteen.

There were washrooms just outside the door. I detoured into one, claiming urgent need. Which was true. At my age it almost always is. But I also wanted to suggest that Teresa wash her face in cold water to help remove the signs of crying. 'I wouldn't want anyone to think we've been bullying you, my dear,' I said, trying to sound as if my image was my chief concern.

The cold water helped. So did Alan's matter-of-fact conversation as we traversed corridors that seemed identical. He asked about artificial intelligence. He asked about applications of the technology. He asked about working conditions in the company, about community life in Victoria, about anything that came into his head. Teresa answered as best she could. I still didn't understand anything at all about AI, but Teresa had calmed down, which was the important thing.

Finally she stopped at an elevator and pushed the call button. 'The executive offices are on the top floor. They're really impressive, and there's an awesome view of Victoria and the harbour.'

Panicky, I looked at Alan. He consulted his watch and opened his mouth, but Teresa continued, 'It's a pity you can't meet Mr Hartford. He's very nice and always glad to greet visitors. But he's away all day today.' Her lip curled. 'It's for a meeting with one of the charities he supports. He's always endowing this or contributing for that. He does so much good for the community! But there's this woman – everyone says she's out to catch him. I can't stand her. She's on most of the charity boards, too, so she sees him a lot. She's too rich, too beautiful, too . . . everything. I don't understand why he doesn't see through her. She's a predatory woman!'

'Oh, dear. What a pity, if Mr Hartford is such a pleasant man.'

'He's too nice. He just can't see that she's got her claws into him.'

'How did you meet this siren?' asked Alan mildly.

'Oh, I've never met her. I've *seen* her, once when Mr Hartford brought her here for a company gala. Tall, blonde, gorgeous. The best face and figure money can buy. Jewels, designer clothes. I can see why most men would be swept off their feet. But Mr Hartford is smarter than that. Elizabeth tells me – used to tell me . . .' She swallowed, but she had herself under control. 'Here's the elevator.'

The executive suite was all that one might expect. I didn't anticipate being allowed into Hartford's actual office, of course, but the outer offices were certainly impressive. I could imagine potential clients being intimidated by the splendour and virtually hypnotized into accepting a deal a little less favourable than they had planned.

To my surprise, though, Teresa persuaded the decorative receptionist to open Hartford's door and let us peek in.

It was much as I had expected. Everything lush, expensive, rather daunting. There was about an acre of desk, set at an angle so Hartford could look at whoever came in, but also could enjoy the view, which was indeed magnificent. The desk was clean and empty save for a photograph in a silver frame.

I raised my eyebrows at Teresa in silent question. *The Siren?*

She nodded almost imperceptibly.

We left, but not before I'd noted the flamboyant signature scrawled across the photograph: Alexis.

'She would have a name like that, wouldn't she?' I commented to Alan when we had made it back to the car.

'Now be reasonable, dear heart. You can't blame her for the name her parents chose for her.'

'I don't feel like being reasonable. Alan, that poor girl!'

My husband is accustomed to following my sometimes convoluted thought processes. 'Teresa. Yes. She's terribly unhappy. I feel almost worse for her than for Elizabeth's family. They have their tribe and their traditions for comfort. Teresa is alone, and far from home.'

'Do you suppose she knows she was murdered?'

'I don't see how she could. That information has not been made public, and won't be.'

'But that means Silas will be blamed!'

'No. I guess I didn't tell you. You know the police often with-hold critical information. Things only the murderer would know, in the hopes that the villain will give himself away. John told me a careful press release has been prepared saying that Miss George's injuries are not consistent with an attack by any native bird, and that a search is being made for a bird that may have been kept as an exotic pet. That's not a lie, by the way. Someone's cockatiel got loose a few days ago, and it is being looked for. Not in connection with Elizabeth George, of course, but the police can't be blamed for what the public infer.'

'Devious.'

'We have to be. We're dealing with a ruthless killer.'

If I hadn't been feeling so depressed I would have smiled. Alan hadn't even realized he had identified himself with the police working the case. An old fire horse . . .

'Do you think you can find the way home, love?' he went on. 'We have a good deal of thinking to do, and I for one could use some good coffee. Paul Hartford may be a generous employer, but his canteen coffee is beyond dreadful.'

I made coffee, good coffee in a French press, and the fragrance made me feel a bit better. There was still some shortbread left, and the snack helped restore some balance to my mind.

'I presume,' said Alan, leaning forward and tenting his fingers, 'that you brought along your trusty notebook.'

'Of course. Where did I put my purse?'

Alan eventually found it in the bathroom, where it certainly had no business to be. He brought it to me and I fished out notebook and pen. 'Though I don't know what I'm going to write down. My mind is a hodgepodge of emotions, with very little that makes sense.'

'Ah. I thought you were too upset to notice much. And it is upsetting, I agree.'

'It's miserable. The whole thing.'

'Yes. But you need to stop wallowing and start thinking. In short, get busy, love!'

His tone ticked me off. I glared at him.

He grinned back. 'Worked, didn't it?'

'Alan Nesbitt, sometimes you make me so mad I could—'

'Yes, I know. But you're not feeling quite so wretched, are you?'

I maintained a dignified silence.

'Good. Now let's think about what we learned this morning. Our little tour was quite interesting, don't you think?'

'Hmph! We found out about Paul Hartford's fancy piece, if you think that's interesting.'

'I think it is, actually. I could stand to know a bit more about her, but if she's on the board of several charities, that shouldn't be too difficult. One look at, say, a symphony program listing benefactors should give us her last name.'

'Well, there can't be too many Alexises, I wouldn't think. Drat the name. You can't even make it plural easily. Alexi?' I made a note: check donor lists.

'And then there's the fact that Hartford certainly knew Elizabeth George,' Alan went on. 'Did you notice the unoccupied office up on the royal tier, near Hartford's suite?'

'I wasn't actually noticing a great deal,' I muttered.

Alan patted my hand. 'Never mind. You're not used to this sort of thing. One never becomes hardened to the tragedy, but I did learn to compartmentalize, set my feelings aside while I was working, and fall to bits later, if I had to. Usually it was when there was a child involved.'

That brought me out of my mood. I shivered. 'Oh, Alan! And all those years after Helen died and you were alone, I can't imagine how hard it must have been.' I took a deep breath. 'Well. So there was an empty office. You think it was Elizabeth's?'

'I do. It was the next but one to Hartford's. It hadn't been cleared out, and there were a few pictures and so on that looked like the work of indigenous artists. And there was a large bouquet of roses. Wilting in the wastebasket.'

I tried to think what that meant. 'Um. They were past their prime and Elizabeth threw them out, and no one has cleaned up the office yet.'

'Some of the roses were still in bud.'

'Oh. So the cleaning staff threw them out – no, that won't work. A cleaner would have taken them away.'

'Almost anyone would have taken them away once Elizabeth had no further use for them. They were lovely, expensive flowers. No, what I think is that they were a gift from someone Elizabeth didn't care for, and she discarded them immediately.'

'You think Hartford?'

'Why not? We know he was a womanizer. There's the Siren, of course, but if rumour is to be trusted, she is pursuing him. Most men prefer to do the pursuing. Elizabeth was an attractive woman, and she was in constant contact with him.'

'That does make sense. And she rejected him, so he killed her?'

Alan shook his head. 'That seems weak. Yes, he would be a man who would not take rejection lightly. But not to the extent of murder. No, I think there's something else behind this. And I remind you that all this is pure speculation.'

'Maybe the Siren killed her. A woman scorned, jealous of a rival for Hartford's affections.'

'Perhaps. But remembering that face, does Alexis look like a woman who would ever be jealous of another woman?'

I had to admit that she did not.

'I'm going to call John and report what we've learned. The facts, not the speculation.' Alan permitted himself a wry smile. 'I don't envy Hartford when the RCMP come to question him.'

'I don't envy the cops,' I retorted. 'That man is dangerous, Alan.'

Neither of us was hungry for lunch, having eaten sweet stuff all morning, but we needed groceries to eke out the bare necessities we'd purchased earlier. While we were out, we bought a couple of newspapers, the *Globe and Mail*, a national paper, and the local *Times Colonist*. On the way home Alan opened the latter. 'Oh, my,' he said. 'His Nibs has entered the realm of politics. "Paul Hartford, owner and CEO of AIntell, Inc., has announced his candidacy as a Member of Parliament for Victoria. This is his first official entry into the political realm, but he has been active in the Conservative party for some time and is well known both here and in Ottawa as a rising party leader. Locally, he is a major benefactor of the Victoria Symphony; last year AIntell was a major sponsor of

Symphony Splash. Among other contributions to the community are his support of the UVic athletic program and his endowment of many scholarships, particularly to students in technology programs. In a statement opening his campaign, Hartford said, 'I believe I can help to make this lovely city an even better place to live. We need to control the petty crime that is marring the sense of peace in our beautiful community, and we must also deal with the major problems of homelessness and drug abuse. In a few days I will outline the steps I propose to take to solve these and other issues, in order to benefit the citizens of our wonderful home.'" Then it goes on to name his other benefactions, a long list. And what do you think of that, my dear?'

'I think I'm glad I don't live here. I'd just as soon vote for Attila the Hun. Or perhaps I do wish I lived here, so I could vote against him.'

'And *I* think he's a very clever man. We've worked it out, haven't we? Without even realizing it. Knowing now about his political ambitions, and his general nastiness, the pattern emerges. Hartford's at the bottom of the disturbances. He creates a problem and then promises to solve it. He may have a little harder time with drugs and homelessness, though. Presumably he didn't create those problems.'

'I wouldn't put it past him.' I gave the steering wheel an angry whack; the car veered and Alan reached over and steadied the wheel.

'Easy, love. Perhaps you might wait till we get home to express your fury?'

'Do you know what I want to do? Besides throw a full-blown temper tantrum, I mean? I want to talk to Amy and see what she thinks about all this.'

'That is an excellent idea. Do we have enough in the way of provisions to invite her to dinner? Or perhaps her and John?'

I took a mental inventory of our recent purchases. 'Everything except dessert, I think. But there's ice cream, and maybe John knows someplace where he could pick up some fruit. Berries, for choice, if there are any ripe ones yet.'

I got busy in the kitchen as soon as we reached the condo, while Alan called John with the invitation for him and Amy.

'We're in luck,' he reported back. 'The early strawberries are just in, and John will pick some up on his way to get Amy.'

'Great. Then I'll make some shortcake. A pity I didn't buy whipping cream, but the ice cream will do nicely. Though I would have enjoyed whipping up the cream. By hand!'

'You could attack some bread dough,' he said helpfully.

'No time. I can attack the chicken with the cleaver, though.'

'I believe,' he said, 'seeing the way your mind is working, that I'll retire to the safety of the living room and read the papers.'

'Coward!'

By the time I had the chicken nicely simmering with wine and herbs and other good things, my temper was under control. Hacking away with the heavy cleaver had indeed been therapeutic, though I thought I'd have to buy Sue a new cutting board. And I'd thought out what I wanted to ask John and Amy.

I put some new potatoes on to boil just as our guests arrived, and we settled down with drinks while the coq au vin finished cooking. 'We've learned some very interesting things,' said Alan, 'but they're not the sort to serve as a first course. Can we think of something pleasant to talk about before dinner?'

'There's always the weather,' said Amy, 'but the trouble is, in summer it's always delightful here, so that topic gets boring. Let's see. They're having sales at a lot of the stores in Mayfair Mall, if you're interested in some bargains in clothes.'

'I'm always interested in bargains,' I said, 'but at my age and figure I don't get wildly enthusiastic about clothes. Although I did buy a gorgeous Cowichan sweater in Duncan. I'd never heard of them before, but they're amazing.'

John and Amy agreed, and that did it for that subject. Silence fell.

'Something smells wonderful,' said John, a little desperately.

'Coq au vin,' I replied. 'One of the things I've made so often I don't need a recipe anymore. And it's almost ready, so I'd better dish it up, and we can give up on trying to avoid what we all want to talk about. Alan, could you set the table, please? I'm sure Amy can help you find whatever you need.'

FIFTEEN

When we were seated, John, unexpectedly, raised his glass. 'I'd like to propose a toast,' he said without a trace of a smile. 'To the truth and those who seek it!' We were all happy to drink to that. 'You shall know the truth, and the truth shall make you free.'

I hadn't realized I had said it aloud until Alan murmured, 'Amen.'

I turned red. Any discussion even remotely connected with religion is almost certain to offend or embarrass someone, and I truly hadn't meant to speak my thought. But Amy smiled at me. 'I might not have put it quite that way, but you're absolutely right. I lived with lies and deception the whole time I was married to Paul. It was exactly like being in prison. A comfortable, well-furnished, plush prison. So yes, here's to you, Dorothy and Alan and John, and everyone else who's trying to free Victoria from the chains of dishonesty and corruption.'

Now that the subject had come up, I was suddenly eager to talk about it. 'Amy, maybe I shouldn't ask, and tell me to shut up if you want, but why did you divorce Paul? I mean, besides the fact that he was intolerable as a husband.'

'The final straw was the usual one, the Other Woman. Or women, actually. He was a very attractive man. Still is, for that matter, if you don't know what's behind the smile. That, and his money, drew them like flies to honey. He was discreet about it at first, but then he took to squiring his lady friends to the charity events he loved to sponsor, flaunting them while I stayed home to look after his daughter. He thought I was so besotted, and so dependent on him, that I wouldn't dare protest. He was wrong.'

'But didn't that obvious infidelity upset those charitable organizations? I would have thought a certain moral tone would—'

Three pitying looks stopped me.

'Dorothy, my dear, a fair amount of slime is often papered over by good deeds,' Alan said gently. 'The end justifying the means. You don't suppose every contributor to charity is doing it to support the cause!'

'Of course I don't! I'm not that naïve! Tax deductions play a big part.'

John shook his head. 'For small donors, individuals, yes. And of course a business will welcome anything it can use to reduce its taxes. But image-building can be far more important. Paul Hartford's image has always been very important to him. He loves big powerful cars, but he bikes to work, to prove how conscious he is of environmental issues.'

'But that's just what I'm saying! Wouldn't all this womanizing spoil the benevolent image he was trying to cultivate?'

'You have to remember who runs the big charities,' said Amy. 'If a man is the chairman of the board, probably he either doesn't care about the morals of donors, or is envious. As for the women – and most of the big guns are women – they just thought that poor Paul had a little wife who'd let motherhood turn her into a drudge, so he had every right to escort someone decorative to the fundraisers. And the beautiful ones probably had dreams of being at his side the next time.'

I finished my glass of wine. 'The more I hear about that man, the less I like him. I suppose you've both known about his political ambitions long before it came out in the paper today.'

John sighed. 'No specifics, but as the paper said, he's been cosying up to the Tories for quite some time. Nobody can prove it, but nobody on the right side of the law would be a bit surprised to learn he's been offering tech help for voter manipulation. You Americans don't have a monopoly in political corruption, you know.'

I sighed. 'I hate to disavow my homeland, but honestly, sometimes I'm really glad I'm officially English now. And before you say what you were about to say, yes, I do know British politics aren't immune, either. I just . . . I suppose I'm an ostrich, but I'd rather not know. Alan will tell you I stand and cry every time I look at the Palace of Westminster, just because it's the home of Parliament, and thus of democratic government. And I know it isn't the original building, and I know not everything that goes on there is admirable, but I get sentimental about it anyway. So sue me.'

'"Without vision, the people perish." Whoever wrote the Proverbs had the right idea. You hang onto your idealism, my love. Just temper it, from time to time, with a bit of realism.' Alan smiled and poured me a little more wine.

'I confess to a certain tendency to idealism myself,' said John. 'Even years with the police haven't knocked it out of me. Along with greed and hatred and all the rest of the sins that you uncover in the slime, you also find genuinely good people, the ones who live their lives by the rules and try to help where they can.'

'But are they in the minority? It often feels like the slime is winning.' The hard knot was back in my stomach. I put down my fork.

'No!' John's voice rose. 'Sorry. Didn't mean to shout. But I have to make it clear: no, the slime is powerful, and its actions – their actions – make the headlines. But the quiet people will win in the end. There are more decent people in the world than thugs. If I didn't believe that, I couldn't go on fighting the battles.'

'And you do go on, even though you've retired,' said Amy. 'No one's paying you to fight the slime, to put yourself in jeopardy, but you keep on. Sometimes I wonder if I fell in love with Don Quixote.'

'Oh, definitely,' John replied. 'Isn't that a windmill I see out there?'

That lightened the mood considerably, and we talked about Cervantes' wonderfully batty hero through the rest of the meal.

But after we'd polished off the strawberry shortcake and I'd made a pot of decaf, I brought up the subject again. 'I really hate to do this, but I – we – need to know more about Paul and his world. I have no understanding of the super-rich, nor of the power-hungry.'

'Power-hungry, right,' said John. His smile held no amusement. 'We call him pH. For Paul Hartford, and power-hungry, but also for the acidity scale. Actually, pH0, because that's the most acidic you can get. Battery acid. We pronounce it Foe, which seems appropriate.'

John and Amy looked at each other. Amy began. 'Dorothy, you have to understand we can't offer an unbiased opinion. Any picture we try to draw of the man will be coloured by the damage he's inflicted on me and my daughter.'

'And on me,' John added, 'not only second-hand but directly. I've always tried to believe there's good in everyone, but if there's any in Mr Paul Hartford, I've never found it.'

'Why?'

They all looked at me.

'I mean, why is he the way he is? Granted he's thoroughly nasty, guilty of every sin in the calendar, and a danger to humanity – and I think he probably is all those things – but why? What made him the way he is? I'm not looking to excuse him, but sometimes understanding a person can make it easier to deal with him. Find his vulnerable spot, and use it.'

Amy shivered. 'His vulnerable spot is his ego. That's obvious. He has to be the best, the finest, the biggest, the most important. When that superiority is questioned, he flies into a fury, and at that point, he's totally irrational. I think, you know, it actually goes back to his childhood.' She looked at John.

'Most things do, for most people, I think,' he responded. 'Raise a child sensibly, with lots of love but also firm discipline, and most of the time you'll end up with a well-balanced adult. In Paul's case, none of that happened. His father was wealthy, so Paul had every material thing that he needed or wanted, but almost no parental guidance. He was sent off to school at the first possible opportunity. Not in BC, of course – way off in Ontario, almost on the American border. No expense spared. No guidance given.'

'That's not quite true, John. Paul never talked about his child-hood, except once early in our marriage, when he'd had too much to drink and got maudlin. He said his father scrutinized his school reports, and jumped on every comment that was even slightly uncomplimentary, every grade below one hundred per cent. I don't think he beat the child physically, only with words. Which can hurt far more, of course.'

'And was he praised for the excellent reports?' I had a sick feeling I knew the answer.

'Of course not. Stellar work was simply what was expected. Anything else was unacceptable. So of course, since diligence won him no rewards, he went off the rails whenever possible. Drink, drugs, women – even then. He had a car, something fast and expensive, and zoomed all over Canada getting into trouble. And Daddy raged and raved – and protected him from the law, because no son of his was going to rot in jail with the common people.'

Alan and I shook our heads in unison. 'I think I have my answer,' I said, a catch in my voice. 'If he'd been beaten, he would probably have become a child abuser himself.'

'Oh, he did,' said Amy flatly. 'The same way he was abused. With words. That was the other big reason I left him. I'm tough. I could take it. But it took years of counselling for Sue to stop being afraid of everything. She never knew, when she was little, when something she would say or do would bring down the wrath of her father.'

'But she's all right now?' I asked anxiously.

'She's better. She has more self-confidence. She's learned that she's bright and capable, and can make intelligent decisions, and all that. I got her away almost in time, before she hit adolescence. But she's nearly thirty now, and has never had a serious boyfriend. Or girlfriend, come to that. I think she's afraid to love anyone, lest she be betrayed.'

There was nothing to say to that.

They left shortly afterward; I was too shaken even to do the gracious hostess bit. Alan poured me a stiff bourbon without even asking. I sipped at it and then put it down. There are some hurts that don't respond to soothing chemicals.

'You asked for it, darling,' said Alan.

'And I certainly got it. A lot more than I bargained for. Alan, if that man were here right now I'd strangle him with my bare hands. And plead justifiable homicide.'

'And I'd claim it was self-defence. He is . . . there are no words, are there?'

'None that I care to use. Alan, to treat a child that way! Cold, pitiless . . .'

'He knew nothing else, remember. It was the way he was treated. And as he would probably have said, he turned out just fine. Wealth, public esteem, all the women he wanted. What more could anyone want?'

'But he does want more. And more, and more. And it will never be enough, because he's looking for the wrong things.'

'He's looking,' said Alan with a sigh, 'for his father's approval, though he probably doesn't know that. He's the poster child for Narcissistic Personality Disorder, so badly in need of Daddy's approval he'll do anything. And he'll never get it, even if he does achieve his political goals. He could become Prime Minister of Canada and it wouldn't be good enough.'

'Is his father still alive?'

'Probably not, given Hartford's age. But even if he is, the man plainly had no idea how to love his son. Once that pattern is set, it seldom changes.'

'So if Hartford senior is still around, he won't really be surprised when Paul is arrested for murder.'

It was the first time we'd laid it out openly. We thought, or anyway *I* thought, that Paul Hartford was responsible for all the 'nastiness', including the murder of Elizabeth George.

'We're a long way from that, Dorothy.'

'I know. Suspicion, even if it amounts to certainty, isn't evidence. So how are we going to get the evidence?'

'"We" are not. That's the job of the police.'

'Okay, then, how are we going to get enough information to lead the police in the right direction?'

Alan put his glass down and raised his hands in the classic gesture of baffled frustration. 'How, you mean, are we going to persuade the authorities that they should arrest one of the most powerful and influential men in the province?'

I put my glass down, as well. 'You know, I keep forgetting that part. We've built up in our minds this picture of a monster, but to most people he's a charming benefactor to mankind.'

'And/or a man with the money and power to manipulate events in his favour. A formidable adversary, my love.' He paused for thought. 'You know, if we're right about Hartford, we've done what John asked us to do. We've identified the culprit. We could hand over our conclusions to John and the RCMP and go home.'

Home. What a beautiful word. Home, where our pets were waiting for us. Home, where the soft rain of England was keeping the grass of the Cathedral Close a brilliant emerald, with no need to waste water, and roses were getting ready to burst into fragrant bloom. Home.

Alan was watching me. I stood. 'We'd better get the dishes done. And then tomorrow, when our heads are in better shape, we decide how we're going to nail Mr pH0 to the wall.'

*   *   *

'I think I want to meet the amazing Alexis,' I said to Alan over the breakfast table after coffee had brought me to full functioning.

'I hardly think she'd be your cup of tea. Nor, for that matter, would you be hers.'

'No. Except that I'm filthy rich, and looking for a way to spread my largesse around in Canada.'

Alan didn't miss a beat. 'Who are you, then? Because Hartford knows quite well that Dorothy Martin isn't a zillionaire. And presumably what he knows, she knows.'

'How does he know what's in my portfolio? His spies can't pry into everything. They're too busy carrying out his nefarious plans. My name is Dorothy Martin-Rothschild, but I don't use the hyphen because it sounds ostentatious. I'm one of those reverse-snob women who delight in looking and acting like a peasant.'

'And where do I fit into all this?'

'I haven't worked that out yet. Give me a break! I've only had two cups of coffee. Maybe you're my boy-toy, kept around because you're so good-looking and sweet to me.'

'I'm older than you are.'

'What does that have to do with it? And you're not that much older. And you are in fact a handsome man.'

He leered at me, and then sighed. 'We're behaving like children.'

'Yes. Acting silly to take the taste of last night's stories out of our mouths. And I actually have no idea how I'm to approach Alexis. How I despise that name!'

'Think of her as Al. She'd hate that.'

'Mmm.' I pushed around the last of my toast. 'I suppose I just need to think of a way to approach her directly.'

'Here.' Alan shoved the morning paper across the table. 'There's a whole section in here about arts events. If there's a gallery opening or a fundraiser for something or other, it would be easy enough to find out if the Siren is going to be there.'

'Yes, but pH0 might be with her.'

'Possibly. Would that matter a great deal? The man already knows we're in town and making nuisances of ourselves. I'd be with you, and I doubt the man would care to try anything drastic in a crowd of the sort of people he needs as supporters.'

'I might not get any chance to talk to Al.'

'On the other hand, you might. And you could observe the dynamic between the two of them. I take it your aim is to work out what part, if any, she plays in all this. You're very good at sensing that sort of thing, far better than I.'

'My feet are getting very cold. What was that you said about going home and forgetting the whole thing?'

'You know quite well you'd risk frostbite before you'd abandon a mission.'

'Oh, very well.' I looked over the listings in the Arts section of the *Times Colonist*. 'Here's one that sounds promising. A gala concert next Wednesday in honour of the new concertmaster of the Victoria Symphony. Champagne reception following the concert. Black tie.' I looked at Alan. 'Do you suppose you can hire dinner clothes here the way you can in England? Or America, come to that?'

'A local version of Moss Bros? I imagine so. Did you bring anything splendid in the way of evening wear?'

'Of course not. I have exactly one garment worthy of such an occasion, that dark blue thing with the sequins, and I wasn't about to drag it halfway across the globe.'

'Then we'll just have to go shopping, won't we?'

'Well . . . but first we have to find out how we get invited to the bash. It's the sort of thing that's by invitation only, I imagine, and it probably costs an arm and a leg.'

'Amy will know all that. And if our underwriters aren't prepared to consider the cost a legitimate expense of the investigation, I'll take it on myself. Who knows, we might have a good time.'

'I very much doubt that. True, none of the charity functions I've attended have been quite this fancy. I've never moved in those exalted circles. But there were some back at Randolph that I, as a faculty wife, had to attend. They were terminally boring. All right, if you'll get in touch with Judith and Edwin, I'll call Amy. We need to get a move on. The shindig's on Wednesday, and today's – what, Alan?'

'I believe that's a Sunday paper, love.'

'Sunday! Oh, good grief!'

A quick search found the church listings. There was a pretty Anglican church not far from us, and with a bit of hustling we managed to get there just as they were finishing the first hymn.

After church, we went home and got back to our phones. I found it surprisingly easy to get an invitation to the gala. Amy knew everybody, and was able to open the right doors. Apparently the only criterion was to know somebody who knew somebody important and/or wealthy, the two categories not necessarily coinciding. That and the willingness to plunk down a sizeable sum to spend an evening with people we didn't know, some of whom we didn't care to know, some of whom we wished fervently to avoid.

Judith willingly agreed to foot the bill, including the cost of dressing up. 'Not jewellery, though,' she told Alan. 'I'm afraid you'll have to make do with fakes.' I could hear the smile in her voice as Alan relayed her words.

Well, I don't wear much in the way of jewels, anyway. Discreet earrings now and then, and a rather nice strand of pearls Alan gave me as a wedding present, that I happened to have brought along with me.

So, with Amy's advice about shops, I set out on Monday morning to try to find an evening gown that would pass muster. I was appalled at the prices I encountered, until Alan pointed out that a Canadian dollar was worth only a bit over half of a pound sterling. 'Still,' I said, pointing to a price tag on a rather nice gown. 'I've never paid this much for anything in my life!'

'You've never posed as Lady Gotrocks before, my dear. I think you'll look splendid in this. Go try it on.'

It did look nice, I had to admit. It had almost a period look, with a floor-length skirt and a high neck that covered up lots of wrinkles and would look good with the pearls. The soft rose satin flattered my white hair, and the bits of lace trim seemed entirely suitable to an old lady.

Not only that, it actually fit, and the cut disguised the extra pounds I couldn't seem to get rid of.

'Yes,' said Alan. 'Quite nice.'

'It'll be perfect for the next time the Queen invites me to a ball. Other than that, I can't imagine where I'd ever wear it again.'

'I'll see what I can do about that ball, when we get home. Meanwhile, buy the thing before your conscience rebels.'

'You buy it. Maybe if I don't actually see the transaction I won't feel so guilty. I have to go find some shoes. They'll hardly show, but I don't think sneakers will do.'

SIXTEEN

Amy and I decided I'd better get my hair done. The casual look I prefer wouldn't fit the image I was trying to project. So I spent a large part of Tuesday in a beauty shop. I hadn't been in one for years – back in England I get my hair cut in a barber shop – and I discovered that I actually rather enjoyed being pampered. I also discovered that the conversations during the ministrations were just as inane as those I remembered from back when I was young. I listened, though. One never knows when some bit of information might be useful.

I decided to go the whole nine yards and get a facial, too. I doubted there was much to be done with a face my age, but what the heck. Judith was paying, and I might as well find out what it was like.

The results, when I got home and looked in a mirror, were startling. I almost didn't recognize myself. The image in the mirror was pleasant, but . . . 'Alan, I miss the wrinkles. I suppose they're not beautiful, but they're me. I've earned them over the years. This face doesn't have any character!'

'They'll come back, love. I miss them too. I'm going to feel quite shy for a few days about living with this gorgeous young woman. Your hair, too . . .' He trailed off.

I nodded. 'It's the silver rinse. I suppose they asked me if I wanted it; I wasn't paying much attention. And again, it's nice, but it's not me.'

By Wednesday night I was a mass of nerves. I had worried all Tuesday evening that my hair would look awful by morning. It didn't. I had worried that my face would react to all the creams and lotions and pummelling and come out red and puffy. It didn't.

'This was an utterly idiotic idea,' I said, my voice muffled in the folds of the gown I was struggling into. 'Why on earth didn't you stop me?'

That was a rhetorical question that Alan wisely made no attempt to answer. He freed the zipper slide, which had caught in my hair, and zipped me up.

'Where are my shoes?'

'On your feet, love. Here, let me fasten the pearls. Now, take a look at yourself. You're beautiful.'

The image in the mirror only increased my panic. 'I'm a fake! I look like . . . oh, I don't know what I look like, but not a person who could ever expect to cope with anything. Alan, I can't do this! Hartford will be there – he's a major patron of the symphony. Why didn't we think of that before? I can't do it!'

He put his hands on my shoulders and turned me around to face him. 'Dorothy, listen to me. You are the same person you were a week ago. No, let me have my say. You look different, but inside you're the same. Intelligent, capable, generous, compassionate. You've assumed a disguise for one evening, and a very becoming disguise it is. Paul Hartford has seen you exactly once and may not even recognize you in your Cinderella-at-the-ball mode. So enjoy the compliments you're going to receive, and keep your mind on your job. I'm proud of you!'

He gave me a careful kiss, so as not to disturb my carefully applied make-up, and asked me to tie his tie.

That restored a tiny bit of my self-confidence. I've always been rather good at tying those pesky men's dress bow ties, a skill learned years ago when my first husband and I had to go to formal affairs on occasion. I was pleased that I hadn't forgotten.

But I was glad to cling to Alan's arm when we went down to meet our taxi. 'I'm scared to death,' I whispered to him.

'No, you're not,' he whispered back. 'I won't allow it!'

'Ohmigosh, I forgot to bring the invitation, and it says—'

'I have it here,' he said, patting his dinner jacket.

'I think I'm going to be sick.'

'I put some ginger tablets in that silly little excuse for a bag you're carrying. Take one.'

'I don't have any water.'

'They're tiny. Anyway, we're here. Buck up, darling. Best foot forward. As one of your favourite fictional characters was wont to say, "Up ze head! Up ze bosom!" Excelsior! And other assorted battle cries.'

'Once more into the breach,' I muttered, and took his arm, doing my best to look rich and confident.

We did not, of course, know a soul in the room. Trying to look as if we did this sort of thing all the time, we presented our invitation to the young woman at the door, were handed programs, and then set out to mingle. Not an easy thing to do, when one is surrounded by strangers clumped in little groups.

The room, essentially just a large empty rectangle with a platform at one end, was laid out for the occasion like a recital hall, with those little gilt chairs that seem required for this kind of do. They are wretchedly uncomfortable and not suited to the weight of some of the attendees. 'Fat cats' do in fact tend to be somewhat overweight. The men, that is. The women are often skeletally thin. 'Do you suppose,' I murmured to Alan, 'that seats are assigned? Or reserved, or whatever?'

'I doubt it. I see some shawls and whatnot marking places up front. Do we have anything we can use to stake our claim?'

'Not really, unless you were to take off your jacket. I didn't bring a wrap.'

'Well, it's very warm in here, but removing one's dinner jacket in this crowd would be equivalent to performing a striptease. Better just hover near the back, and when everyone sits down, we can slip in.'

At that point a grey-haired woman sailed up to us. She wore a 'little black dress' that probably came straight from Paris, and understated diamonds whose value I estimated at approximately our total net worth.

'You must be Amy Hartford's friends,' said the woman in a pleasant voice, extending a hand. 'I'm Patricia Underwood. She asked me to look after you. And you, my dear, are looking absolutely splendid!'

There was a small note of surprise in her voice. I smiled as I shook hands. 'I suppose Amy told you to look for the poor relation.'

'She told me nothing of the kind! She did say that you had almost certainly not brought formal wear with you and would have to find something off the peg. Don't say another word. You must be the world's canniest shopper! I knew you because I know everyone else, not for the way you were dressed, which is perfect. Now, there are some people I'd like you to meet.'

Not Paul Hartford, I prayed, but as she led us around introducing us, I scanned the growing crowd and didn't see him. He'll probably come in late in a blaze of glory, I thought unkindly.

And then I found myself face to face with Alexis.

'Alex, my dear, I'd like you to meet Dorothy Martin and Alan Nesbitt, visitors from England. Dorothy, Alan, this is Alexis Ivanov, chairman of this event and patron of the Symphony.'

I hope my jaw didn't drop. I've met some very attractive women in my time, but this woman was more like her picture than seemed possible. I'd assumed Photoshop manipulation, but I was wrong. She was a perfect Hollywood glamour picture, back in the days when Hollywood oozed glamour.

She said something. Alan and I said something. Then she floated away to talk to someone important, and Ms Underwood led us to seats next to hers in the second row, not in the inconspicuous nether regions where we would have preferred to be.

'I gather from your smacked-in-the-head look that you'd heard about Alex, but never seen her in person,' said Ms Underwood in an undertone.

'I . . . yes. I've seen a picture. It doesn't do her justice.'

'Her name would imply a Russian background,' said Alan, his tone making it a question.

'It isn't her own name. That is, not her birth name. I don't know who she is or where she comes from. She simply appeared on the social scene in Victoria and knocked everyone flat. All the men, that is. The women—'

The murmur in the hall was dying down. Alexis had stepped onto the platform and was gesturing for silence.

'I'm sure you'll all be relieved to hear that I'm not going to make a speech. Paul is usually the speech-maker, but tonight he is in Ottawa. I imagine you can guess what he might be doing there.' Laughter, not entirely kind in tone. 'So I simply welcome you all to this splendid occasion. I won't go on and on about our new concertmaster either; her stellar biography is in your program. Please welcome her to her new musical home, Miss Kwan Mei!'

The violinist was a diminutive young woman who walked on stage with the confidence of one who was sure of her ability. She took a bow, nodded to her accompanist, and launched into a fiery piece played in a demanding tempo. It could have been an exercise just in technical skill, but in the hands of this talented young woman it was music – bold and exciting and at the same time reassuring. We applauded until my hands hurt, and Alan had to remind me that there was more to come.

There certainly was. Miss Kwan had chosen a beautifully varied program, including the familiar and not so familiar, from the Renaissance through to the contemporary. When she was finished and had taken bow after bow, she stepped forward to speak.

'First, I want to thank you for trusting me to lead your wonderful orchestra, and for your reception here tonight. I hope we will have many happy years to love music together.' Applause. 'Second, I want to introduce to you my accompanist, Arthur Grant.' Applause. 'I think you will agree that he is an extremely accomplished musician. He is also an extremely pleasant man, and just before the concert tonight, he asked me to marry him – and I said yes.' More applause as Arthur joined Mei and they embraced – a bit awkwardly because of the violin.

After that, anything Alexis could add was anti-climax. She finished her remarks, a model of the obvious, and invited us to enjoy the ensuing buffet. Waiters, right on cue, began circulating.

'Now's my only chance to talk to her,' I muttered to Alan. 'Run interference for me, will you?' For Alexis was surrounded the moment she stepped down from the platform, mostly (of course) by men.

'I'll do my best, love. But my riot-control skills have got a bit rusty.' He moved forward, and then checked. 'What on earth?'

Alexis had separated herself from the crowd and was making her way rapidly to a rear door, accompanied by a young man.

'Who's he? Where's she going?' I turned to Ms Underwood. 'I thought she'd stay to schmooze. Oh, I'm sorry, that's rude.'

'But accurate. Yes, normally she would stay to woo the high-fliers. That's what these affairs are for, as of course you know. And to give her her due, she's very good at squeezing a bit more out of them. I can't imagine what she's up to.'

'And the man with her?'

'I don't know. One of her staff, I suppose.'

I frowned. 'Staff?'

Ms Underwood smiled gently. 'Alex is a philanthropist, and that profession, on her scale, requires a considerable workforce. Quite apart from the management of her portfolio, which is a full-time occupation in itself, there are records to be kept, applications for aid to be processed and reviewed – oh, yes, she employs a staff.'

I felt about two years old. 'Yes. Well. Never having had what any of this crowd would consider wealth, I didn't know.' I looked at Alan, who hovered, ready to step in if I needed support.

I pulled my head erect. 'On the other hand, I have a husband who loves me dearly, and I him. I have a wonderful old house to live in, sufficient money for our needs and a bit extra, beloved friends, and a lifetime of happy memories. I am in fact wealthy in any sense that counts.'

Alan kissed my cheek, and Ms Underwood pressed my hand warmly. 'My dear, I believe you are far richer than most of the people in this room. Now you must excuse me. In the absence of our hostess and schmoozer-in-chief, I need to talk to some people who have only money, and see if I can't extract a bit of it. Do enjoy the champagne; it's sure to be excellent. They don't serve plonk to people who know the difference.'

We circulated with the others, smiling at people we didn't know, trying to get to the buffet tables without being overtly impolite, but it wasn't easy. It was just about dinner time, and everyone had the same idea.

A man came up to us. We didn't know him, but of course we didn't know anybody. 'Hello. I understand you're visitors to Victoria. Pat Underwood told me you might be feeling a bit lonely. I'm the current conductor of the Victoria Symphony. Well, interim conductor. I hope you enjoyed the concert.'

'How could we not? That young woman is spectacular, and so is her accompanist.'

'Thank you,' said a soft voice at my elbow. I looked to see the violinist and her fiancé. 'Oh, and here they are! My dear, you're wonderful! I'm delighted to be able to tell you so in person. I didn't recognize that first piece the two of you played, but it was amazing!'

'It was commissioned for the occasion,' said the conductor. 'One of our wonderful benefactors, Paul Hartford—'

The scream interrupted him. It reverberated through the room, seeming to come from all directions at once, to go on and on.

A crowd is sometimes slow to react. When at last the terrifying sound ceased, there was silence for a moment, and then a rising clamour and finally a surge toward the doors.

'One moment.' The man who had been at our side a moment before was on the platform. He had found a microphone from somewhere, and his voice commanded, 'I'm told there has been a terrible accident. Two police officers are with us tonight, and they asked me to say that you may all leave – in an orderly fashion, please. We know who is here, since you all had invitations. If anyone is no longer at the address Ms Ivanov has for you, please inform one of the door attendants before you go. I'm so sorry this splendid evening had to end this way. Good night, and please drive safely on your way home.'

'But what *happened*?' My urgent whisper to Alan was echoed all over the room. No one seemed to know.

'From the way this is being handled, I would say a death. Very possibly a murder. Will you be all right for a moment? I need to speak to one of those police officers.'

Alan is a tall man, and his long career as a senior policeman has given him an air of authority. He made his way through the crowd with ease, and spoke to the man on the platform, who looked startled and then pointed to a man who was speaking on his mobile phone, while barring the door to a side room. He looked irritated when Alan tapped him on the shoulder, but then his expression changed.

Alan returned to me. 'My dear, I must stay here for a bit. Do you mind taking a taxi home? I'll be there as soon as I can.'

'So it is a murder.'

'Yes. Paul Hartford has been stabbed to death.'

SEVENTEEN

I sat down on one of the hard little gold chairs. It offered little comfort, but I needed a breathing spell. My mind refused to process the news. I had cast Paul Hartford as the villain of the piece, a murderer or at least an *agent provocateur*. Now he himself had been murdered. Presently I could begin to think again. Just now my thinking apparatus was clearly marked Not Open for Business.

I didn't want to go home. For one thing, it wasn't home. None of the familiar comforts were there. No nice squishy chairs. No animals to cuddle. Most important, no Alan. I couldn't toss ideas back and forth with him, compare notes, argue, hash out a solution. At least not until the Victoria police decided he had done all he could to help. Or maybe it was the RCMP, or whoever. The principle was the same. I was alone for a while.

But I didn't have to be. I picked up my cell phone. 'Amy? Oh, I'm so glad you're home! May I come over in a few minutes? Or could you come to us? Oh, good. It's important; I'll explain when I see you.'

I didn't want to tell her over the phone that her ex-husband was dead. She had despised him, but he was the father of her daughter, and some ties are never really broken.

I asked one of the departing guests how to get a taxi, sounding as English as I could. 'Oh, my dear, you'll have a terrible time getting one, with most of this crowd trying to do the same. We brought our car. Can we give you a lift somewhere?'

My eyes teared up. The kindness of strangers can do that to me, especially when I'm under stress anyway. 'Oh, if you could, that would be wonderful! I'm in one of those condos just over the bridge – staying with a friend.'

Of course the woman and her husband wanted to talk about what had happened, and I had to pretend I knew nothing. Fortunately it was a short drive.

Then I remembered that Alan had the keys. I had begun to panic when Amy drove up. I went to her car. 'I've stupidly locked myself out. Do you have a spare key?'

'Of course. But where's Alan?'

'I'll explain inside. These shoes are killing me.'

Well, they weren't, but it's an excuse any woman can use at any time. I kicked them off the minute we got inside, and gestured to the liquor cabinet. 'I'm going to get out of these clothes. Help yourself to whatever you want. Back in a jiffy.'

I didn't take the time for a full change, just pulled off my gorgeous dress, hung it up, and put on a robe and slippers.

Amy was sitting on the couch with an empty glass in front of her. She pointed to another. 'I waited for you. You looked as if you could do with something yourself. Bourbon, right?'

'Right.' I sat down gratefully, took a swig, and took a deep breath. 'Amy, you haven't seen the news, have you?'

'No. It doesn't come on till ten, you know.'

'I thought there might have been a special bulletin. I don't know any way to say this except to say it. Paul Hartford was killed tonight.'

She had picked up her glass. She set it down again, very carefully. She opened her mouth, but no sound came out. She cleared her throat and tried again. 'Will you say that again?'

'After the gala, Paul's body was found backstage somewhere. He had been murdered.'

'I . . . see.' She sounded politely interested.

Uh-oh. Not a normal reaction. 'I'm going to make us some tea. Sit still.' I switched on the fire as I passed it. The room wasn't cold, but if she was suffering from shock she needed to be kept warm.

I switched on the kettle and went to our bedroom, where I thought I remembered seeing an afghan draped over a chair. I brought it back and wrapped it around Amy's shoulders. Her hands were icy, though the room was growing uncomfortably warm.

The kettle whistled. I stuck tea bags in two mugs and poured in boiling water. Not the way I prefer to make tea, but this was a time when speed trumped tradition. Nor could I find a tray anywhere. Milk, sugar and the two mugs went into a shallow glass baking dish I found in a cupboard.

I put quite a lot of sugar in Amy's cup, stirred it, and handed it to her. 'I think it's too weak yet to add milk.'

'Thank you, but I don't care for sugar.'

'Drink it. You need it.'

'But won't you tell me—'

'Not another word until you've got that inside you.'

She sipped and made a face but obediently drank, slowly until it cooled. When it was gone, I handed her my cup, which by that time was very strong indeed. 'Milk this time. *And* sugar.'

She managed about half of that one before setting down the cup and shuddering. 'Dorothy Martin, you make a terrible cup of tea.'

'I know. The caffeine and sugar were medicinal. You're in shock, Amy. Or you were. I think you're beginning to be better.'

'I'm warm, anyway. Too warm. Would you mind turning off the fire? And then tell me everything you know about all this.'

'Are you sure you're okay?'

'I don't know. I don't even know how I feel. You'd think I'd be . . . I don't know, relieved, I guess. He was a truly dreadful person. And yet . . .'

'He was your husband, and the father of your child, and you can't help remembering the good times.'

She made a face. 'There weren't many of them, except just at first, when I was blown away with his charm. Before I discovered it was all fake. Is there by any chance any Scotch?'

I looked her over. Her face was no longer dead white. Her breathing was regular. She had shrugged off the afghan. 'Well. My medical degree is a little out of date. And it was from the University of Google, anyway. But I don't think you're in clinical shock anymore, so a little alcohol probably won't hurt you.' I poured Amy a small tot of Alan's Glenfiddich. 'I'm only giving you a little till we see how you react. Besides, Alan would have something to say if I let you use this superb stuff like medicine.'

She managed to smile at that, so I sat down with my own drink and began. 'You want to know what happened.' I made it a question.

'I think I need to know.'

'Yes. Well, my own knowledge is sketchy in the extreme. Alan will probably tell us more when he gets home. You know we went to the gala.' I began to describe the evening to her. 'It all went exactly as I had anticipated. Pretty boring, to tell the truth, especially since we didn't know anybody. Your Mrs – Ms? – Underwood is delightful. How do you know her? If it's not a rude question. I mean, you don't move in quite those circles, do you?'

'Hardly. Not since I left Paul. No, Pat Underwood is one of the deep-pocket ladies, but she's unusual in that she really cares about the causes she supports. She's a big patron of the library, but she doesn't just hand out largesse. She comes to our events. She takes home bagfuls of books and somehow finds the time to read them, and argue about them. I think she's going to buy us the new computer system we need, but first she has to find out all about it, why we need it, what we plan to do with it, why we should spend money on that instead of new books.'

'Hmm. Sounds like a bit of a nuisance.'

'She would be if she were just being obstructionist, or trying to show off, but it isn't that. She cares passionately about the welfare of the library and wants to make sure we're not just jumping on some faddish bandwagon.'

'Or,' I said, taking another sip of my bourbon, 'giving in to some high-pressure salesmanship?'

'I begin to understand why John's niece thinks so highly of you. Yes, of course you're right. Paul's company stands to make a sweet little profit on the new system, and of course he wasn't shy about pointing out the advantages of dealing with a local concern. Easier to negotiate face to face, support the local economy, make sure the system is tailored exactly to our needs. I'm sure you can fill in the blanks.'

'And it all sounds reasonable.'

'Yes. Paul always does sound reasonable on the surface. Did.' She suddenly found a need to hide behind her glass. I waited.

She found a tissue in her purse and blew her nose. 'I'm sorry.'

'Oh, don't be silly. You don't have anything to be sorry for. You're not English, to be embarrassed at any display of emotion, so come off it.' I didn't know her well enough to be that bossy, but I thought perhaps it would do her more good than sympathy. Which I wasn't sure was appropriate anyway.

'The trouble is, I'm not sure what emotion I'm feeling. Sorrow, relief, fury . . .'

'Or perhaps fear? Someone killed Paul. We don't know who, we don't know why. Speaking for myself, fear is certainly a part of my reaction. I don't know what's happening, and one always fears the unknown.'

Amy nodded slowly. 'Yes. In my own mind, I was quite sure Paul was somehow behind all the terrible things that were happening. And now he's a victim, and I don't know what to think. Go on telling me what you know. Don't worry, I'll be all right.'

'I can't remember where I left off.'

'You'd met Pat.'

'Oh, yes. And she was very nice to us, and introduced us to people, including the chairman – chairwoman – of the evening.' I hesitated, not sure how much Amy knew about Alexis.

'The Dragon Lady?'

'Is that what you call her? Alan and I have nicknamed her the Siren.'

'Also appropriate. That describes her fatal allure. I concentrate rather on her talent for destruction.'

I decided I didn't need to tiptoe. 'She isn't very popular, it seems.'

'Not among women. In fact I don't know a single woman who would choose to be in the same room with her. Men flock to her, of course.'

'There seem to be a few sensible ones. Alan, for one, doesn't care for predatory females.'

'Nor does John. But they're the rare exceptions. She goes around playing Lady Bountiful and oozing charm all over the place, and they just fall over like ninepins. I can almost – could almost, I still can't get the tenses right – could almost feel sorry for Paul. She was leading him a merry dance, and he simply couldn't see that she was using him. He actually bragged to me about how she couldn't resist his appeal.'

'But why? I mean, she seems to have quite enough money of her own. At least she gives it away lavishly. What does she need of his? Or is it just the thrill of the chase? Ensnare one more poor helpless male.'

'Oh, no. It isn't the money. She only goes after men who can get her what she wants. In one case it was control of a company. That little affair broke up a happy marriage, and incidentally increased the Dragon Lady's wealth a great deal. But that wasn't the object of the game. She wanted that company. She craves power, and doesn't care who she hurts to get it. She wants Paul so she can get at the ultimate power. He intends – intended – to be Prime Minister one day, and she meant to ride right along with him to Ottawa. Well, now she won't get that wish, will she? Unless she can find some other likely horse.'

'Would he actually have stood a chance in politics?'

'Oh, yes. He made a lot of friends over the years, pulled a lot of strings for them. He could call in those favours. He'd been funnelling donations to the Tories for a long time, had contacts in Ottawa. And he was well-liked in Victoria, again thanks to all the glad-handing and the under-the-table deals. He could easily have been elected MP, and from there it's only a small step to a cabinet seat and then the head of the party.'

'I see.' Canada, in some ways, had begun to seem so much like America to me that I had been thinking of the path to power in my homeland: local politics, state office, the legislature, the presidency. Now I realized that in the Parliamentary system, things worked the way they did in England. Get elected to Parliament, become more and more important in your party, and eventually when you head that party, and it attains a majority, bingo, there you are in Number Ten Downing Street or whatever the Canadian equivalent is.

'Do you suppose that's why he's dead? Someone didn't want him to succeed in politics, didn't want it so badly that it was worth killing him?'

'I suppose it's possible. But if he had lots of friends in high places, he had lots of enemies, too. Without even thinking about it, I could list off ten people who hated him like poison. Twenty. More.'

'You may need to do just that.' Alan had entered the room unheard. 'The police would find that an interesting list.' He picked up the bottle of whisky and poured some for himself. 'It's early days yet, of course, but so far it seems they haven't the slightest idea who killed him.'

EIGHTEEN

I stood up, wobbled a little, and realized I'd been drinking on an empty stomach. Not a brilliant thing to do.

'I'm going to figure out something to eat,' I said firmly. 'We didn't have supper. I was counting on that lavish buffet that we never got to taste. There must be something edible in the kitchen.'

'There's a great pizza place not far from here,' Amy suggested. 'And they deliver.'

'Heaven smiles,' I said devoutly. 'Why don't you order for us? You know what they do best. We like everything, even anchovies.'

'Better order quite a lot,' Alan suggested. 'John's coming over when he can get away.'

I opened a can of nuts to stave off starvation until our meal arrived and poured water for everyone, and we sat down at the kitchen table. Somehow just Alan's presence had changed the atmosphere. Or maybe it was turning on the lights; evening had settled in without my noticing, and the room had grown dim.

'So,' I said, reaching for a handful of cashews, 'tell all.'

Alan ran a hand down the back of his neck. 'Not a great deal to tell. I tried not to get in the way while the scene-of-crime people did their work. It was quite frustrating for them, of course. Hartford was killed, or at least was found, in a side passage of a corridor leading to a service area. The caterers had been back and forth all evening, probably twenty people walking everywhere and touching everything. All their shoes had to be examined; all their fingerprints taken. Meanwhile they needed to deal with the uneaten food, salvaging what they could. They couldn't throw anything out, because until the autopsy we won't know the cause of death.'

'But I thought . . .' I looked at Amy and shut up.

'Yes, there was the one obvious injury. But one can never assume that the obvious is all there is.'

'What injury?' Amy's face was pale again.

'I don't think you want to know,' I began.

She looked determined. 'Dorothy, I'm not a child. Many things about Paul's life were not pretty. It doesn't entirely surprise me that his death was ugly, which is what you're implying. I need to know. How did he die?'

'Apparently,' said Alan in his driest police manner, 'from a deep wound inflicted with a knife.'

'He was stabbed.' She spoke with no expression whatever.

'Yes. We will not be certain of the cause of death, as I said, until the medical examiner has done his work.'

Amy drank water. 'And how soon will that be?'

'I don't know. It depends partly on the backlog of work. But as the deceased was an important figure in the community, they'll probably try to get it done promptly.'

'I don't think they'll find any other cause of death,' said Amy after another drink of water. 'For a man as cordially hated as Paul Hartford, somehow being stabbed to death seems a predictable end.'

Well, that was a shocking remark, or it would have been if we had known less about the man. In the circumstances we let it pass. A terrible epitaph, but quite possibly a true one.

John and the pizza arrived at the same moment. Alan got some beer out of the fridge and the gathering took on the air of a rather macabre party. There was too much to say, but as none of it made pleasant conversation, there were long stretches of silence, punctuated by trivialities. Finally John set his beer glass down with a thump.

'Amy, it's time we spoke the truth. I'm not having any nonsense about speaking no ill of the dead. The fact that he's dead doesn't change the fact that the man was a bastard. He treated you and Sue unforgivably. He was a liar, a cheat, an immoral man in every possible sense of the word, and we're all better off now that he's gone. If the various police forces wish my help, I will cooperate in trying to track down his killer, but only because a murderer must not be allowed to go free. For the sake of an ordered society, not in this case for the sake of justice. Alan, you're free of any obligation you think you might owe me. Free to go straight back to England if you want – and I wouldn't blame you.'

Alan glanced at me. I shook my head, and he cleared his throat. 'John, I agree with every word you've said, but Dorothy and I have had this out. We can't leave you with this chaos to resolve, if for no other reason than our love for the beauty we've found here. The ugliness must be swept away. If we can help with that chore, we're yours to command.'

'Besides that, we're just barely getting to know you two,' I put in. 'When the mess is cleared away, we can have some fun before we have to leave. Now eat up. This pizza is too good to waste, and I don't like it cold the way I used to when I was young.'

Now that we didn't have to keep up the pretence of emotions we didn't feel, we could get down to business. 'Amy, you probably knew him better than anyone else in this room. Do you have any idea who might have done this?'

She sighed. 'Not seriously. I know plenty of people who hated him. I mean, really hated him, not just the dislike we usually mean by that word. Some, like John, hated him on my account.'

'But on my own, as well,' he said.

'You said that before, John.' I looked at him intently. 'You never explained.'

'No, because it sounds petty.'

'It was not petty! Each individual incident, maybe, but as a whole, no. Let me explain, John.' She took his hand. 'When John and I first began to take an interest in each other, of course Paul knew about it. He had his spies everywhere, and they kept a close eye on me. Paul was trying to find a reason to take Sue away from me. Even though we'd been divorced quite a while by that time, he was obsessed with the idea. I had something that belonged to him, you see, and that enraged him.'

'He also wanted to make damn sure she wasn't enjoying herself.' John finished his beer. Alan poured him another. 'He never accepted the divorce settlement. He wanted to see her begging on the streets. So seeing us going about to plays and concerts and nice restaurants fed his fury, and he did everything he could to end our relationship.'

Amy took up the narrative. 'First it was flat tyres. A series of them. Every time John took me someplace, we would come back to the car to find at least one tyre slashed. We started walking or taking cabs, so he changed his tactics and tried to catch us in compromising situations.'

I choked on my beer. 'In this day and age? What could you possibly have done that would be labelled "compromising"? You're both mature adults, for heaven's sake!'

'Yes, but he wanted to prove me an unfit mother, you see, so he could get custody of Sue. She was still in her late teens then. Barely, but Paul could have made capital out of that. Setting a bad example for an impressionable young girl – you can write the script.'

'So until Sue was old enough to be her own custodian, legally, Amy and I took great care never to be alone together, anywhere.'

Amy giggled. 'It was like being a teenager again. We travelled with the pack. I did so long to spend time with John, just talking and really getting to know him, but we didn't dare.'

'That's not all I longed for, believe me!' said John, and we all laughed. I was remembering the days before Alan and I married, when only his position in the community kept us from . . . well, the young always think they're the only ones who know about passion. They're so wrong.

'I know, it sounds funny now,' John continued. 'It wasn't funny then. And when none of his juvenile tactics drove us apart, he started a smear campaign. I was still with the Mounties then, and my superior officers started getting anonymous letters accusing me of all sorts of things, from minor dereliction of duty to serious corruption.'

'They came to the library, too. Nobody took them seriously. Our co-workers knew us too well to believe the claims, but in John's case, the RCMP had to make at least a cursory investigation.'

'And that was infuriating,' he said, 'because it took precious staff time away from real problems. In the end I decided to resign, to free the department from the nuisance. They didn't want me to.'

'No, his boss said he was too valuable to lose, and I told him it would look like an admission of guilt. So for quite a while it looked as if Paul had us exactly where he wanted us.'

Alan shook his head in sympathy. 'Damned if you do, damned if you don't. Stay on and keep the department in turmoil, or resign and let Hartford go to the tabloids with "No smoke without fire". Clever villain, I'll give him that.'

'But not quite clever enough,' John said with satisfaction. 'We knew, of course, who was behind all the persecution, but we hadn't been able to prove it. No witnesses, no fingerprints, no DNA left behind. It was a surgically clean operation, until one hot summer day. It can get hot here, and that day there'd been a thunderstorm, and we lost power in parts of the city for almost a whole day. One of the places affected was the AIntell building. No air conditioning.'

'Paul always did hate the heat,' Amy chimed in. 'His temper was never under very good control, but when he was too warm he lost it completely, raged and stomped about – which of course made it worse.'

'So that day,' said John with satisfaction, 'that day he sat down and wrote an especially vitriolic letter about me. Had to write it by hand, since his computers were down. Of course that made him furious, too. His whole life revolved around the world of technology, so he took it as a personal insult when his machines wouldn't respond to his bidding.'

'Laptops?' I ventured. 'Mobile phones?'

'Of course. But he'd been out of town for several days, and all his devices needed recharging – and of course there was no power to do that.' John was laughing by now.

'"How all occasions do inform against me!"' I quoted. 'Here he was, raging furiously, and unable to do much about it. One can almost feel sorry for the man.'

'But not quite, although in this case his rage was his undoing. He wrote the letter, wrote it with a pen held in a sweaty hand, and instead of giving it to one of his lackeys to hand-deliver, as usual, he put it in an envelope and sealed it and stamped it and mailed it to the RCMP.'

Alan got it first. 'So when it arrived, it was positively covered with his fingerprints and sweat and saliva.'

'Enough DNA to convict him of any crime. In this case, of libel.'

I frowned. 'Is it libel if it isn't published?'

'It was published, Dorothy, in the sense of being written and disseminated. A defamatory statement doesn't have to appear in print to be libel. So of course the crime lab people couldn't wait to run the tests, and as soon as we had the results we knew we'd get, my lawyer went and had a little chat with Hartford.'

'You sued him?' Alan asked.

'No, we blackmailed him,' Amy replied. 'Our lawyer told him that we had sufficient proof of his "persistent, pernicious defamation" and that we would refrain from legal action only if he ceased his persecution. He tried to bluff, saying we wouldn't dare make the letters public, but Mike, our lawyer, convinced him that he would be hurt more than we would if his libellous actions became known. "Your spiteful, childish accusations" Mike called them. And really, they were couched in language that would have shocked Paul's many admirers. He refused to admit to anything, of course, but then *his* lawyer told him he'd better back off. And he did. There were no more letters, and he was always sickeningly sweet when he ran into either of us in public. I know he hated us even more because he'd lost again: the divorce settlement and Sue, and now this. I'm sure he was planning something diabolical, but . . .'

'Has it occurred to you,' said Alan slowly, 'that his decision to seek political office might in part have been based on his desire for revenge? "She thinks she's so clever! I'll show *her*!" or sentiments to that effect?'

Amy considered. 'I'm not sure. Certainly he was childish enough to relish giving me that sort of slap in the face. But I'm not sure it wouldn't have been too subtle for his thought processes. And think of the humiliation if he'd lost.'

'Would it have occurred to him that he might lose? If I'm reading him right, he was too egotistical even to consider that outcome.' I picked up my beer glass, found it empty, and decided I'd had enough.

'You're right, of course,' said John, making the same discovery and shaking his head to Alan's offer of more. 'And he was very probably accurate. In politics, along with money and influence, sheer self-confidence can take even a total rotter a long way. Amy, love, if this hurts you, I'm sorry, but I think this community, and this country, has had a very narrow escape.'

'I agree. John, I can't help remembering the time when he was sweet to me. But knowing what I know now, that it was never about me, I realize that even the memories are lies. I'm not going to grieve for him, only for what might have been, if he'd been the man I once thought he was.'

John took her hand and said softly, '"Of all sad words of tongue or pen, the saddest are these: It might have been."'

NINETEEN

I woke in the morning still in that mood of melancholy, and it wasn't dissipated by my coffee, excellent though it was.

Alan saw my expression. 'Did I put salt in it, instead of sugar, love?'

'What? Oh, the coffee. No, it's fine. It's just . . . what a waste, Alan! Another terrible waste.'

'Yes. An intelligent man, a success at business, born to privilege – he could have done so much good. Instead he destroyed lives everywhere he went.'

'Including his own, in the end. Alan, who killed him? And why?'

My husband sighed. 'You know the list of motives as well as I do. Pick one. Hatred, envy, lust—'

'Any of the seven deadly sins, in fact. Literally deadly, in this case. But in my mind, it all boils down to the one motive: fear.'

'That's your hobby-horse, isn't it? All crime stems from fear.'

'Because all of the other motives hark back to that one. We hate someone because we fear what he can do to us. We envy him because he has more than we do, and we fear he'll stand in our way of getting what we want. Lust, the same thing – fear of not attaining our desire. So the question is, who was afraid of Paul Hartford, so afraid that it was necessary to kill him?'

Alan spread his hands. 'I'm just a common or garden-variety copper, ma'am. I'll leave the philosophy to you. What I want is evidence. And let me tell you, my dear,' he said, dropping his pose, 'we seem to have precious little of that. I've had a call from John this morning. The forensics people were at it all night.'

'And?'

'Nothing. All those people rushing around. No one saw anything. No one heard anything. The passage where Hartford was found was not in use last night. It was seldom used, in fact, as it led to a storage area – the sort where things are put that just might come in handy sometime.'

'Only they never do.'

'Indeed. So there were no lights on.'

'How, then, did it happen that his body was found? One would think it might have lain there undiscovered till morning, or whenever the cleaning crew come in.'

'That may have been the murderer's plan, but he, or she, reckoned without human nature.'

I waited.

'We all heard the scream. It came from a woman on the catering staff. A very young woman, a student at UVic who does this sort of thing for a little pocket money. Her boyfriend was also working.'

'Oh. A dark hallway, a lull in the pace of the work—'

'Exactly. I gather she literally fell over the body.'

I shuddered. 'That happened to me once, as you'll recall. It was horrible!'

'This was probably even worse, love. Although there wasn't as much – er – mess as one would have expected.'

'Oh, I don't want to know. As heartily as I despised that man, I hate to think of someone – there was only the one stab wound, didn't you say?'

'Yes, but it seemed quite deep. And there were no obvious signs of his having defended himself, which suggests that he was unconscious when he was attacked.'

'A blow to the head first? Alan, this begins to sound an awful lot like that girl Elizabeth's death. Unconscious, then stabbed. Only in her case it was made to look like a raptor attack.'

'And this time there was no apparent blow to the head, though of course the autopsy will tell us more. But you're right. A knife of some sort as the weapon in both instances.'

I wished I hadn't eaten quite so much pizza the night before. I swallowed. 'I gather they haven't found the weapon.'

'No, and they don't expect to. Water, water everywhere. If I had just stabbed someone, I'd throw the weapon into the sea straight off.'

'What about the one used to kill Elizabeth George? The ocean is farther away from that crime scene.'

'A lot of water around, though. Streams, lakes. And sad though it is, I suspect that investigation will be shunted aside for a bit. Given limited resources, and the relative perceived social importance of the two victims . . .' He spread his hands.

'Of course. Will anyone except us be going on the assumption that the two deaths are linked?'

'I don't know, love. If John were still officially involved, perhaps. As it is, I'm sure he'll do the best he can, but . . .' Again he trailed off.

It was ever thus. The high-profile cases get the attention, not only of the police, but of the media, who push hard for a resolution. As they should, of course, but sometimes the pressure can force the police into a quick, easy arrest that turns out to be entirely mistaken.

Which reminded me. 'Have you read the paper this morning?'

'Haven't brought it in. I imagine there won't be much of a story. This all happened very close to their deadline. Do you want to check the local news on TV?'

'No. There might be pictures.' I shuddered again and got up to pour myself a glass of water. On second thought I added a little bicarb.

'So what,' I said when I was back at the table, 'can we do for the good of the order? I can't stand to just sit around and do nothing, but I'm not sure how the real police will feel about us butting in. It's not like back home where everyone knows us and knows what we do.'

'I've been thinking about that. I think we can be most useful by simply talking to people. Asking questions. Finding out who Hartford's friends were, and his enemies. Don't forget that talking to people is where you excel, my dear.'

'We tried that before and didn't learn a whole lot.'

'Yes, but now we're under fewer constraints. Hartford, poor sod, is no longer a threat. We can be more direct.'

'His friends are still alive. His goons. Does his death cancel out his orders to give us grief? At least, we're still assuming they were his orders, right?'

'I'm not sure we're safe in assuming anything at this point. Hartford's death has thrown a very large spanner in the works. We may have been all wrong about everything.'

I swallowed that unappetizing thought, and groaned. 'But that would mean we have to start all over!'

'Better that than continue to go round in circles.' His voice held not the slightest hint of sympathy.

I glared at him.

'In any case, it's not starting entirely from scratch. We know a great deal about the cast of characters now. We know about the tangled webs of motives, of personalities. We know where to look.'

'But it's all so . . . so dreary!'

'Dreary!' Alan threw his arms in the air. 'Great God in heaven, woman, look out the window! Has there ever been a more beautiful day since the earth was made?' He opened the door to the balcony. A subtle flowery scent drifted in. Birds were singing their hearts out. Somewhere children laughed at play. 'We've been given a problem to solve in a paradise on earth, with all our expenses paid, I might add, and you call it dreary!'

I fidgeted, wishing I had a cat to pet, or some knitting, or something, anything, to look at and occupy my hands.

'Not to mention that you have a husband who adores you,' he added. 'Snap out of it, darling, and let's go adventuring. The game is afoot!' He reached out with both hands, pulled me out of my chair and into an embrace, and gently pushed me to the door.

I ask you, who can stay in a snit after that?

He handed me into the car with the care one might have afforded Queen Elizabeth. 'I'll drive this time, shall I?'

'Certainly. Since you seem to know where we're going.' But I said it with a smile, and he understood that I had recovered. I hate to admit it, but I do occasionally need to be told off. Alan almost never chides me – but when I need it, he does the job thoroughly.

'We're going to AIntell, to stir up the hornet's nest.'

'I would imagine it'll be pretty well stirred up already. Paul Hartford was more than just the CEO of that place. You think it'll be open for business, then? I'd have thought they'd close down, out of respect.'

'We'll see, won't we?'

Alan negotiated the short drive to the AIntell offices competently, neither veering onto the wrong side of the road nor missing any traffic signals.

The offices were plainly open for business, though I doubted much business was getting done. Cerberus was not at his gate;

in fact the security station stood open and unmanned, but a uniformed Victoria police officer, an attractive young woman, appeared in seconds and courteously but firmly informed us that no one was being admitted.

Alan, obviously prepared for this, said with equal firmness (and equal courtesy), 'We are here at the request of Chief Superintendent McKenzie, who is working with the RCMP and the Victoria police in the investigation of Mr Hartford's murder. You'll want to see our identification.' He pulled out his passport and handed it to her as I got mine from my purse.

She studied them carefully. 'I've been given no instructions to admit you. Wait here, please, while I check.'

'What if she won't let us in?' I whispered while the officer moved into the security office, pulled out her mobile and made a call. 'That was splendid improvising, but will it work?'

'It wasn't entirely improvising. John *is* working with the police, and he *has* requested our help. He didn't specifically ask us to come here, but I doubt we'll be thrown out.'

Sure enough, in a very few minutes the young woman was back. 'The Deputy Chief Constable would like to talk to you. He'll be down in a moment, if you'll wait in the office, please.'

I had looked up the command structure of the Victoria Police Department when we arrived. The Deputy Chief Constable was the head of the operations branch of the department. Hartford's murder was, as anticipated, getting VIP handling.

And greatly to my surprise, we got the same. Alan stood as the Deputy Chief came into the room. They shook hands. The man then shook hands with me. 'I have heard good things about both of you, from McKenzie. I have great respect for him; the Mounties lost a good man when he decided to retire. He has told me, sir, about your distinguished career in England, and the very great help you, Mrs Martin, have been able to provide. If you had been born a few years later, ma'am, I believe you, too, would have been a credit to the force – in whatever country you chose to serve. As it is, I'm very glad you're here to help.'

'The old story, I suppose,' said Alan in his most deprecatory manner. 'Understaffing is a pandemic among police forces everywhere.'

'Indeed, but I don't want you to think this is just a matter of welcoming an extra two minds and pairs of hands. You two are uniquely placed to help us. You have no official connection with either VicPD or the RCMP. You are known to only a few people with any connection to the case. Yet you have the background and experience required for such an investigation. If you're willing to operate entirely off the record, you can be of inestimable help.'

'There is one possible fly in the ointment, sir,' I put in. 'You're probably aware that we were attacked a few days ago by some men we think might have been working for Paul Hartford.'

'The attempted kidnappings, yes. I regret to say that, though we have a good idea who your attackers were, we have not yet been able to track them down.'

Ah. So they *had* taken us seriously. 'Well, that's just the thing, you see. Those men know who we are. And although we think they won't try to do us any more harm – if they *were* Hartford's goons, that is – if they spot us asking questions it could compromise our usefulness.'

'Yes, I see your point, and had in fact taken that into consideration. We believe that those men are far away by now, Mrs Martin. You have forgotten what a very large country Canada is, and how much of it is still largely unpopulated. If a man doesn't care overly much about the amenities of life, he can disappear into the bush and never be found. But just in case we're wrong, and the men are still around, I have a ploy in mind. If you're willing, that is. Do sit down, Chief Constable, and I'll explain.'

'I prefer Mister these days, sir. Or Alan.'

'Splendid. And I'm Derek. Now what I have in mind is to spread a discreet rumour that the two of you are high-powered English narcs, operating entirely incognito, here to get to the bottom of our drugs problem. That will explain your presence in almost any venue and scare off anyone who might think about doing you harm.'

'Hmm,' said Alan, scraping his jaw. 'What if this series of events, culminating in Hartford's murder, is connected with the drug traffic?'

'Then it won't work. No one connected with drugs will give you truthful answers to any questions about the traffic. But we are reasonably certain there's no connection. Hartford was almost certainly profiting from drugs, of course, but in a round-about way – contributions to the Conservative Party in return for discreet silence, that sort of thing.'

I made a noise of disgust. 'Is there any way that man wasn't corrupt? What an utterly, thoroughly appalling human being!'

Derek smiled grimly. 'We've never been able to connect him with prostitution. Oh, he enjoyed his women, but he didn't traffic in them. So far as we know.'

'So why, with all respect,' I asked, trying to keep my temper under control, 'was the man not charged with his crimes? If you knew he was involved in all these disgusting rackets?'

'Dorothy, you know the answer to that.' Alan sounded weary. 'The answer has been the same since time began, or at least since a justice system was established. The police very often know about criminal activity that they can't bring home to the villain, even though they know quite well who that is, because there is no proof. A court requires evidence, good solid evidence. Further, being a despicable human being is not a crime, except in the highest court of all.'

'Which Hartford is presumably facing right now.' I shivered. 'Now there's a sobering thought. Derek, now that the probable culprit in what Alan and I have been calling the "nastiness" is dead, will that investigation die as well?'

The Deputy Chief sighed. 'There never was much of an investigation, sadly. There seemed to be no pattern, and as McKenzie will have told you, most of the incidents were too petty to warrant taking time away from what seemed to be more serious matters. But the matter of Varner's hawks, and then the death of Miss George, raised the issue to a new level. And now, of course, with the death of the supposed engineer of those crimes as well as the rest, it's all hands to the pump.'

'Yes.' Alan stood up. 'And these hands had best begin pumping.'

Derek pulled out a business card and scribbled something on it. 'Here. This will admit you anywhere you need to go. Meanwhile I'll go and crank up the rumour mill.'

'All right, Deputy Martin, where first? This is your bailiwick, you know. The Conversation Department.'

'I'd like to find that woman we talked to before. Teresa something.'

It took a while, since no one was at his or her desk, and normal working procedure had been shattered, but we were finally directed to a cubicle in what would, in the old days, have been the steno pool. Teresa was sitting next to a box which contained a pitiful collection of personal belongings: a couple of pictures in small, cheap frames, a comb and mirror, an apple, a roll of breath mints. That was all, except for a nearly empty box of tissues. The rest of them were in the waste basket, crumpled.

She looked up when I tapped on the edge of the wall. Her nose and eyes were red; tears had left stains on her cheeks. 'Are you going to let me go now?' Her voice was toneless.

'We're not the police, Teresa,' I said gently. 'We met the other day when you gave us a tour of the building. But' – I gestured toward the box – 'you're moving to another office?'

'I'm leaving the company. Just as soon as the cops will let me, I'm out of here.'

'Oh, dear. I'm sorry to hear that. I was hoping to talk to you about what's happened.'

'There's nothing to talk about. Someone killed him. The next Prime Minister of Canada, and they killed him. I'm leaving the country.'

'But where will you go?'

'Anywhere. The States, first, as soon as I can get a visa. Then – who cares? First they killed my only friend, then they killed Mr Hartford, the best boss anybody ever had. It doesn't matter where I go or what I do.'

I sat on the edge of the desk, the only unoccupied surface in the room. 'Have you told your family what you plan to do?'

'They don't care. They dumped me when I moved away. Nobody cares what I do. Nobody cares if I live or die.'

Uh-oh. Here was another casualty of Paul Hartford. Unless something or someone intervened, this young woman was going to destroy her life, either directly by means of suicide or slowly via drugs and/or alcohol.

I pushed myself off the hard edge of the desk. I didn't have to explain to Alan. He was already on his phone. 'Let's go down to the canteen and have some coffee, Teresa. You can wait to be released just as well down there as up here. It's all right; we know the police officer in charge.'

She was too lethargic, too sunk in her misery to object. She didn't notice when we headed for the front door instead of the canteen, but she did rouse once we were outside on the way to our car.

'Where are you going? The canteen is inside.'

'I know. They make terrible coffee. I make very good coffee. It's not far.'

Teresa struck me as an intelligent woman. If she'd been in her normal frame of mind she would, I think, have screamed bloody murder when two almost-strangers carried her off to some unknown destination. And rightly so. But she was very far from normal and made only a token protest when Alan helped her into the car.

'Home first, don't you think?' I murmured to Alan.

He nodded and got into the driver's seat, while I sat in the back with Teresa. Her tears had begun to flow again, unnoticed. I pressed a couple of tissues into her hand and let her cry.

TWENTY

'm no therapist, but over the course of a rather long life I've come to realize that common sense and plain human kindness can deal with a lot of problems. Once we got Teresa into the house I sent her to the bathroom to wash her face and tidy up generally. When she came out I had hot coffee waiting for her.

'Now then. Sugar, cream?'

'I don't care.'

Well, she looked better, but that was all. I added both to her coffee and put it in front of her. 'Drink it. It'll do you good. But careful – it's hot.'

I heard Alan answer the door, and in a moment he brought John McKenzie into the kitchen, along with a woman I'd never seen before. In her forties, she looked like everybody's favourite aunt.

She took over. Sitting down at the table, she smiled at Teresa. 'Hello, Teresa. You've never met me, but my name is Mary Carmichael, and I understand you're feeling a bit low.'

John gestured with his eyebrows, and the rest of us left the room.

'Who is she, John?' I asked quietly when we were in the living room out of earshot.

'A therapist the police use from time to time. She's often called in when there's a suicide threat, either spoken or apparent. You believe this girl is suicidal?'

'I'm no psychologist, but yes, I believe so. She's in a state of complete apathy, says no one cares about her – but not as if she's seeking pity, just stating what she thinks is a fact. And God help us, it may be a fact, for all I know. She says her family rejected her when she left home, and her one good friend here was Elizabeth George. And she idolized Paul Hartford, so now his death on top of Elizabeth's has swept the rug out from under her.'

'Yes, I see. Look, I have to get back into the fray. They've brought me back into active status in the circumstances, but I'll keep in touch. Mary came in her own car, so she has transportation.' And he was out the door.

'What now?' I asked Alan. He shrugged. We waited.

Finally Mary called us into the kitchen.

'Teresa tells me she's feeling pretty despondent just now, and we neither of us think it's a good idea for her to go home alone to her apartment, where she knows no one. There are facilities where she could be looked after till she's on her feet again, but I'm not sure that's the best thing, either. So we're shamelessly begging. John McKenzie tells me you've an extra room here. Would it be at all possible—?'

I didn't let her finish. 'We'd love to have Teresa stay with us for a day or two, if that would help.' I hoped my response was prompted by compassion rather than sleuthly curiosity, but I couldn't be sure.

I walked Mary to the door while Teresa sat, still impassive, still apparently unable to make any decision on her own. 'Shall I try to talk to her about her feelings? I don't really know how to deal with this sort of thing.'

'If you can get her to talk, you can certainly listen. That may be most of what she needs just now, someone to listen. She is not, in my opinion, clinically depressed, just overwhelmed by circumstances. I'm licensed to prescribe meds, so I'll get something that should cheer her up a bit. And I took her keys, so I can get some essentials from her flat and bring them back here. I'd just as soon she wasn't left alone for the next couple of days. If that creates a difficult situation for you and your husband, she'll have to go into care. You understand, this is a suicide watch situation.'

I nodded. 'That's why Alan and I brought her here. It seemed to me that it wouldn't take much to push her over the edge. And that's where the tricky part comes in. Alan and I had planned to work with the police in investigating Paul's death, and Elizabeth's. We may have to talk to a good many people, and I don't think it would be a great idea to take Teresa along.'

'Possibly not. Although, since both those deaths have had such a profound effect on her, she might be willing, even eager, to help you solve them. Look, Dorothy – may I call you Dorothy?'

'Please.'

'All right, then. You must understand, there is no magic formula for dealing with someone who is profoundly unhappy, even to the point of considering suicide. Every person is an individual, with her own needs. John tells me you're a kind and sensible person. I think you can play it by ear.' She pulled a card out of her purse. 'Here's my card, in case you need me. Any time, day or night. I'll be back shortly with Teresa's things and her keys, and if you have qualms or questions then, feel free to ask me. I'm on retainer to the VicPD, by the way, so there's no question of a fee. Good luck, and thank you.'

I took a deep breath and went back to the kitchen.

Alan was drinking coffee and placidly reading the newspaper, every now and then commenting to Teresa about something he'd read. The scene was so calm, so normal, that my anxiety level lowered a trifle. I hoped it was having the same effect on Teresa. At least she'd stopped crying.

'Hmm,' said Alan, 'they're having a sale of Cowichan sweaters at the Moss Street Market this afternoon. Too bad you already bought one.'

'Yes, but I was thinking of picking some up as gifts for people back home. Jane would love one, I know – if they make them big enough for her.'

Jane Langland, our next-door neighbour, pet-sitter and all-round angel, was getting on in years and was often cold. She was also rather a large lady. As I sat trying to estimate her measurements, Teresa spoke. She had been silent for so long that I jumped.

'You have a Cowichan sweater?'

'Yes, I bought it when we went to Duncan the other day.'

'Elizabeth had several of them. She was Cowichan, you know. Did I tell you?'

'I think perhaps you did.' No need to mention that we knew it from other sources.

'She was going to make me one. She was a very good knitter. Her grandmother taught her how to make them, spinning the yarn, everything.'

'They're certainly amazing. Teresa, does your tribe have any similar crafts?' I wanted to get her off the subject of Elizabeth.

It wasn't a fortunate question. 'I never really knew my grand-father's people. My father was ashamed of my mother's mixed blood and never let me visit my grandparents. They came to see us, of course, but not often. My grandfather was proud, and he knew he was not welcome in our house. That's why I loved it when Elizabeth told me about her people. They are not my tribe, but they are of the First Nations, as I am. Sort of.'

I said a quick prayer for guidance, and made up my mind. 'Look here, Teresa. I know you're missing Elizabeth terribly. Would you like to go up to Duncan and meet some of her people?'

'You know them?'

'No, not directly. But I have met one wonderful Cowichan woman, the one who made the sweater I bought, and I know she, and the rest, would welcome any friend of Elizabeth's.'

I was sticking my neck out, and I knew it. I was pretty sure the Cowichan people would welcome Teresa, but not certain. She was, after all, of mixed race. And I didn't know if I'd be harming Teresa's fragile emotional balance. But if we were to help the police get to the bottom of Hartford's murder, I was convinced we had to know more about Elizabeth's. And taking Teresa to meet Elizabeth's family was one really good way to gain an entrée to that very private community.

Alan gave me a look I couldn't interpret. I looked at Teresa. 'What do you think?'

'If you think they won't hate me, I'd like to meet them.'

'Why should they hate you?'

'I'm part white. The biggest part.'

Alan cleared his throat. 'There are no guarantees, my dear. It's been my experience that most people respond well when they are treated with respect and accorded the dignity they deserve. The First Peoples here have been badly treated by whites for generations, but they have preserved, or regained, their way of life by sheer persistence and the dogged knowledge that they were in the right. I think, when they know that you also have been treated badly, they will open their hearts to you. But as I said – no guarantees.'

'Elizabeth knew your heritage, and she was kind to you,' I offered tentatively.

'It wasn't kindness! Not "be nice to the poor little Métis", not at all! We were friends. We liked each other!'

The tears were flowing again, but she was angry, which was a great improvement over apathy. 'Then why do you think her people wouldn't be friendly, too? She must have told them about you.'

'She did! She wanted me to meet them. We were going to . . .' She faded out.

'Then let's go. Right now. We can get some lunch on the way.'

'I'm not hungry.'

'But we are.'

The doorbell rang. I'd forgotten Mary was going to bring some clothes and things for Teresa. I let Alan answer while I kept our charge talking. 'Have you ever been up to Duncan, Teresa? It's a very pretty little town. A bit touristy, but pleasant. You'll like it.'

Her momentary excitement had faded. She shrugged.

Mary came into the room, smiling. 'I've brought you a few night things and a change of clothes, love. Alan tells me you're going on a jaunt this afternoon. Have a good time, and don't wear yourself out.'

I saw her to the door. 'I wasn't sure if this was a good idea or not. Do you think it's okay?'

'The important thing right now is to keep her occupied. She may very well nap in the car on the way up. Strong emotion is exhausting. If she does, wake her gently, and make sure she eats something. She won't want to, but when she smells food she'll probably be hungry. Just follow your instincts – and remember, I'm never farther away than your phone. But I don't think you'll need me.'

Teresa said almost nothing on the way to Duncan, and when I looked back after a while, she had indeed fallen asleep. We were pulling into a car park in Duncan before I had the heart to wake her.

She was a bit groggy, but went with us into the café without argument, though saying she wasn't hungry. Alan and I ignored that and ordered hamburgers for all of us, and when they came she took a tiny bite (with a fork) and then another, and before she was aware of it had eaten about half the sandwich.

'I guess I was hungry after all,' she said with a tiny smile.

'Good. Now before we do anything else, I want you to meet the lady I told you about, the one who knitted my sweater. And before that, we both need to head to the washroom.'

'Oh. Am I a mess?'

'Your hair is a bit mussed, and you could use some lipstick. Come along.'

I wasn't going to let her out of my sight. She seemed a lot better, but a washroom is a great place to swallow too many pills, or stick in a needle full of oblivion. Not that she probably had with her any of those tickets out of the world, but I was taking no chances. She was coming with me now so she couldn't say she needed later to go off by herself. And if she did, anyway, I was right behind her.

I was afraid the dignified old woman wouldn't be at the shop today, but I needn't have worried. She was in the same place, knitting needles working away. If there were a few more lines in her weathered face, if she was a little slower to look up and speak to us, I didn't wonder why. I cleared my throat. 'You won't remember me, and I didn't learn your name, but we met a few days ago. You told me a lot about your people, and I bought one of your wonderful sweaters.'

She inclined her head. 'I do remember. You may call me Laura. You could not pronounce my tribal name.'

'Then, Laura, I want to say, first, how very sorry – how *very* sorry – I am about the death in your family.'

Another inclination of the head.

'And I want you to meet someone who was one of Elizabeth's good friends. This is Teresa, who works for the same company. The two women became fast friends in part because Teresa, too, is of the First Peoples.'

Teresa, her eyes bright, bowed to the old woman, who studied her face intently and then nodded. 'Elizabeth talked to me about you. She said you had been rejected by your white family because of your native heritage. You are not of our tribe, Teresa, but you are of our people. Elizabeth loved you. If you wish, you are welcome to visit our village and meet her family.'

By now both were weeping quietly, and, I admit, so was I. I fished a packet of tissues out of my purse and offered them around. Laura declined and simply let the tears trickle down her lined cheeks.

'We had thought,' I said when I had blown my nose, 'of going to the village this afternoon, if you thought we wouldn't be intruding.'

'One of my sons will take you there,' she said. 'But first, Teresa, I will measure you for a sweater. It would be too warm for you now, but winter will come. I will knit it myself. Come here, and tell me what pattern you would like.'

'I can't afford one,' Teresa whispered to me.

'Shh! It's a gift. Don't even mention money, or you'll insult her.'

Careful measurements were taken. Teresa was shown the various traditional patterns from which she could choose. Details were settled. Laura's son Harold was fetched away from a workshop in the back, where he had been carving an elaborate totem.

'This is Elizabeth's friend Teresa,' the matriarch said. 'She is of our people. She is from another tribe, the Cree, but she loved our Elizabeth. She is as one of us. Take her to the village and let her know her family.'

'I shouldn't take you away from your work,' Teresa began, but the young man shook his head and smiled. 'What Grandmother says to do, we must do.'

'Grandmother? She said—'

'She called me her son. We are all her sons. You will soon be her daughter. I believe she is actually my great-great-aunt, but she is mother to our tribe.' He turned to me and to Alan, who had been lurking in the background. 'You are her friends, yes?'

Teresa nodded firmly. 'Very good friends.'

Whom she has met exactly twice, I thought, but I was glad she thought of us that way.

'We brought her here for a visit,' said Alan. 'Teresa lives in Victoria, where we are visiting for a few days.'

'And would you like to come with her to our village?' Harold asked.

'I think we'd better follow you there,' I said, 'because Teresa has no other way to get home. Also because we would like to meet your people, if we may.'

'Before we go,' said Alan, 'I'd very much like to see what you're working on, if you don't mind. I've always been interested in wood carving.'

Well, that was the first I'd heard of it, but then Alan had lived a lot of life before we met and married. Teresa and I accompanied the two men back to the workshop.

It was untidy, as all wood shops are. Slivers of wood were everywhere, and the air was rich with the scent of . . . was it cedar? It reminded me of my father's workshop when I was little. I felt instantly at home.

'You see,' Harold was saying, 'I rough out the shape with a chainsaw, but the fine carving must be done by hand. Be sure not to put your hand down anywhere. A knife might be hidden under shavings, and they are razor-sharp.'

Most of the knives weren't hidden, though, but neatly hung in a rack where Harold could find them easily. They looked lethal, bright steel set into wooden handles, smoothed with long use to fit their user's hand.

'Harold.' The voice was not loud, but it was demanding. 'We'd better go. Grandmother does not wish us to delay.'

As we left the shop, I grabbed Alan's arm and pointed.

'Yes, I saw,' he said very quietly.

'Is it—'

'I think so. I'll have to talk to Harold, but not just now.'

No. Now was definitely not the time to talk, in front of Teresa, about the knife that was shaped into a long curve, pointed at the end. Much like the length and shape of a raptor's talon.

Nor about the stain that had seeped into the wooden handle.

TWENTY-ONE

I went in Harold's car while Alan followed in ours. I wasn't letting Teresa out of my sight for one second, no matter how much better she seemed. Nor was I ready to talk about that knife. I wanted to get some thoughts clear in my head first.

So I sat back and listened to Harold and Teresa as they began to get to know one another.

There had been no time to tell him about her fragile emotional state, but he seemed to understand. He chatted about the countryside we were passing through, about his own love of wood from a tree to a finished carving. He talked about the Cowichan ways of relating to nature, and asked about her heritage.

'I was brought up as a white girl,' she said. 'My mother wasn't ashamed of her background – her father was the one who was a native – but Father was very prejudiced. Mother tried to teach me a little about Grandfather's way of life, but she had to be secretive about it, because Father would be furious if he found out. I think I missed out on a lot.'

'I think you did,' said Harold quietly. 'There are many ways to live one's life, and the way of the white man is only one of them. It is good to know both ways, so you can choose – or take the best of both. I went to university and learned how to manage a business. The shop is mine, and it has given me a good living. But once it was going well, and I knew that I could keep it going well, I went back to my first love and studied wood-carving from the masters.'

'Your tribe?' Teresa asked.

'Yes, but the masters through the ages as well, and not just workers in wood. I learned from Michelangelo a way to see the sculpture inside the wood – for him it was marble – and then cut away to find it.'

'That seems like . . . like magic to me,' said Teresa in an awed voice. 'I could never do that.'

'Have you ever tried?'

'No. I never even thought of it. I'm not any kind of an artist.'

'How do you know?'

'Oh . . . well . . . I've never done anything like that. I just . . . I went to university for a little while, but I didn't seem to fit in. So then I took a secretarial course and, when I couldn't get a good job at home, I came here. I'm a pretty good secretary – or I was. I quit my job today.'

Don't ask her why, I prayed from the back seat.

'Did you not like your job?'

'I . . . well, no. I don't suppose I did. I was reasonably well paid, for a beginner, and there were good opportunities. And then there was Elizabeth – and the owner of the company was wonderful – but with both of them gone, I . . .' Her voice broke.

'You liked some of the people you worked with, but not the work itself. That is not good. You must find work you enjoy.'

'You make it sound easy! I've never been able to pick and choose. I have to eat, you know!'

She was getting annoyed. Good! So much better than apathy. I was beginning to like and respect Harold a good deal.

'It is not easy, and you are very young. I think you need to talk to Grandmother. She is very wise and will help you. One thing I can tell you, though. You were made to be happy in your life, and for that you must find the work that you were meant to do. And now we are here. I will show you how we live.'

Teresa was quiet on the way home, but it was the silence of thought, not of despair. She made only one remark, perhaps talking mostly to herself, 'It's a very different way of living, isn't it?'

When we got to our condo, she went in with us, but sat down in the living room, a determined look in her eye. 'You know, you don't have to keep me here if you don't want to. You thought I was about to kill myself, didn't you?'

Honesty was best. 'We thought it was a possibility, yes,' I replied. 'You were very distressed.'

'Yes, I was. I thought my world had come to an end. I don't think that anymore. Harold and the others showed me that there's a whole different way of looking at life, a way I hadn't even imagined. I'll be all right now.'

'I'm sure you will – now. But you're going to be lonely from time to time.'

'That's nothing new. I think I've been lonely all my life. I didn't fit in. Now I've found a place where I might.'

'And that's a good thing,' said Alan. 'But it won't solve all your problems immediately. Suppose you have a bit of supper with us and then spend the night. It's getting late. And I don't know about you, but Dorothy and I are tired. It's been a long day.'

'We-ell . . . but in the morning—'

'We'll see what the morning brings. Meanwhile, come help me make some sandwiches or something.'

At least I think that's what he said. It had in fact been a long and disturbing day, and the relief from severe worry about Teresa was knocking me right out. Alan had to wake me so I could eat my supper.

The first words out of my mouth the next morning were, 'We never got a chance to talk about that knife.'

'You must have been dreaming about it, to have it pop out before you're even properly awake. Here, have some coffee. We won't talk about anything more taxing than the weather until you've come to full consciousness.'

I obeyed, but I couldn't stop thinking. The coffee did clear the misty tangle of ideas, so when I put my cup down I was able to be articulate. 'Alan, he couldn't possibly have done it. Not Harold. He's just not a murderer. Oh, where's Teresa?'

'Still asleep. I looked in on her a few minutes ago. She's all right, and we can speak freely. By the way, I called Mary last night to tell her about the trip to Duncan and the village. She's going to come over in a bit to see Teresa and assess her condition. Then if she approves, we'll take the girl home.

'But about the knife. It's certainly the right size and shape to have inflicted the wounds that killed Elizabeth. And that stain certainly looks like blood. We'll have to tell John, and he'll tell the RCMP, and they'll take it in for analysis.'

I opened my mouth to protest. Alan held up a hand. 'There's no option, my dear. Here we have a weapon that could have been used. We have a man with strong views about tribal culture. It isn't a great stretch to posit a quarrel between them, about her "selling out" to the white man, a quarrel that escalated, a knife he happened to be carrying – it's all too possible.'

'It's flat-out *im*possible. He's a gentle man who would never, ever raise his hand to a woman.'

'If we're looking at our instincts, I agree with you. Looking at the evidence, I cannot.'

'I need more coffee.'

I was annoyed with Alan. Not quite angry, because he was right, and I knew it. The knife had to be taken and the stain analysed. And when it turned out to be wood sap, or Harold's own blood from an unfortunate slip, it would work in his favour. But I was right, too. A man of his character ought not to be subject to police scrutiny. Especially a man of his background, to be investigated by the white police, would be painful, raising racial memories better forgotten.

So often life presents a conflict not between good and bad, but between the better of two bad – or two good – choices. I sighed. 'But we won't tell Teresa.'

'Certainly not!'

'Won't tell me what?'

She had appeared quietly at our door.

There were times in my teaching career when I had to think fast. Ditto Alan as a policeman. 'Oh, we were talking about where we wanted to take you tomorrow, but we wanted it to be a surprise, a little treat for you. Now I suppose we'll have to ask, have you ever been to Butchart Gardens?'

'No, but you don't have to show me around. I told you, I'm over wanting to . . . you know.'

So she'd reached the stage of being embarrassed about it. That was a good sign. 'Well, we're glad of that! Not that I really thought you'd be that stupid. But you're going to have a lot of time on your hands until you get another job, and we enjoy your company, so think about it.'

'What would you like for breakfast?' asked Alan, the breakfast chef.

'I usually just have coffee and toast.'

'Now see, that's another reason you've been down in the dumps. Low blood sugar will do it every time. Alan will make you one of his superb breakfasts, even though the sausages and the bacon here are quite different from what he's used to.'

She started to protest, then held up her hands in surrender. 'At this rate I'll not only be depressed, I'll be fat!'

'Fat has something to be said for it,' said Alan. 'Dorothy has taught me how to make French toast, and though it's unknown in England, I've learnt to quite like it. Do we have any syrup, love?'

'I think I saw some in the pantry.'

Alan's French toast has to be tasted to be believed. I ate far too much, and was wishing I'd put on trousers with an elastic waist, when Mary arrived. It didn't take her long to pronounce Teresa well enough to go home, but she took me aside while the girl was packing up her things. 'I was pretty sure this was just a matter of temporary despondency, and she's come out of it nicely. But until her life improves quite a lot – new job, new friends – she could easily slip back. It becomes a pattern, you see. I plan to keep in close touch with her, and I hope you'll do the same.'

'I think she's going to want to go back to the Cowichan village. She was strongly attracted to the people there, and the way of life. She's never had a chance to explore her tribal roots; her white father wouldn't even acknowledge them. Do you think it's okay for her to get involved with the tribe?'

'Did they accept her?'

'Very graciously.'

'Then I'd say yes, it will probably be very good for her. Does she have any money, do you know? To live on for a little while, I mean, until she can find another job.'

'I don't know, but I'll ask. I think she trusts us enough not to be insulted by the question.'

Alan drove Teresa to her flat and reported back that it was small but comfortable, and was furnished simply but tastefully. 'I did ask her if she was all right for groceries until she received her final pay cheque, and she assured me she was fine. I think she was telling the truth. There were no signs of scrimping or making do. By the way, did you really intend to take her to Butchart? I'm not sure she's a garden aficionada.'

'No, I just said the first thing that came into my head when she came in that way. If we take her anywhere, I think it will be back to Duncan to visit with the old lady – and Harold, of course.'

'Did you get any feeling of sparks flying there?'

'No-o. I don't think so. No. I think they've begun to think of one another as family, brother and sister or that sort of thing. She needs family, poor dear.'

Alan nodded soberly. 'And we're about to launch a police investigation of her new brother. I called John about the knife, and he's going to go pick it up. He wants us to meet him there.'

'But why? Alan, I'd much rather not. It feels like . . . like betrayal.'

'He says we've developed a bit of a relationship with the Cowichan. Our being there might ease tensions a bit.'

'Or destroy any chance Teresa might have for finding her place in the world!'

I grumbled all the way to Duncan. Alan was patient. 'You're making too much of this, you know. We're not rapacious settlers trying to take their land or otherwise defraud or abuse them.'

'We're white. Not only that, we're English, or you are, anyway. Racial memories go back a long way.'

'And do you think the old grandmother, Laura, is an unreasonable woman who will blame us, and Teresa, for the mild and reasonable actions of the RCMP? Who are, incidentally, working to try to find the murderer of a member of her tribe?'

'Oh, if you put it that way—'

'What other way is there? You're fond of saying "Put it back to front". All right. Suppose you're living in a place where your race, or at any rate your nationality, is in the minority, and where it has in the past been subjugated. Things are different now. You have a good deal of self-determination and economic independence. A member of the once-ruling race, a person in authority, comes with a courteous request to look at and perhaps take away an object that may have been used in a crime. How do you react?'

I tried to consider it rationally. 'I think I'd feel intimidated and somewhat afraid.'

'Belligerent? Obstructive?'

'No, because I've learned – my people have learned – over the generations that cooperation is safer. We have also learned, however, that in cooperating we lost nearly everything we had, including our identity.'

'Agreed. So we will walk softly and be respectful. And Dorothy – this has to be done, if only to prove that Harold's knife had nothing to do with Elizabeth's death.'

'Which I don't for a moment believe that it did.'

'Yes, dear.'

The 'I don't agree but I'm not going to argue' response. I hate it, and maintained a stubborn silence for the rest of the trip.

'Lunch?' Alan suggested when we reached Duncan. 'I told John we'd meet him at the café.'

'I'm not hungry.' And that was actually true. My stomach was clenched at the thought of the ordeal ahead.

'Then have some coffee with us.'

But John didn't want anything to eat or drink, either. He wanted to get the distasteful business behind him as soon as possible.

Business was brisk in the crafts shop. Laura was busy measuring a woman for a sweater. She looked up and nodded and then went back to what she was doing. Alan went to a clerk and asked for Harold.

'He's in his workshop. You've been back there before, haven't you? Go ahead, then.'

I stayed in the shop, looking at sweaters and jewellery and small examples of Harold's carving. I stayed well away from the door to the workshop. I couldn't stand to hear the conversation.

It was brief. John came out with a couple of plastic bags in his hand; Alan followed. Harold didn't come out.

John and Alan didn't hurry out of the shop, but they didn't linger, either. I followed, taking a deep breath when we got outside.

'Now I want something to eat,' said Alan.

'And something to drink,' said John. 'How about this one?'

It was a brew pub. I offered no opinion, but went along with the men. I was still too edgy to be hungry, but perhaps some cider would taste good.

TWENTY-TWO

It was dark and cool inside, and busy. We found a table in the corner and ordered drinks while the men looked at the menu. The drinks came, and the men ordered food. I took a long pull at my cider and said, 'Well?'

'Could have been worse,' muttered John into his beer. 'The guy was polite. Handed over the knife with no protest.'

'Picked it up before we could stop him,' growled Alan.

I frowned. 'But it's his knife. His fingerprints would be on it no matter what.'

'Unless someone else used it and then wiped it clean,' argued John. 'Then Harold's new prints might be the only ones.'

'But what did he say? Was he upset?'

'It's hard for us, for white men, to read a native man's face. He didn't *sound* upset. He said the knife was his, that he used it seldom, but it was useful for certain kinds of detail; that the last time he used it he had been careless and let it slip, and it gouged his other hand.'

'So that explains the stain.'

'If true. He did show us a scar on his left hand, below the thumb, just where a knife might go if you were pulling it toward you through tough wood and it slipped. But there were many scars on that hand – as one might expect with someone who routinely uses very sharp tools. Most of the scars looked old – again, as one might expect. Presumably as a craftsman becomes more skilled he is able to handle his tools more deftly.'

'But he handed it over willingly?'

'He asked us to be very careful of it, as it was an unusual tool and had been quite expensive.'

'Did he ask why you wanted it?'

'We said straight off that we were investigating the death of Elizabeth George,' said Alan, 'described the knife we'd noticed, and asked if we might see it. He's not a stupid person. He got the point. And he willingly gave us a DNA sample, for matching purposes.'

I lifted my glass, noticed the cider was all gone, and put it down again. 'Did he . . . ask about Teresa at all?'

'No.' That was all Alan said, but his face was full of sorrow.

The waiter brought our food. Alan had ordered me a sandwich – he of the low-blood-sugar mind-set. I hadn't known I wanted it, but it was grilled salmon and smelled good, so I took a bite. Another bottle of cider also appeared in front of me without my request. That man of mine looks after me, even when – maybe especially when – I'm annoyed with him.

'What's done is done,' I said when I had forced down as much food as I could, past the lump in my throat. 'What now?'

'I have to take this to the crime lab,' John said. 'I should have done it straightaway. Chain of evidence, you know. But it's been right here in my pocket the whole time, and you'll bear witness that nobody has tampered with it.'

'Anyway, it's irrelevant to the crime,' I said firmly.

'Yes. Well. I'd best be off.' He finished his beer, nodded to both of us, and was gone.

'And what about us? Are we off to chase yet more wild geese?'

'No, I'd thought about wild hawks. Or semi-tame ones, rather. I think it would be profitable to go visit Silas Varner.'

'Good grief! What on earth for? He won't let us in anyway, without John.'

'Perhaps. But I'm having this feeling, stronger and stronger all the time, that he and/or his birds are pivotal to this whole problem, and I'd like to talk to him.'

'The best of British luck. And just how do you propose to storm that fortress?'

'I bought him a present. Two presents, in fact. And no, you can't see them. Possess your soul in patience.'

'Hmph. Do you remember how to get there?'

'No, but John told Sadie a day or two ago. Come along, darling.'

Alan drove very slowly once we left the paved road, but I was still regretting that second cider when Sadie announced that we had arrived at our destination. He let me out before he buried the car in the hedge, as John had done. When he joined me, Alan was carrying a large bag with the logo of the crafts store.

We began to walk up the rutted drive. I was frankly a little scared, and was gripping Alan's arm. Without that firm support, I probably would have screamed when the shout came. 'Who's that? What are you doing on my property? Git!' He had come, silently, from around the back of the mews.

'It's John McKenzie's friends, Mr Varner. I've brought you something I think you might like.'

'Don't need nothin'. Don't need charity.'

'I didn't suppose you did. This isn't something you need, just something I think you'll like. Here, take a look.'

He held out the bag. Suspiciously, the old man took it.

'Careful, part of it's breakable.'

Silas reached into the bag and pulled out a bottle of Alan's favourite Scotch, Glenfiddich. 'Hmph. Reckon you think I'm an old sot.'

'No, I happen to enjoy that label myself, and I'd hoped we might share it. But look at the real gift.'

Silas handed Alan the bottle, with some disdain, and reached into the bag again.

I was stunned. So, from the look on his face, was Silas.

It might almost have been alive. It was not realistically carved, but there was power in those wings, fierce determination in those eyes, strength in those talons. It was no longer a lump of wood. It was a hawk, just about to take flight.

Silas swallowed. A tear started to trickle down his cheek; he brushed it angrily away. It wasn't, I thought, easy for him to utter words he probably hadn't spoken in years.

'I–I s'pose you might as well come in and set a spell.'

And that, from Silas, was the equivalent of a gilt-edged invitation.

While he looked for a place to put his new treasure, I looked around. His hovel smelled (as did Silas). But the place was surprisingly tidy. The one decrepit chair, an old recliner, had a patched blanket draped over it. A small table right next to the chair was cleared off, I presumed for his next meal. A shelf on the wall held a few plates and mugs; a pump evidently provided his water. There was a Franklin stove in one corner and a Coleman stove in another – heating and cooking taken care of.

The walls were bare boards, no plaster, no drywall, and here and there a chink where daylight shone through. The roof was similar. There was no floor, only the beaten earth. This single room comprised, apparently, his entire living space. I could see no closet, no storage place for extra clothes. Perhaps his only clothes were the ones he had on, which would explain the body odor.

There was no bed. He must sleep in his chair.

He was not to be counted among the homeless, only because he did have this permanent place to sleep. Yet many who lived in homeless shelters had far better accommodations than this.

And yet. And yet. Everywhere one looked there were piles of books. I spotted the Harry Potter series; their multi-coloured spines were unmistakable. There in a corner was *Huckleberry Finn*, over there a formidable tome that looked like a textbook on ornithology. An unabridged dictionary propped up a stack of Canadian history books; a biography of Winston Churchill teetered precariously on top of *The Wind in the Willows* and *Anne of Green Gables*.

'Reckon there's not much settin' room. You take my chair, ma'am. Plenty of stacks of books,' he added, nodding at Alan. 'An' there's no glasses, but the cups are clean.'

He put the carving down on the floor opposite the cracked, dirty window, where it would get whatever light there was, and got three mugs from the shelf. Two were chipped. He poured a generous measure of Glenfiddich into each and held up the nicest one. 'Water, ma'am? Don't need to worry, it's good clean well water.'

'Yes, please, just a little.'

There were no more cups, so he pumped the water into a small bowl and poured some into my cup, which he handed to me carefully. Apparently assuming Alan would take his neat, he gave the other chipped cup to him and raised his own. 'I'm . . . uh . . . mighty obliged.'

He leaned against the wall and drank. Alan and I sipped. I couldn't think of a thing to say.

He cleared his throat, wiped his sleeve across his mouth, and glared at me. 'You bin lookin' at my books.'

'Uh . . . yes. You have some of my favourites.'

Alan put his cup down on the floor, the only place he could find except for the stack of books next to the one he was sitting on. 'Silas,' he said quietly, 'you are an educated man. Why do you pretend to be a backwoodsman?'

Long pause. Silas cleared his throat again. 'That's what I am. Now.' His voice had changed; his hillbilly accent was gone. 'The old days are dead. Let them be.'

'And yet you kept this.' Alan held up a piece of paper, somewhat dirty, with one corner missing. 'I wasn't prying. It fell out of a book when I straightened the stack.' It was a diploma from the University of Victoria: Master of Science, Magna cum Laude, dated some forty years ago.

'Yes. Makes a good bookmark.'

Alan and I were silent. I sipped my Scotch (which I don't actually like) and waited.

'You're asking yourselves how I ended up a bum.'

'You're not a bum, Mr Varner,' I said firmly. 'I believe you're living the kind of life you want to live. I'm sure you have a story about how things changed for you, and we'd like to hear it, but only if you care to tell us.'

'And then you'll tell the world. You're working for John McKenzie.'

'No,' said Alan, 'not exactly. We are working with him, yes, at the request of his niece back in England, who is a friend of ours. John was, and is, distressed about the series of incidents, petty at first but then increasingly serious, which were disturbing the peace of this island. Of course you know about the release of your birds. Do you know about the rest?'

'McKenzie told me.'

'Ah. Those incidents are the reason Dorothy and I are here. I am a retired English policeman. My wife, who has no formal training but is a talented natural detective, has worked with me for years in unofficial investigations. We believe that all the incidents in the series, up to and including the death of Elizabeth George, were directed, if not performed, by one man. We believe that you are not in any way culpable.

'But I have become increasingly convinced that you and your birds are somehow at the heart of the matter. I can give no reason for this belief. There is no evidence, and I would be embarrassed to mention it to John. It's just a . . . I suppose my American-born wife would call it a "hunch". I talked Dorothy into coming here today in the hopes that if we could learn more about you, it might lead us to some connections – somehow.'

Silas shrugged. 'Can't imagine how. My story's old. I mostly don't tell it because I don't want people feeling sorry for me. Got that?' He looked as fierce as one of his hawks.

'I think pity would be misplaced,' said Alan drily. 'As my wife says, you live the way you want to. Fifty years ago you would have been called a flower child.'

'Fifty years ago and more, that's exactly what I was. I grew up in Nelson, little town in the Kootenays. Silver rush town in the glory days. When I was a teenager, it was a haven for American draft dodgers. Not far from the border, you see.'

'The border with Washington?'

'No, Idaho. East of here. That was the Vietnam era, remember, and the boys came in droves. The Kootenays are a good climate for growing pot, and the town was more-or-less wide open then. I got into it in a big way – live off the land, love beads, protest marches – the whole shtick.

'Then I met a girl who changed my life. I didn't fall in love with her, or anything like that, but we got to be friends. I met her one day when I was out in the woods looking for birds; I'd always liked them, and I was getting kind of interested in them. She was a serious type, and she told me straight out I was wasting my life, that I was too smart for all that. She brought me books, books about birds.' He pointed to a stack I hadn't noticed, resting on a very large, fat book. The cover was obscured by the books on top, but the spine read, *Birds of America*.

'Audubon?' I couldn't keep the awe out of my voice.

'A reprint, of course, but a good one. Even way back then, it cost Cathy way more than she could afford. She had some kind of crummy job, I forget what. Anyway, she bought me that book and told me I had to read it, and long before I'd finished I knew I had to learn a lot more about birds.'

He picked up the bottle and gestured to both of us. We shook our heads. I would have loved some plain water, but I didn't want to interrupt him, now he'd got started.

'Well, Cathy was right about one thing. I had a good mind, even though I hadn't done anything about it. My father had told me the same thing over and over, but of course coming from a girl my age, it sounded true. There was no money, so I knew if I was going to university it would have to be on scholarship.

'I went back to school – I'd dropped out – and worked like a madman. They didn't call it the GED then, but it was the same idea. I did so well on all the exams that the teachers at the high school urged me to apply to UVic and take their entrance exams. And when I aced those I applied for a scholarship, and got it.'

He poured himself a little more Scotch. 'Those were good days. I took my degree in biology, went on to the master's in ornithology, started applying for jobs. I didn't want to teach, wanted to be out in the field. Park ranger, something like that. I applied for a few jobs that looked promising. And then I met a girl.'

Uh-oh. His face went dark. We were getting to it.

'We got engaged. In about five minutes. She was . . . well. Doesn't matter. I'd almost quit smoking joints, but she got me into it again. Wasn't legal then. I landed a job, a good one, and was just packing up to go live near the park when the RCMP came knocking at my door.'

He looked at the mug in his hand and threw it to the floor. The tough pottery didn't shatter, but the handle came off. He ran his sleeve across his mouth again. 'Turned out my "fiancée" was living with a guy who'd just started dealing drugs. He'd got in a shipment of cocaine, and when he thought the authorities were getting a little too close, the woman I thought I loved stashed the stuff in my flat – our flat, the one we shared. When the cops came, she told them where to look.'

There was nothing to say. Silas had forbidden pity, and what I felt, in any case, was rage. *Judas also ran*, I thought, but didn't say.

'It's an old story, from Samson on up. My flat smelled of pot. I had a reputation as an anti-authoritarian hippy. My fingerprints were on the box Delilah put the stuff in. It was an open and shut case. I got five years. Could have been a lot more, but it was a first offense and all that. While I was "away", Delilah stole everything of value that I owned. There wasn't much. She did leave my books; they had little or no cash value.

'In prison, I read everything I could about raptors. Those fierce, independent killers appealed to me. I decided I was, somehow, going to get myself some birds and train them. When I got out, nobody would hire me. I found this shack to live in, planted some vegetables, wrote a couple of books about raptors. They brought in a little money, still do. Not much, but enough to see to my birds. I scavenged building materials wherever I could, to build the mews. Found a couple of red-tails. I knew how to look after them, how to train them. Harry and Ron are my fourth set. First ones were David and Jonathan. Got these just after I read the books. Should have named Ron Voldemort. He's a vicious one. Good bird.'

'Always males? I read somewhere that females make the better hunters.'

'Won't have a female living on my property.' He pushed himself off from the wall, picked up his broken mug, and set it down in the dry-sink by the pump. 'Need to mend that. So now you know my story, and much good it may do you. Don't see how it has anything to do with all the crimes.'

'Nor do I, but I do have a question or two, if you don't mind. And could I have some water, please?' I handed over my mug and he filled it from the pump. I drank thirstily of the clear, cold water. 'Mr Varner, there are two important people in your story whom you have not named: your betrayer, whose name was presumably not Delilah, and her lover.'

'I call her Delilah. I've blocked her real name from my memory.'

'Do you have any idea where she is now?'

'Don't know, don't care. If she kept up with her dealer friend, they're probably both dead by now, though they were younger than I. The drug scene doesn't lead to a long life.'

'And her lover? The drug dealer? Did you know his name?'

'At one time I did. He wasn't actually a dealer, not professionally. He was dabbling in it. He was young and rich and out for kicks. Maybe what happened to me scared him out of it.' He shook his head. 'No, I can't recall. Peter, maybe? One of the saints, anyway, because I remember thinking how inappropriate the name was.'

Alan coughed, perhaps choking on his drink. 'A saint. Paul, perhaps?'

TWENTY-THREE

'So there we have the connection,' I said when we were back in the car. I drove; Alan was feeling the effects of the whisky a bit. He'd had to have another wee tot while he convinced Silas that his personal saga was safe with us.

'He didn't remember the last name, Dorothy. And Paul is not exactly an unusual name. You'll note he didn't make the connection with the Paul Hartford who's been all over the news.'

'And how would he have heard the news? No radio, no TV, no newspaper, not even a phone.'

'He does go into town occasionally. I think he keeps informed somehow.'

'Nevertheless: a rich young guy named Paul who was a bit of a rakehell, who thought himself above the law? Alan, I'm convinced, and you are too. You're just being a cautious policeman. Your instincts told you to get Silas's story. Well, now we have it.'

'Very well, tell me what you suppose we have. And while you're about it, perhaps you can work out how we will find any evidence to support our opinions.'

'Evidence is your problem. You're the policeman. What we have here, now that we know Silas's story, is a human tragedy, with Paul Hartford – or no, with his father at the centre of it.'

I paused to negotiate an especially awful stretch of dirt road, and to think. 'Once upon a time,' I began.

Alan grinned. 'The proper beginning for a fairy tale.'

I ignored him. 'Once upon a time there was an evil king. He was very rich and very powerful, and he had one son. The young prince was handsome and charming, and very intelligent as well. The king his father gave him everything he wanted, everything except love. So of course the prince grew up badly spoiled, but his charm and good looks, and his superior brain, continued to get him everything he wanted – except what he wanted most, his father's approval.

'He reached out for happiness, looking in all the wrong places: alcohol and drugs and easy sex and thrills. He got involved in crime in a small way, but a drug deal that would have brought him a lot of money went wrong; he managed not to get arrested, but the shipment was seized, and he had to flee in a hurry to avoid the boss who would have shot off his knees – if not worse – for losing all that crack.'

I stopped to sip some water from the bottle in the cup holder.

'So the naughty little prince grew up. He went to university and did brilliant work. He founded a tech company that began to make money hand over fist, so it was easy for the prince to cultivate a benevolent image, strewing largesse to the peasants. He married a beautiful, malleable woman, but she proved to be not quite so malleable as he had supposed. They had a daughter, but the marriage grew more and more contentious when the wife wouldn't do exactly as the prince demanded. He was not accustomed to being thwarted; he found her attitude intolerable and began to find consolation elsewhere, which was easy for one with his wealth and charming good looks.

'At last the wife had had enough and sued for divorce. The prince fought, of course, but as his infidelity was well known in the community, the wife won her suit along with a handsome monetary settlement and the custody of the daughter.'

I had a little more water, and continued. 'All that is proven fact.'

'Except for the part about the drugs deal in his youth.'

'Easy to prove. Now I'm getting into the realm of speculation, or psychology, if you prefer. I think the divorce was a tipping point for Paul Hartford. After a lifetime of instant gratification, he suddenly ran up against opposition, and something snapped. He had to get even. First with Amy, and of course with John for "taking her away", so the persecution campaign began. Then he conceived the idea of standing for Parliament, in part because it would so annoy Amy. Then he, or one of his sycophants, dreamed up the really brilliant series of petty crimes, a problem he could solve when elected.

'But I'm sure it was his own idea to persecute Silas. He would never have forgiven him for that long ago drug deal.'

'Dorothy, you're getting your motivations mixed up. It was Silas who was wronged, Silas whose life was ruined by Paul. Surely it's Silas who would find it hard to forgive Paul, not the other way around.'

I shook my head. 'For a person with normal reactions, you'd

be right. But Paul Hartford wasn't normal. That deal would have made him a lot of money, and perhaps led him on to greater and greater things in the world of crime. Silas was stupid enough to get caught with the drugs; Silas messed up the whole deal; everything was Silas's fault.'

'And what about Delilah?'

'Ah, yes, what about Delilah? She messed up, too. First by taking up with someone other than him. He was allowed to have many women; his women were supposed to be loyal to him.'

'The King of Siam syndrome.'

'Exactly. "The honeybee must be free . . . but blossom must not ever flit from bee to bee to bee." I wish we knew what Delilah's real name was. I'm willing to bet, given the psychology involved, that something very unpleasant happened to Delilah. And Silas, Silas who has carved out a minimalist way of life that suits him, Silas must be hounded by his neighbours; his birds must be accused of something they didn't do; he must be made miserable. All of this accomplished, of course, by one of the flunkies of Clean-Hands Paul.'

'A flunky who goes too far and, trying to imitate a raptor attack, kills Elizabeth George.'

'Right. Case closed.'

'Without a scintilla of evidence.'

'Right. But we'll find some.'

'And have you forgotten that Paul Hartford is now beyond the reach of human justice?'

'No. He's being dealt with. I trust as he deserves. No, but whoever actually set Silas's birds loose, whoever actually killed those chickens, whoever killed Elizabeth – that person, or probably those people, are at large. They must be found and dealt with as *they* deserve. Here on earth.'

'Red light, love!'

I had been too caught up in my own rhetoric to notice, but thanks to Alan I stopped in time.

'And where,' he said quietly when we were under way again, 'where in this scenario of yours do you fit the murder of Paul Hartford?'

* * *

We talked about that all the way home, tossing ideas back and forth and coming to no conclusions whatever.

'I don't know about you, but I'm ready for some tea and/or a nap. I didn't have a lot of whisky, but it was too much for that time of day. And Silas's story was exhausting.'

'Indeed. But for me, it will have to be tea. Or coffee. No nap. I need to see John as soon as possible. He can get to work, or get his colleagues to work, on finding proof of what we think happened in Paul's early life – even though it sheds no light on the ending of it.'

'I think it does, though. Or it might. Why don't you just call John? Then you could relax a little.'

'I don't want to talk about Silas's story on the phone, Dorothy. You know a mobile is roughly as private as Trafalgar Square, and we promised not to spread it about.'

'Oh, right. Well, this time you're on your own. I'm having some tea and some down time. Are you okay to drive?'

'I will be once I've had some good strong coffee.'

I thought of the line about coffee not sobering anyone up, but just producing a wide-awake drunk, but decided not to mention it. Alan was far from drunk, only a bit muzzy, and coffee probably would erase the effects of the Scotch.

I had my tea and settled down for a lovely nap, wishing I had some comforting animals to share it with me. I missed them so much. When I wake up, I thought, I'm going to call Jane and see how they're doing. And then I remembered that it was past bedtime in England. Well, morning will do. And that was my last conscious thought.

I slept for only an hour, but it was enough. I woke full of bright ideas, eager to tell Alan, who came home just as I was tidying my hair.

'Alan!'

'Dorothy!'

We spoke at the same moment, each sounding excited, and laughed. 'You first,' we both said.

'Ladies first,' said Alan, though he was obviously bursting with news.

'Oh, you probably have something more exciting than I do. It's just, we never asked Silas if he saw anything, the day Elizabeth died. It did happen not far from his place, and he does go out with his birds almost every day. What if he saw something, but didn't think it was important? Or more likely, decided to keep his mouth shut just because he hates getting involved in anything outside his narrow little world. I think it's important, Alan.'

'And so do I, and we will certainly ask him. We, I think, certainly not the police, not even John. He trusts us. But I have some good news.'

'Tell!'

'The lab rushed through the blood sample from the knife. It's unquestionably Harold's. It was also certainly not used to kill Elizabeth George, although it fits the wounds perfectly. They gave the knife a very thorough going-over. There was no other blood anywhere, and no traces – sweat, skin fragments – of anyone else ever handling it. Harold's fingerprints were all over it. It's his knife. He made it himself, or at least made and fitted the handle, and it's never been out of his hands until we carried it off. And as he has a very complete alibi for the presumed time of the murder – oh, yes, they checked that out as well – he's unmistakably in the clear. Now the police are looking for where the killer might have obtained a knife with a virtually identical blade, for something like it was certainly used on the poor girl. Well-chosen to imitate a raptor's talons, but not quite close enough.'

'That is good news for Harold! Has anyone told him yet?'

'John was headed up there to return the knife, with apologies.'

'And then someone has to tell Teresa.'

'You're not thinking, Dorothy. Teresa doesn't know Harold was under suspicion. She doesn't need to know. She's feeling a little more secure in her world now, knowing she has a family, at least by adoption, who will back her up. I'm going to call Mary this evening to see how Teresa's getting along, but I think we should give her her privacy for the time being. Don't forget she's in mourning, not only for Elizabeth, but for Paul.'

'And that makes me absolutely furious! A nice girl like that, grieving for that, that . . . I don't usually use the words that describe him best.'

'I sometimes do. Bastard, I think, is a fairly mild descriptor. But Teresa only knew the charming side. Let her hold onto her illusions a while longer. It will all come out eventually, but it will be piecemeal, easier for her to assimilate. Let her be.'

I sighed. 'I suppose you're right. She's so fragile right now – best not to rock the boat.'

'I learned something else from John, too. The coroner is quite sure that Hartford was killed not long before he was found – but not *where* he was found. There wasn't enough blood. His clothes soaked up some of it, of course, but he would have bled copiously.'

'It was the stab wound that killed him, then? Not the blow to the head?'

'The blow to the head, it turns out, was minor. Perhaps enough to stun him, but not enough to render him unconscious. The knife, on the other hand, or whatever was used, hit the aorta. Death occurred in a matter of seconds.'

'The aorta! Then his murderer must have been covered in blood.'

'Not necessarily, not if he or she was standing behind Hartford. The man's own body would have shielded his attacker to a considerable extent.'

'Wouldn't that be awfully awkward, though – to stand behind a man and stab him in the chest?'

'It would depend on the circumstances. Let's say his attacker hit him on the head from behind, and then he fell backward, into his attacker's arms, so to speak. Then it would be easy for the attacker to thrust a knife into his chest, below the ribs, just in the right place to slit the descending aorta. And before you say you thought the aorta was right next to the heart, I thought so too, until early in my career. An ME in Penzance explained to me that the aorta originates at the heart and then branches into several directions, one going straight down to, and through, the diaphragm into the abdomen.'

I shuddered. 'So any knife thrust just there would . . . what a horrible picture. At least he died quickly. But – God forgive me – I'm not sure he deserved that merciful an ending.' Alan just looked at me, and I was ashamed. 'I know, I know – judge not, etc. Anyway, so have they figured out where he *was* killed? I'd have thought there'd be marks from dragging the body and that sort of thing.'

'That's one of the odd things. There are no such marks. They're inclined to suspect that it was done in the kitchen itself, not far away at all. For one thing, it bears all the earmarks of an unpremeditated crime, and they think the weapon was a thin kitchen knife, a boning knife or something of that sort.'

I nodded. 'They're very sharp and would certainly make a formidable weapon.'

'Yes. But while the use of that sort of knife makes the kitchen seem a likely place, offset that against all the activity that was going on there that night. Food being prepared, waiters in and out – what?'

I had held up my hand. 'Food was not being prepared, not in the sense I think you mean. No one was actually cooking. The food had already been prepared in the caterer's kitchen. It had to be removed from boxes and placed on platters. The food that was to be served hot had to go in the oven or on the stove for a little while. But while all that meant a lot of activity, it was mobile activity. Almost no one would have stayed in one place in the kitchen for more than a minute or two at a stretch. And when you're on the move and in a hurry, intent on your job, you're not going to be very observant.'

'You're right, of course. Still, a violent murder is unusual enough to be noticed, even when busy, wouldn't you think?'

'Sarcasm is the tool of the devil! Tell me, what is this kitchen like? Big, small, well laid-out, well equipped, what?'

Some men would have been hard-put to answer such a question, but Alan knew his way around a kitchen. His first wife died a good many years before he and I met, and he had grown accustomed to cooking for himself, and quite enjoyed it. He considered.

'Quite big, somewhat bigger than I would have expected, and very well equipped. I didn't notice all the details, but there were at least two six-burner stoves, two large commercial stainless-steel fridges, two large upright freezers, cabinets stocked with tableware, two large stainless steel islands – you get the picture.'

'What about supplies? A spice cupboard, that sort of thing?'

'Perhaps. I didn't notice any of that. As you so rightly observed, no actual cooking was going on.'

'Right. So you didn't happen to see the pantry.'

Alan looked puzzled. 'A butler's pantry, do you mean?'

'Oh, for Pete's sake! Here we go again, two countries divided by a common language. The – what is it in Brit-speak? – the larder. Is that right? Where they keep the staples, flour and sugar and dry beans and rice – all that.'

His brow cleared. 'Yes, larder. No, I didn't notice one. There was probably a door somewhere, but I confess I wasn't thinking about dry beans.'

'Sarcasm again. My point is this: there's a larder. There has to be. A commercial kitchen could not function without one. Now without knowing the layout of the kitchen, I'm speculating entirely in the dark. But if the larder is near an entrance to the kitchen – and it would almost have to be, for big bags of flour and so on to be brought in – and if it is near a knife rack, it would be relatively easy to stab someone in there without attracting attention, and to move the body out when no one was paying close attention. Add a folded tablecloth, perhaps from one of the drawers in the kitchen, and you could easily drag the body over a smooth surface, such as the tiles or linoleum I assume floors the area. Then you close the pantry – sorry, the larder – door again, and you have all the time you need to wipe away bloodstains.

'So the point is, has anyone searched the larder?'

'I don't know the answer to that. But John will know.' He picked up his phone. 'But love, you know there are a good many holes in your proposed account. Yes, given . . . oh, hello, John. Dorothy has some questions for you. Do you have a moment?' He put the call on speaker and handed me the phone.

'John, I have a lot of questions, and some of them are pretty involved. I'd like to get together when you have a little time. Yes, I know that may not be for a while, but as soon as you can. For now, though, I have only two. First, is there a pantry – larder – stores cupboard – whatever you call it in Canada – off the kitchen in the event centre? And second, if there is, has it been searched carefully for bloodstains or anything else interesting? Yes, I'll wait for a call back.' I clicked off. 'He doesn't know, but he'll find out. Alan, do you think they'd let us in if we went over there to take a look for ourselves?'

'At the crime scene? I would say, not a chance. There have

been quite enough people contaminating that scene without adding our footprints and DNA.'

'Well – what about just taking a look at the kitchen? I really want to see the layout. I know you're a good cook, Alan, but you haven't spent most of your life in a kitchen. And I'll bet most of the cops swarming over the place haven't either. I might see something odd that they'd miss.'

'I don't think they'll buy it, but when John calls back you can make your request.'

John sounded very tired when he called back. 'Yes, there is a pantry, and no, they hadn't searched it, as it is always kept locked when an outside caterer is using the kitchen. At your suggestion they will search it now, though they don't see the point. Nor do I, I confess. And I'm sorry, but I won't be able to meet with you until tomorrow at the latest. Things are very . . . difficult just now. I must go.'

'This is getting to him, Alan. You heard.' I'd put the call on speaker phone.

'Yes. And to me, I admit. I know you had a nap, but I didn't, and I'm worn out. We're neither of us as young as we like to think we are. I'll call Mary to check on Teresa, and then, my dear, suppose we have an early night, and by tomorrow perhaps things will seem brighter.'

I doubted that.

TWENTY-FOUR

A lan brought me coffee and news in the morning.

'Well, my dear, you are vindicated.'

'Mmm?' I couldn't even think what the word meant.

'John phoned me just now. They went over the larder and found a few traces of what could certainly be blood. They're waiting for lab results now, and questioning the staff all over again about that locked door.'

'Good.'

Alan smiled and went away to fix breakfast. He hadn't expected wild delight, not first thing in the morning.

I finished my coffee, showered and dressed, and came to the kitchen wide awake.

'Alan, did I dream it, or did you tell me they found bloodstains in the pantry?'

'I did. By the way, it's a "pantry" here as well. Frightful, what's happening to the Queen's English. Do you want bacon, or just eggs and toast?'

'Just toast, please, love. And more coffee. Did you ask John if I could go and take a look?'

'I did. I doubt he'd have even asked those in charge if you hadn't been right about the larder – pantry. Even so, he said they weren't happy about it. You may go and stand at the door and look – under supervision.'

'That's all I need. I just want to work out escape routes.'

'My dear, you were wasted as a schoolteacher. You should have been a writer of shilling shockers. Escape routes, indeed.' He poured more coffee for both of us and put down a plate of hot buttered toast. (I've persuaded him to make it that way for me. He still prefers his English-style, crisp and dry and cold.)

'I was asleep last night by the time you came to bed. I trust Mary's report on Teresa was good?'

'Fair. The poor child is still very unhappy, but is coping. She's going to start a cyber-search today for another job.'

I snorted. 'Cyber-search indeed. In my day we checked out the classifieds in the newspaper.'

'*Autres temps, autres mœurs*. Trust me, love, the Internet is the way it's done nowadays.'

'There are times when I feel very old.'

It was still quite early when we got to the event centre, but the place was buzzing with activity. I had expected to see only the police. 'What's going on?'

'It's a public venue, love. John told me there's a big wedding this evening. The caterers aren't allowed in the kitchen yet, to their loudly-voiced dismay, but they're setting up the tables. The police have promised them the kitchen at the first moment possible. You'll need to take your peek quickly. And perhaps we'd best go in the back. You're not going to be very popular if you can go to the kitchen and they can't.'

'Right. The back works best for me anyway.'

We had to show our IDs to get in. The harassed constable at the door raised eyebrows at our English passports, but John stepped up just then.

'It's all right, Sam. They're English detectives, here at my request.'

That was certainly stretching a point, in my case at least, but it got us in.

John led us from the back door to the back kitchen entrance. 'You can look in any of the kitchen doors, so as to see the whole layout from different angles. Please don't get in anyone's way – they're frantic, trying to wrap up before the wedding caterers have to start working.'

'Hmm. Then after the caterers do start swarming over the place, presumably we could too.'

'So far as the police are concerned, yes,' said John, sighing. 'But I wouldn't advise it, Dorothy. The caterer, the one in charge, I mean, is already furious to the point of apoplexy about being kept waiting. I wouldn't want to upset him further.'

'I won't. I just want to stand on the side-lines and watch. Meanwhile, I'll peek in the doors.'

There were four of them. The one nearest us opened into the back hallway, more of a vestibule, really. Then there were the doors into the main room, where the events actually took place. These were the traditional swinging doors 'in' and 'out', for the convenience of waiters carrying trays. That counted as one entrance. Then there was what might be termed a side door, from the kitchen to the main front-to-back corridor. That led to the small 'backstage' area and on into the main room, and, almost as an afterthought, to that awkward little passage to the storage room, the place where the body had been found. Finally there was the one I couldn't examine right now, an overhead garage-type door leading directly from the pantry to the loading platform outside, for the convenience of trucks making food deliveries. It wasn't so convenient for caterers bringing in things like tables and chairs and boxes of china and crystal; to get to the main room they would have to go through the kitchen or, with the kitchen forbidden to them for now, in through either the back door and the passage to the backstage, or the big front entrance.

I took all that in and then gingerly opened the kitchen door nearest me and stood in the doorway.

There was lots of activity, but it wasn't the sort one usually sees in a kitchen. I supposed the floor had been examined first, because the officers went about their work without watching where they stepped. The pantry door was to my left, closed and sealed with police tape. That was obviously still off limits until the forensics people had done their work. Well, the caterers wouldn't need it, since they would bring their own supplies. I scanned the room.

Aha! There was a substantial knife block on one of the islands, whose stainless-steel surface was otherwise clear. There were no knives in the block. I wondered why the police hadn't taken block and all. Perhaps it was a built-in part of the island. Unusual, but sensible in a facility that was used by outside groups.

Cupboards. Drawers, none of which were big enough to hold tablecloths. Good. I hoped they were stored in the pantry.

Sinks. None was close to the pantry. That would have made it more awkward to clean up bloodstains, or anything else, for that matter. But perhaps the pantry served also as a broom closet, with a mop and pail handy. That would be unusual, though. In the States, I thought I remembered dimly, cleaning supplies in a commercial kitchen could not by law be stored near food.

A big commercial dishwasher, the conveyor type, stood against one wall, taking up a lot of space. You could wash a knife in that monster, and it might not have blood even in the cracks anymore. But you couldn't do it inconspicuously. If the monster was anything like the one in my college dorm kitchen all those years ago, it made a lot of noise in operation, and produced a great deal of steam. No, the murderer had probably taken the knife away. Tricky, given the shape of the thing, and the razor-sharp blade. It would slit through any pocket lining like butter. Well, maybe it was wrapped in something.

Assuming, of course, that the weapon was indeed a boning knife. I was breaking Sherlock's rule and speculating way ahead of my data.

Alan tapped me on the shoulder. 'Seen enough?'

'Until I can get into the pantry, yes. Parts of my theory are working out very well, but I wish the pantry were closer to the place the body was found.'

'I've had an idea about that. Did you know that there's an outside door at the end of that inconvenient little hallway?'

'Good grief! The place is just lousy with doors! Why on earth did they make it so hard to keep secure?'

'If you look closely, you'll see it wasn't built all of a piece. It's been added onto over the years. I don't know the history of the building, but it's my guess that it began life as just a village hall, or something of that sort. Then when they began to hold larger and larger events here, the kitchen was added, or expanded. Then they added the stage, and then I would suspect that the fire officials stepped in and said they have to have another exit close to the stage.'

'It's not much of a stage – just a platform, really. No backstage, no flies – they couldn't stage a play here, or anything of that kind.'

'No, just lectures and limited musical performances. They couldn't fit in a full orchestra, but a dance band or, heaven help us, a rock group would work. But my point is that there is a door at the end of that virtually unused passageway. So if I were going to murder someone in the pantry, I'd take the body out through the loading-dock door and back in again by way of the forgotten door.'

'Wouldn't it have been locked?' I asked, frowning.

'Probably, but it can be opened from the inside.'

'You're positing an accomplice.'

'Well, love, I don't see how it could have been done by one person. That is, if it was done the way you suppose. It isn't easy to move a body, and Hartford was a solidly muscular man. If one has to do it in a hurry, and by stealth, the task becomes much harder.'

'Do the police accept my theory?'

'According to John, they're giving it due consideration. The stains on the pantry floor tend to support it. On the other hand, they could be something besides blood, and there's the locked pantry door to deal with.'

'I do wish I could see the pantry.'

'That won't happen until those stains are analysed. It's being rushed through. This is, as you of course realize, a high-profile case.'

'Yes, just because Hartford was such an "important" man. Never mind that he was an egomaniac and a sociopath! While the murder of Elizabeth George, an ordinary good person, gets put on the back burner.'

'Simmer down, love. You know quite well that the police can only do so much, and they do have to pay attention to public opinion. They'll find Elizabeth's killer soon. Especially if, as we believe, he or she was one of Hartford's minions. They're likely to be in considerable disarray now that their boss has fallen victim himself.'

'Yes, I suppose. How soon do you think they'll be done here? The police, I mean?'

John joined us. 'In another hour or so. Of course the pantry will still be sealed off. Now look, both of you. I've been on my feet for longer than I wanted to be. I can't keep up this pace the way I used to. It's getting on for lunch time. Suppose we go find something to eat, and compare notes. Unless you want to look around some more, Dorothy.'

'No, I've seen what I need to see, until I can get in the pantry. Lunch sounds like a good idea.'

John knew of a good Chinese place not far away, so we got a table in a secluded corner, ordered a huge platter of dim sum, and fell to.

'I don't know what most of this is,' I said when I had taken the edge off my appetite, 'but it's delicious.'

'Yes, I thought it would be a good antidote to our conversation, which may not be so delicious.'

I nodded. 'John, Alan and I have lots of theories, and a certain amount of support for them, but nothing in the way of real, solid evidence. But before we even get into that, how's Harold? How did he react to the return of his knife?'

'With the reserved dignity that I've come to expect from the indigenous peoples. Many of them, perhaps most, have good reason to fear and despise the white invaders who stole their lands and their way of life, and whose diseases wiped out whole tribes. But they are a proud and wise people who realize that showing their real feelings is not only demeaning, but can be dangerous. So they are courteous, but distant. It is remarkable, I think, that Laura and Harold were so accepting of Teresa. The pure-blood peoples are not always so kind to the Métis.'

'I think the old lady – I have the greatest difficulty thinking of her as Laura – I think she has lived so long and seen so much that she's become wise. An elder of her tribe, except I don't suppose women can be elders. Anyway, she took to Teresa right away, and apparently what she says, goes. I am so glad you were able to give Harold a clean bill of health. I have the feeling things might have got a bit ugly otherwise.'

'You could well be right. The trouble is, having lost Harold as a suspect in Elizabeth's death, we have no one else. The only other faint possibilities, Silas's birds, have been exonerated completely.'

'Well, that's one of the things we wanted to talk to you about. We had a long talk with Silas yesterday and found out a good deal about his background – very interesting.'

Alan and I gave him a précis: Silas's early life, his education, his ambitions cut short by Paul Hartford's criminal activities. 'We are not certain it was Hartford,' Alan cautioned. 'The description of his way of life fits, but we have no more than that to go on.'

'Alan may not be certain,' I retorted. 'I am. But as I said, there's no proof you could take to court.'

John drummed his fingers on the table. 'As it happens, there might actually be some evidence. One of the things we do, as of course you know, Alan – "we" being the police – one of the

things we do when investigating a homicide is an extensive search
into the victim's background. That's much quicker and easier
now than it used to be in the days before the Internet. And we
– well, they, but I'm counting myself in for the duration – we
found out quite a lot about Paul Hartford. He was' – John hesitated – 'not an entirely admirable character.'

'Which comes as no surprise to anybody,' I said sourly.
'Especially you and Amy.'

'His character, no. Nothing we could learn about his character
would shock us. But I confess I was somewhat surprised at how
near he'd skated to the wrong side of the law. And sometimes
just slightly over the edge. One of those incidents might well be
the one you've just described.'

I leaned forward eagerly, so eagerly that I knocked over my
cup of jasmine tea. 'Really! Tell.'

'Don't get all excited. It won't lead anywhere, except to shore
up your ideas. It was a long time ago, in the eighties. There was
a drug raid on one Silas Varner; he was arrested for possession
of a considerable quantity of cocaine, the drug of choice back
then. He had no previous criminal record, though he'd been on
the radar for a time years earlier, when he was part of the hippy
scene in Nelson. So they brought him in, and he was tried and
convicted even though he swore up and down he had nothing to
do with it, that it was planted there by a woman.

'Well, one of the officers working the case had some doubts
about it. The evidence was there, quite enough to convict Varner,
but the officer knew a little about the "back to the land" crowd
and didn't think Varner fit the profile of a drug dealer.'

'He doesn't,' I said firmly. 'A little pot, okay, maybe. When
he was young. But he really is tied to the land, to nature. Even
back then he wouldn't have wanted to poison himself with that
rot.'

'Well, this young officer – what was his name? I've lost it,
but he was of your mind. So he started keeping an unobtrusive
eye on the woman in the case.'

I nodded. 'Delilah.'

John smiled. 'Is that what Varner called her? Appropriate. I
gather she was a . . . er . . . the sort of woman who preys on
men. I never saw a picture of her, but the descriptions were

graphic. At any rate, when she started using a little too much of the poison herself, and became unreliable as a dealer or go-between, her partners in crime threw her to the wolves – so of course she did the same to them. And one of the people she accused of being in the game was—'

'Paul Hartford,' Alan and I chorused. 'So,' I continued, 'now you – they, I mean – can bring her in and get her to tell her story.'

Alan shook his head. 'For one thing, Dorothy, what good would it do? Hartford can't be called to account for anything now. And for another . . .' He paused, looking at John, who nodded.

'You guessed it. The woman's been dead for years, an overdose. Perhaps an accident, perhaps suicide, perhaps murder lest she say too much. At any rate . . .' He raised his arms. 'Too late. Way too late.'

TWENTY-FIVE

The waiter came and cleaned up the spilled tea, and brought some more. We went ahead with our dim sum. 'Now that you have some real evidence against Hartford, won't it make it easier to round up some of his hangers-on? The ones who presumably have been carrying on his campaign of minor terrorism?'

'But we have no real evidence of Hartford's criminal activity,' said John patiently. 'We have a very old report of some remarks by a woman who is now dead. No court on earth would admit that as evidence of anything. And as we keep having to remind ourselves, Hartford is dead. What he may or may not have done many years ago is moot.'

'But we know what he did!'

'Dorothy, you know as well as I do that the police often know quite well who perpetrated a crime, but cannot find enough hard evidence to make a case. It's one of the great frustrations of the job.'

I shoved my plate away. 'Okay. Yes, I get that. And much as I'd like Hartford shown up as what he was, I suppose it wouldn't do any good in the end. At least now he'll never be an MP, thanks be to God! But the people who did his bidding, his bully boys – they need to be tracked down and prosecuted. Elizabeth George and her family, her tribe, deserve justice.'

John started to speak, and I held up my hand. 'I know the police are working on it, except right now most of their resources are being devoted to the Hartford murder. And I get that, too. But there's one tiny lead to Elizabeth's murderer that we haven't followed up yet. I'll swear that Silas Varner saw something, or someone, when he was out with his birds that day. If Alan agrees, and if it's okay with you, I'd like to go up tomorrow and talk to him about it. Who knows – it might be some use.'

Before we went to bed that night I remembered that I'd intended to call Jane, but again I'd left it too late. Morning would do.

* * *

So the next morning Alan and I went to the early service at the sweet little church we'd found, and then headed up the now-familiar road to Silas's refuge. 'I wish he had a phone,' I grumbled as mile unrolled after mile. 'I would hate to make this trip for nothing.'

'It's a beautiful drive. If the old man isn't at home, we can always drive back to Duncan for some lunch, and shopping.'

'It's Sunday. Don't know if the shops will be open.'

'The restaurants will be, anyway. Live in the moment, love.'

Duncan, as we passed through it, presented a festive air. The streets thronged with people, and maple leaf flags hung from every building, every lamp post, gaily red and white.

'What on earth?' asked Alan in puzzlement.

'I don't . . . oh yes, I do! Canada Day! John said it was July first, and that's Wednesday. I'll bet they're starting a bit early, just as we do in the States for the Fourth.'

'There'll be no lack of things to do, then, if Silas isn't home.'

He wasn't. We bumped slowly over the terrible road, parked in the bushes, and walked up his drive, or the rutted path that did duty for a drive. There was no noise from the mews, so we walked around the back to their open-air enclosure and peered.

There were two windows I hadn't noticed before, one into each side of the mews. Both were open, hinged at the top and hooked up to the outside wall. We could easily see that the birds were not there.

'Drat! He's taken them out to hunt.'

'Yes. He did tell us he flew them almost every day. He'll be back. I'll go up to the house and leave a note for him, Dorothy, shall I, while you wiggle the car out of the shrubbery. We can have some lunch in Duncan and come back. If you want to do that, of course.'

'You bet I do. Do you suppose, if we gave him a mobile, he'd use it?'

'I very much doubt it. He wants to keep the world at bay as much as he possibly can.'

It was early for lunch, but even so, with the crowds thronging Duncan, it was a while before we could get a meal. Then, not knowing how long Silas might be out, we roamed a bit, doing some window shopping, but not entering any of the shops, which were filled with tourists eager to spend their money.

'I have a certain sympathy with Silas's misanthropy,' I said after a large man, hurrying out of a shop, cannoned into me and nearly knocked me flat. 'People *en masse* are sometimes not very lovable.'

'I agree. Shall we go back and see if he's returned?'

We stopped at a bakery and picked up some cookies and a loaf of wholegrain bread as a present, and set off.

We were lucky this time. Silas had returned, and greeted us with what, for him, was cordiality. He looked a little less shabby than usual, and for a wonder, he didn't smell.

'Saw your note,' he said, sounding embarrassed. 'Cleaned up a bit. Come on in. Mind the rabbits.'

Rabbits? Then I saw the canvas bag sitting on the dry sink. Several paws protruded. I averted my eyes.

'Don't s'pose either of you ever ate rabbit stew,' he said with a grin.

'You suppose wrong,' said Alan. 'My father was a fisherman, but my grandmother lived on a moor, and rabbit was an important part of her diet, especially just after the war when food was in very short supply in England. She was a good shot, and a good cook. Her rabbit stew was some of the best food I ever ate. Did your birds catch those for you?'

'Yes, one each. Didn't want to eat them – weren't hungry – just enjoyed the catch. And ma'am, before you get to feelin' bad for the rabbit, or judgin' my hawks, have you ever seen a cat catch a mouse just for the sport of it?'

'Yes, of course. I was just being foolish. Hunting is the way of the world.'

Silas nodded. 'Ever since Eve ate that apple. Before that, maybe everybody lived in peace together and ate grass or whatever. In this world, it's kill, and eat, for survival.'

Well, Silas knew a lot about survival. Alan cleared his throat. 'Mr Varner, we have a few more questions for you.'

'You can call me Silas. Reckoned you didn't come just for my company.'

'No,' I said. 'But another time, if you'll allow it, we'd like to come just for your company. This time, because we feel guilty about pestering you so much, we brought you a treat. I know you can cook, but when we were here before I didn't see any way for you to bake, so we brought cookies and some bread.'

'I'm partial to good bread, and I don't know when I've last had cookies. Home-made?'

'Well, no. A bakery in Duncan. But they're good – I sampled one on the way here.'

'I'll make some tea to go with them.'

We settled as we had before, on piles of books with me afforded the only chair, and munched companionably for a little while. Then Silas took the lead.

'Questions, you said. Let's have 'em.'

'Just one, really. Dorothy and I both had the feeling that you knew something about the day Elizabeth George died. We have, by the way, pinned down the way she died, or rather the police have. She was attacked with a knife used to carve wood, one with a shape that looks quite a lot like a bird's talon. That's why she was at first thought to have been attacked by a raptor, but only for a few hours. The coroner knew at once that no bird had caused those wounds, and we have now identified the knife.'

'Well, not quite, Alan. At least, we know the kind of knife it was, the size and shape of it, but we haven't found the actual weapon.'

'Explain that.'

Alan explained carefully.

Silas snorted. 'Couldn't ever have been the boy. Oh, man, but he's a boy to me.'

'You know him?' I was stunned.

'I know a few of the Cowichan. Like them better than most white people. That boy wouldn't have hurt one of his own. They don't.'

'Actually, nobody ever thought he did,' said Alan, 'but there was the knife, and the police had to be sure. Now they're trying to trace where someone else might have bought one just like it.'

'Not so many places they could find one. They've asked the boy?'

'I'm sure they have. It would be the obvious place to start.'

'But they're not goin' all out on the search, are they? This other guy bein' so important and all?'

Alan sighed. 'You're probably right about that. They have only so many forces. They're doing what they can. We're doing what we can to help. But don't expect miracles.'

'That's why we're here,' I said. 'We think you can help, too, if you will.'

He changed his position, leaning against the wall. Crossed one ankle over the other. We waited.

'Saw someone,' he said finally. 'Was out with my birds. I saw the woman. She walks the woods a lot. Walked. Didn't bother her, don't think she saw me. I get along with the tribes hereabouts. They respect the land and a man's privacy.'

A long pause.

'There was a man. Didn't like the looks of him. Looked like a city feller. Not dressed for the woods. Sneakin' around. Thought he was maybe lookin' for my birds. They're trained to come back to me when I want 'em. I brought 'em in, headed back, didn't see the man again.'

'Did you see him near Elizabeth?' I asked, my hands shaking.

Slowly he nodded. 'Not to say close. Not so's she could see him. But he was watching her. Following her, maybe.'

I let go the breath I didn't know I'd been holding.

Alan asked the critical question. 'Can you describe him?'

'Knew you'd ask that. Not well enough to be any use. He was tall, but a little hunched over. Walked like his feet hurt him, but maybe he just didn't know how to walk in the woods. Had on city shoes.'

'And the rest of his clothes?'

'Ordinary. City clothes. Looked like suit pants, grey. Had on a tan windbreaker he didn't need; it was a warm day. Wear that in the woods in hunting season, young idiot, I thought to myself, and you're dead.'

'He was young?' I asked quickly.

'Ma'am, they're all young to me.'

I laughed ruefully. 'I know what you mean. The rest of the world keeps looking younger and younger. My doctor looks about twelve. But truly, do you have any idea how old this man was? What colour was his hair, for instance? Did he move like an old man? An old man with sore feet, I mean?'

He considered. 'No. Forty or so, if I had to say. But not to swear to, mind. Don't know about his hair. He was wearing a cap. Like a baseball cap, but pretty much the same colour as his jacket. Stupid.'

'Stupid if he was out in hunting season,' said Alan, 'but clever if he didn't want to be seen in the woods in June.'

'Would you know him again?' I asked.

'Maybe, if I saw him walking away. Backs are as good as faces; better, sometimes.'

And that was all Silas could tell us. 'You know we'll have to report this to the police,' Alan said as we left. 'And they'll probably send someone to talk to you. I'm sorry.'

'Don't mind if John McKenzie comes.' Silas paused. 'I want them to find her murderer.'

'He meant you to be blamed, you know,' I said.

'Me or my birds. Or both. That's one reason I want him caught.'

We left then, but not before I'd given Silas a small piece of paper. 'Mr Varner, I know you don't have a phone. But you say you go into town occasionally. If you should ever need us, here's the number of my mobile, and this is Alan's. Just in case.'

'He wants the man caught, for the sake of vengeance. But that's only one reason,' I said to Alan as we headed home. 'He cares about the native people, doesn't he?'

'They share a lot of values – love for the land, living in harmony with nature.'

'And aversion to the men who have taken all that away.'

'Not away from Silas. He's taken it back. You know, I'm developing a good deal of respect for the man. He's a philosopher, in his way, and he's living out his beliefs. His way of life wouldn't suit me. I enjoy my creature comforts, but I can see the appeal.'

'So can I. But I'll never give up my indoor plumbing.'

We waited until we got off Silas's impossible road, and then stopped to make some phone calls. Alan, of course, had to report to John our conversation with Silas. And I finally remembered to call Jane.

'Jane, it's Dorothy. I'm sorry I'm calling so late. What time is it there, anyway?'

'Not late. Still in Canada, are you?'

'Yes, and still embroiled in an investigation. Two, in fact.'

'Heard about the politician getting murdered. Didn't much like the sound of him.'

'No, well, he wasn't a very nice man. I'm surprised the news got all the way across the Atlantic, though. He was a pretty big frog here, but it's a smallish pond.'

'Commonwealth nation. Mother country pays attention. And billionaire's always news.'

'Oh, I suppose. I keep forgetting he was filthy rich. I suppose I shouldn't say it, with him lying there in the morgue, but he really was awful. An ego as big as Canada, a womanizer, a bully – I can't really be sorry he's dead.'

'Knew him, then?'

'Not well. I know some people who did know him and had reason to loathe him. Amy, his ex-wife, among others. She's going to marry John McKenzie, the man we came here to help. I don't know that we're doing much good, though I guess we've made a little progress. I suppose Alan and I will have to go to Hartford's funeral, for Amy's sake, much as I hate the thought. I just hope I don't run into Alexis.'

'Alexis?' She sounded incredulous.

'Alexis Ivanov, she calls herself. Ridiculous name! His current mistress. Or I suppose I should say former, now he's dead. A bombshell, hard as nails, filthy rich herself, and leading him a merry dance, from all I hear. She runs everything charitable in Victoria, or at least everything cultural. I doubt she cares about providing for the homeless or treating addicts or anything that would mean getting her hands dirty. And yes, I know St Peter will get me for that.

'But I didn't call to bore you with our troubles here. How are the kids?'

'Missing you. So am I. Cats sulk most of the day. Watson howls.'

'Oh, dear! We had no idea we'd be gone so long, but the mess just got thornier and thornier, and we can't leave John in the lurch. Are you sure you can cope with the animals, or would you rather take them to the vet to board?'

Jane snorted. 'Nonsense.'

'Well, look, this call is going to bankrupt me. Tell the kids I love them and I'll see them soon, and do call me if it gets to be too much.'

TWENTY-SIX

Alan and I exchanged information about our calls on the way home. I hadn't much to contribute except worry about the animals, which Alan dismissed. 'They'll be fine, you know. How could they not be, with Jane looking after them?'

'You're probably right. What did John have to say?'

'Glad for the information, sketchy as it is. They'll start looking at AIntell employees, since they seem likely candidates to be Hartford stooges. The trouble is, there are so many of them.'

'Is there anything new on his end, the Hartford murder?'

'The stains on the pantry floor are definitely human blood, perhaps Hartford's, but the DNA analysis isn't complete yet. Oh, and they've solved the mystery of the locked pantry door. The skivvy whose job it is to lock it lost the key. Swears she went to lock it before she went home that afternoon and it wasn't in the door. She tried the door and it was locked, so she thought her boss or someone had taken it and didn't worry about it. Now she's afraid she'll lose her job, and she's a penniless UVic student who desperately needs the money.'

'Yet more collateral damage.'

'Perhaps. The key was in the lock later, of course, so the girl can't prove she didn't just forget.'

'Was it tested for fingerprints?'

'Not until several people had handled it. It doesn't have a good, smooth surface in any case, so prints don't show very well.'

'So – one step forward, two back.'

'Seems that way, doesn't it. Let's try to forget it for a while, love, and enjoy this beautiful evening.'

We grilled some salmon and sat on the deck of our borrowed condo and watched a glorious sunset, but I kept thinking about an intelligent girl who loved her native land, loved nature, and would never again see a sunset.

Morning brought the news that Paul Hartford's body had been released, and the funeral was scheduled for tomorrow. 'It would have been more usual to wait until Wednesday, but as that's the holiday, and they didn't want to put it off until Thursday, they're going ahead with it,' Alan reported, after a phone call from John. 'It's to be at Christ Church Cathedral.'

'Of course. All the pomp and circumstance possible.'

'Be fair, darling. It's the biggest Anglican church in town, and the world and his wife will be there. It's by invitation only, but I'll wager no one will send regrets.'

I snorted. 'Precious few will feel regret, is what I'll wager. But that means we won't have to go.'

'I'm afraid we will. John said Amy has specifically requested that we be there.'

'Drat! I just hope that Alexis person won't come.'

Alan just looked at me pityingly.

I couldn't settle to anything that morning. I kept going over and over what we knew and what we suspected, and couldn't think of a single useful line to pursue. The police were, we knew, working frantically to try to find a thread, a single lead that would take them nearer a solution to either murder, but especially Hartford's. It was totally unacceptable that the man should go to his grave with his murder unsolved, but it looked very much as though that would be the case.

I put together a salad for our lunch, but neither of us was hungry. I wanted to *do* something – but what?

I was listlessly piling the few dishes in the dishwasher when my mobile rang. Expecting John, I answered.

'Dorothy? Nigel here.'

'Nigel? Nigel *Evans*?'

'How many other Nigels do you know? Can you hear me all right? You're breaking up a bit.'

'I . . . yes, I can hear you. But look. Are you calling on a landline?'

'Yes, from my office.'

'All right, hang up and call me on this number.' I walked over to Sue's phone and read him the number. 'That's the landline here, and it will be clearer. Did you get that?'

He read the number back to me, and while I waited for him to call back I called to Alan. 'Come and show me how to put this phone on speaker.'

The call came through, loud and clear. 'Ah, that's better,' said Nigel, close to five thousand miles away. 'Mobiles have their disadvantages. Now Dorothy, I called because Jane called me, and this might be important. You talked about someone named Alexis Ivanov, a really rich babe who likes to run the world?'

'Yes, but I'm sure that's not her name. How could it be?'

'I saw a picture of her in *The Times*, in the report of Hartford's death. I was interested, because of course he was a kingpin in IT, so I read the thing through, and I'm sure I recognized her. It's rather a distinctive face, isn't it? Not to mention the rest of the package! Anyway, if she's who I think she is, her name is Alice Ingram and I knew her at King's.'

'King's? Oh, King's *College*.'

'Yes, I did do a few things there besides sing and get into trouble.'

Nigel had been a member of the famed King's College Choir until his youthful peccadillos had caused the authorities to boot him out.

'She was a student there?'

'For a bit. She didn't last much longer than I did, but for different reasons. She was brilliant, and very social. Even then she had lots of lovely lolly, and threw it about. Parties in her rooms, all that. I didn't know her well, of course. I didn't move in those circles. But I knew she was from Canada, can't remember where. She got into campus politics early on, and was running everything she could, as a first year, mind you. Then something happened. I don't know exactly what; I'd been sent down by that time. She simply dropped out of everything and disappeared. Someone said it was a tragedy of some sort. I thought you might want to know.'

Alan was blowing a long, slow whistle. I said, 'Nigel, if you weren't so far away, I'd kiss you. Tell that lovely wife of yours I'll collect when we get home. And give her and the kids my love.'

'So. A mystery about the lovely Alexis.' Alan produced a pretty good imitation of a leer.

'There's always been a mystery about her, as far as I'm concerned. I knew that name couldn't be real. And I'm willing to bet her background plays into what's been happening here.'

'My dear, she's Canadian. That covers some thirty-seven million people or so. The odds—'

'Less than nineteen million, if you figure that roughly half of them are male. Then you can reduce that to the ones who have assumed a false name, and have been educated at Cambridge, and have moved to Victoria, and are richer than God, and I think the odds diminish considerably.'

'Still. Assume that Alexis is in fact this Alice Ingram. It would be easy enough to check her passport, if the police had any reason to do so. Why does that make her a candidate for involvement in the recent tragedies?'

I raised my hands helplessly. 'Alan, I don't know. Call it intuition, if you like, though I'm not sure I believe in that. I only know that I want it checked out. Do you think John can do that?'

'Perhaps. I'll try to persuade him to look into her background, but I think it's an awfully slim lead.'

'Slim is better than none.'

The next morning I dressed carefully, wishing I'd brought something a bit more subdued. 'I hate black, and I look awful in it,' I groused. 'Anyway, I'm not mourning the loss of Paul Hartford. Why should I look as if I were?'

Alan ignored me, knowing I was really talking to myself.

Alan suggested we take a cab to the church, knowing parking would be at a premium, as indeed it was. Not only cars, but the vans of TV crews crammed the space in front of the cathedral. We pushed our way through and gave our names to someone at the door, who passed us on to an usher, who seated us up near the front, where John and Amy were waiting for us. I would much rather have stayed inconspicuously at the back. I would much rather have stayed at home.

Since I was here, however, I might as well see if I couldn't get something out of it, some information, whatever. I looked around, trying not to be obvious about it. There was Alexis, in the very front pew, next to a youngish man I didn't know. Bad taste, I thought. She was his mistress, not his wife. Or perhaps not even that, if the rumours were true. Just his 'great and good friend' as *Time* magazine used to put it. Though that usually meant . . . oh, we were starting. The organ struck up a mournful

voluntary and a subdued commotion at the back of the church
indicated that the coffin was being brought in and the procession
assembling. A voice intoned, 'I am the resurrection and the life,
saith the Lord . . .' The procession made its way up the long
aisle, accompanied by a waft of incense. *Pulling out all the stops*,
I thought sourly, and then reprimanded myself. Criticism of a
man's funeral is reprehensible, no matter how little one liked the
man.

We sang a hymn, coughing a little as the clouds of incense
dispersed. Prayers. Scripture readings. The Twenty-Third Psalm.
(*If they don't read that at my funeral*, I thought, *I'll come back
and haunt them.*) Hymn. We stood for the Gospel (and more
incense) and then settled down for the homily.

The priest (the dean of the cathedral, according to the service
leaflet) climbed to the lofty pulpit and repeated a phrase from
the Gospel: '"Everything that the Father gives me will come to
me, and anyone who comes to me I will never drive away."
Again: "Anyone who comes to me I will never drive away."' He
leaned forward, grasped the edge of the pulpit, and went on. 'I
will also quote from another source which many of you will
know well, may perhaps have had to memorize back in school:
"I come to bury Caesar, not to praise him." It is, of course, from
Marc Antony's funeral oration for Julius Caesar in Shakespeare's
play, and I'm quoting it, along with Jesus' words, because they
are both appropriate for this occasion.

'We are gathered here for the funeral of Paul Hartford, a well-
known and complex man. As a parish priest I hear many things,
most of which I must never repeat, so I know that Paul was not
universally beloved.'

There was a stir of anger in the congregation. 'Yes, I know
that I have offended some of you. It is the usual practice at a
funeral to speak nothing but good of the deceased, but I believe
that such hypocrisy will not do here, today. It will not do, my
friends, because we in this community are badly in need of
healing, and only the truth will heal.'

I exchanged glances with Alan; he frowned and shook his head
– whatever that meant.

'There is in every human being a mixture of good and evil.
We are all sinners with the potential of becoming saints. So it

was with Paul. Though he was officially on the parish rolls of this cathedral, I seldom saw him in the pews – but he donated very generously to the parish.

'He was also a generous donor to many other institutions here in Victoria and elsewhere. Some of you, sitting here today, may owe your education to Paul Hartford through his scholarship program at the University of Victoria. Thousands, every year, enjoy the Symphony Splash, often co-sponsored by Paul's company, AIntell. He has contributed greatly to the cultural life of this city, and I hope we are grateful.

'But there was another side to Paul, a darker side. His private life was not always conducted in a way that accorded with Christian precepts, and by those actions, he hurt a great many people. If you saw only his public persona, you may not know some details of his life, which, I assure you, I am not about to reveal. My point is simply that, while there were many reasons to love Paul Hartford, there were also many reasons not to do so.

'And this is where I come to the quotation from the Gospel according to John. Jesus assures us that those who come to him, those whom the Father has given to him, who belong to him, will never be driven away. Note that word: *driven* away. Jesus will not drive us away. Our own perverse and sinful actions, even, will not be able to drive us away. We belong to him. From the day of our baptism, we were "marked as Christ's own forever". Nothing, *nothing* can change that.

'Of course not all of you here today are practicing Christians. Perhaps most of you are not. Whatever your beliefs, I urge you to generosity of spirit. Only thus may the divisions in our community be healed. If you loved Paul, be understanding to those who did not. If you did not, I beg you not to judge him. Which of us, if judged fairly, would escape censure? Paul Hartford is now in the hands of one who will judge him with perfect justice and with perfect mercy and grace, knowing him as we could never know him, understanding him as no human ever could. Let us love one another and leave judgment to God. Amen.'

The congregation responded with a somewhat dazed 'amen' and rose to our feet for the recitation of the Creed.

I stood and knelt, sang and responded through the rest of the service, but my mind was far away. I had to be nudged to go up for communion. When at last it was over, and John and Amy offered us a lift, I was glad to sit in silence.

We fetched up on John's patio. He put some sandwiches and a pitcher of something frosty in front of us, and sat down.

'Well,' said Amy.

'Yes.' Alan nodded. 'The most remarkable funeral I've ever attended.'

'The most remarkable sermon, at any rate. What was your reaction, Dorothy?'

'I don't quite know. I was torn between remorse and . . . well, anger, I guess. How dare he hint at Paul's miserable actions without condemning them? And yet we're not supposed to judge, and he did in fact do a lot of good. He hurt you and Sue so badly, Amy, and so many other people along the way. But at least half the congregation thought he was a knight in shining armour.'

'Yes, he did good, but for all the wrong reasons, for self-aggrandisement and political capital.' That was John, and he sounded as if he, too, was thinking aloud.

'Does that matter, though? The students he sent through school didn't care why he gave the money, only that he did.'

'I don't know if it matters,' said Amy, 'and if you don't mind, I'd rather not talk about it. Paul is dead. Marc Antony talked about that, too. "The evil that men do lives after them; the good is oft interred with their bones." I was one of the ones who had to memorise that speech. Let Paul's good and evil be buried with him, and we can go on with our lives.'

'Not judging him?' It was a real question; I was still disturbed.

'Trying not to judge him, hard as that is. Meanwhile, let's drink to happier times.'

John filled our glasses, and we raised them. I added another toast. 'To John and Amy!'

That one we could drink with enthusiasm.

TWENTY-SEVEN

'**B**ut isn't it sometimes a duty to judge?'

Alan and I were sitting in our living room pretending to read the paper. We had been silent until my remark popped out *a propos* of nothing.

'For a policeman, you mean. Or anyone engaged in investigating crime. I'm not sure it is, actually. It's our duty to judge and weigh evidence, to see where it leads and whether it justifies lodging suspicion in some particular quarter. It's the duty of the courts, then, to judge whether the suspects we turn up are really guilty.'

'But you do actually judge, don't you? Or did, I mean, back when you were an active policeman?'

'Of course. I think, though – I hope – that I was judging my own judgment, if that's the way to put it. Did I do the right thing in bringing this particular person before the judge?'

'In the problems I've been involved with,' I responded, 'I wasn't so detached. I ended up truly despising the villains, and rejoicing that they'd been caught. I suppose . . . no, I know that I should be more forgiving, but I have a really hard time with that.'

'So does everyone else, love. Don't beat yourself too hard. And stop feeling guilty for your feelings about Paul Hartford. He was a genuinely bad man, who tried to win favour with philanthropy which he could well afford. Who knows, maybe somewhere deep within he was trying to placate his own conscience. We'll never know, but we can leave it be. How about some coffee?'

The phone rang – the landline, which was unusual. 'Probably a telemarketer,' I said, glancing at the display. 'No! It's from England!'

It was, in fact, Nigel.

'I did a little research today,' he said after greetings had been exchanged, 'into the mysterious Miss Ingram, and I think you might be interested in what I found out.'

'You bet I would. Wait a sec, I want Alan to hear this, too. Now.'

'I decided the best place to go would be her college records.'

Alan frowned. 'Surely those are confidential.'

'They are. But they've all been digitized recently, and there isn't a firewall ever made that I can't penetrate. Only in a good cause, of course.'

'I certainly hope so!' I said warmly, and Nigel chuckled at the other end.

'Don't worry. I'm a reformed soul these days, and "strictly legit". So I went into Alice's records and learned some very interesting things. For a start, she was born in Vancouver. The city, not the island.'

'So she's a native of these parts!'

'We-ell, except I gather one uses the word "native" to mean something rather different in many parts of Canada. At any rate, she went to school in Vancouver, an expensive girls' school, and won a scholarship to King's. Which she turned down, because she said her family had quite enough money to send her there, and she didn't want to take the place of someone who really needed it.'

'That's in her records?'

'Including a digital copy of the letter she sent. All right. Everything was going along swimmingly, laudatory notes from her professors and all that, until 23 May, when she was nearly finished with her first year. She abruptly dropped out of school, citing a family emergency.'

'The records didn't say what?'

'No. But having the date I could start doing some research in Canada, old newspapers and so on. It took a little while, but a newspaper story sent me to court records – don't worry, Alan, they're available under public access laws, so I didn't have to hack anything. And what I found was that Alice's sister, a sixteen-year-old named Lucia, had been killed in a hit-and-run accident. The newspapers had played it up; the two girls were very close, partly because the younger sister had cerebral palsy. Alice had apparently protected her fiercely from the bullying of her school-mates, helped her to fit in, all that. Reading between the lines, it seemed Alice had been torn about going so far away for university, but Lucia insisted.

'Well. It wasn't too hard to identify the driver of the red Lamborghini, so he was eventually tracked down and charged, but his attorney successfully claimed that the identification was doubtful, and there had been procedural mistakes, and so on – all the tricks that a smart lawyer can use. So the charges were dropped. But, speaking of procedural mistakes, the record of the whole business was never expunged. Would you care to guess the name of the man in question?'

'No.' Alan's voice was harsh. 'Tell us.'

'Paul Hartford. You did really guess, didn't you? Hello? Anyone there?'

I cleared my throat. 'I . . . there's nothing really to say, is there? Thank you for the information, Nigel. I think.'

I stood with the receiver in my hand until Alan gently took it from me and put it back in the cradle.

'Alexis. All this time, Alexis hating him and plotting revenge.'

'You go too fast, Dorothy. Alice Ingram had reason to feel extremely bitter about Paul Hartford, who escaped any punishment at all for taking her sister's life. We still don't know that the woman calling herself Alexis Ivanov is really Alice Ingram.'

'Nigel recognized her.'

'From a newspaper photograph. Remembering a woman he knew – what – seventeen or eighteen years ago? People change, Dorothy. Photographs are unreliable, especially in this age of Photoshop and similar electronic wizardry.'

'It can all be checked. Did you persuade John to get that going?'

'I tried. I don't know if he was able to persuade the authorities.'

I suddenly noticed how tired and discouraged Alan looked and sounded. 'It's hard for you, isn't it? Trying to work this way with no access to the tools you used to have at your fingertips.'

'Somewhat frustrating, yes.'

'Poor dear! It's different for me, of course. I never did have any authority, so I just go bumbling around asking questions and annoying people, and somehow the two of us usually get there in the end. And back in England there are lots of people still on the force who are willing to help. Here . . . well, we're both strangers in a strange land.'

'Yes, and there are barriers. But your strength, my love, has always been dealing with people. You usually get along well with

them, all different sorts of people, and they confide in you. That's
no different here than anyplace else.'

I sighed. 'I told you I had a strange feeling about Alice/Alexis.
Now I know why. I think I'll call John and tell him what we
know now, and I'll bet he'll push forward that background check
on Alexis.'

But I couldn't reach John. Both his phones, the mobile and
the landline, went to voice mail. Frustrated, I tried Amy, who
answered on the first ring. She was at the library, of course.

'Amy, I can't reach John, and I have something important to
tell him. Do you know where he is?'

'He went straight back to the police station. They're having a
conference to talk over the whole mess, from the first theft of
plants through to Paul's death.'

'What do you think they'd do if I asked to join that conference?'

She hesitated. 'If it were just John, he'd say yes like a shot,
but . . .'

'But it's all the law and the prophets. Well, I think I'm going
to chance it. This is information they'll be glad to have, and they
need it right away.'

'Is it . . . no, I won't ask.'

'I'll tell you, I promise, but I need to get going. I'll call soon.'

I told Alan where I was going. 'Do you want some moral
support?'

'I think I might have a better chance on my own. Relying on
their chivalrous response to a lady in distress. But I'd love to
have you drive me down. I don't know where I'd park.'

'Right. I don't even know where the police station is, but I
trust Sadie will get us there.'

Sadie got us there all too soon. 'You're sure?' Alan asked.

'Quite sure.' I extricated myself from the car, telling myself
that it was just old joints that made my progress so slow, and
walked into the clean, attractive modern building.

A pleasant-looking woman in uniform, sitting behind a glass
window, asked how she could help me. I had my speech all
prepared. 'My name is Dorothy Martin. I have some information
for Chief Superintendent McKenzie, of the RCMP, on the Hartford
murder case, and it's urgent that I speak to him immediately.'

'I'm afraid Mr McKenzie is in conference with several other officers and can't be disturbed right now. I'd be happy to take your information and give it to him as soon as he's free.'

'Oh, no, that won't do, I'm afraid. May I see someone else connected with the case? At once, please.'

I had expected the run-around, and had sworn I'd meet it with devastating courtesy and iron determination. My experience teaching sixth-graders stood me in good stead. The guardian at the gate realized, after another exchange or two, that I was prepared to stand there until I got what I wanted, or pigs started flying over the Inner Harbour. She picked up the phone, turning away from the window so I couldn't hear, and then turned back. 'Sergeant Moore will be down in a moment, if you'd care to take a seat.'

I smiled, showing as many teeth as possible. 'I'll stand, thank you.'

When the officer walked into the lobby, I was delighted to recognize him as the man who had taken our statements the day Alan and I were so ineptly accosted in Chinatown. 'Oh, I'm so glad it's you, Sergeant. I absolutely must see John McKenzie, or someone on the force who's involved in the Hartford murder case. Would you give him this note? I'm sure he'll see me when he's read it.'

The sergeant was taken aback. 'They're in a confab, absolutely not to be disturbed.'

'They'll want to be disturbed by this. Look, trust me. You know I'm not a dithery old lady. I promise, I *swear* you won't get in trouble for delivering this message. You could, however, get in serious trouble for *not* delivering it.'

It hung in the balance. I fixed him with my best you-do-it-or-get-sent-to-the-principal look, and he capitulated. 'Come with me,' he said, resigned. 'They'll flay me alive and demote me to constable. I've always wanted to spend out my time till retirement writing parking tickets.'

The working area of the station looked a little more familiar than the lobby. By comparison with the English ones I'd seen, however, it still seemed too new, too sterile. Sergeant Moore led me down a hallway to a door marked Conference: Private and pointed firmly to a chair outside. 'Wait here.' His manner was as adamant as mine. I capitulated. For the moment.

He squared his shoulders, tapped on the door, and walked in. 'What the hell—' I heard before the door closed.

In a moment the door opened again. The sergeant came out, followed by John. 'Dorothy, what does this mean?' He held out the note I'd given the sergeant.

'Exactly what it says. The woman Alice Ingram has an extremely powerful motive for harming Paul Hartford. If, as I believe, she and Alexis Ivanov are one and the same, the police need to talk to Alexis immediately.'

John looked at me, looked at the note, looked at me again, and made up his mind. 'All right, Sergeant. You did the right thing. Dorothy, come in and tell us all you know.'

TWENTY-EIGHT

I've faced more intimidating assemblages in my life – but not many. None of the faces in the room were friendly; several were actively hostile. John gestured me to a chair, but I preferred to stand. Looming over the rest gives one a psychological advantage.

'I will be brief. My husband and I are here in Victoria at the request of Mr McKenzie, whose niece is a friend. My husband is a retired chief constable in the English county of Belleshire, and he and I have become involved in several investigations since his retirement. As you may be able to hear in my voice, I am American by birth, but am now a British subject, living in Sherebury. The information I'm about to give you comes via the head of IT services at Sherebury University, a man I've known for years.'

I explained it all: Nigel's connection with Alice Ingram, his recognition of her, his research and its results. 'It is, of course, not proven that Alice and Alexis are the same person, but the likelihood is so strong that I urge you to find out as soon as possible. I'll be happy to answer any questions, if I am able.'

'This Nigel Evans,' growled one grey-haired man, one of the hostile ones. 'Is he to be relied upon?'

'Unquestionably. Since you will probably check up on him, I will tell you straight off that he was sent down from King's College for various infractions, but of college rules, not municipal laws. When I first met him, many years ago, he was suspected of involvement in a murder case, but was proven to be entirely innocent. He would not hold the responsible position that he does if the university officials had any question about his integrity. I tell you this lest you accuse me of hiding the facts, but I repeat that I would trust Nigel with my life.'

'Alexis Ivanov is a highly respected member of our community,' said one of the other men.

'Yes. So was Paul Hartford. As the homilist said this morning at his funeral, there was another side to him.'

'Yes. Thank you, Mrs Martin,' said the deputy chief constable, who was apparently chairing the meeting.

It was a dismissal. I nodded gravely to the chairman and allowed John to escort me from the room, where Sergeant Moore was waiting to take me downstairs.

'Thank you, Sergeant, for taking me at my word. It took courage. No skin lost?'

'None. I may even get bumped up for using my own judgement. Did you accomplish what you wanted?'

'I'll know that when I find out what they're going to do.'

'Good luck, then!' He sketched a salute and was gone, and I phoned Alan to come pick me up.

Home. Too restless to settle to anything. Waiting for something to happen.

My mobile rang. Maybe this was John with news!

No. Amy.

'Dorothy, John asked me to call. He and the rest are running all over. They've verified Alexis's identity as someone named Alice Ingram, and are now out looking for her. He didn't tell me much more than that. How about supper, so we can talk? I could get some deli stuff and bring it over.'

'That sounds perfect. I'm dying to talk it all over with someone!'

She rang off after ascertaining that we had no food allergies or hatreds, and I busied myself with setting the table. Anything to keep busy.

She arrived, several bags in hand. Alan poured drinks and we went out on the deck to enjoy the weather – perfect, as usual.

'Okay,' said Amy, 'I want to know all you know. Pretend John didn't tell me anything, because he was actually too rushed to make a lot of sense. I've gathered that Alexis has a Past, which anyone with any sense could have guessed.'

'She does, but not quite the sort you might imagine,' said Alan. 'The outline is this: she was born in or near Vancouver to a wealthy family; her name was Alice Ingram. After school at Crofton House she was accepted at King's College, Cambridge.'

Amy whistled soundlessly.

'There she excelled, both academically and socially, for less than one year. In May of her first year her younger sister, back in Vancouver, was killed in a hit-and-run accident for which, it was finally discovered, Paul Hartford was responsible. He was never prosecuted for the crime.'

Amy picked up her glass of wine and drained it.

'My assumption is that Hartford Senior paid for the best lawyer available, and perhaps some money was spread in other directions as well. We all know judicial corruption exists.

'Now, we know at this point nothing of what transpired until, years later, Alexis Ivanov bursts like a Roman candle on the Victoria social and cultural scene. We do know, because you've just told us, that the transformation of Alice into Alexis took place at some point, but we'll have to wait for more information to know why and how and when.'

He lifted the wine bottle to pour Amy a little more, but she put her hand over her glass. 'No, thank you. Is there iced tea or something?'

He went in to the fridge, and I took up the tale. 'So Alan's told you what we know for fact. My department is speculation. I think that Alice – I'm going to call her that, it's so much easier – that Alice nursed a grudge all those years. Or more than a grudge, really, a burning hatred against Paul Hartford. The sister, incidentally, was severely handicapped, and the two girls were very close. So here she is, bitterly mourning her sister, while he goes merrily on his way, getting richer and richer all the time, and making a name for himself as a thoroughly nice chap. That would have fanned the flames for Alice, of course.'

'How long ago would this have been?'

'Seventeen or eighteen years ago. I'm not certain as to the exact year, but of course the records would show.'

'Then it was just about when Paul and I divorced. I can see him tearing around, just looking for trouble.'

'Yes, well.' I cleared my throat. 'While he was chasing money, Alice, too, increased her wealth. I don't know how; I suspect she took what money her parents gave her and invested it wisely, and as money will, it bred more money. You've told us she was ruthless in pursuing wealth and power – that company she acquired by dubious means, for example. At any rate, she became very wealthy indeed by some means. She also became very beautiful, and I hate to admit it, but I don't think her beauty owes much to spas or plastic surgeons or even Estée Lauder and her ilk. It's in the bone. Of course she's tended it assiduously. It's her stock in trade.'

Amy made a face. 'Unwillingly, I agree. She's a natural Venus.'

'She's also intelligent and single-minded. We can't prove it – yet – but I believe she moved to Victoria and started throwing money at cultural organizations with one purpose in mind: to meet and cultivate Paul Hartford, to ensnare him, and ultimately to destroy him.'

'You think she killed him, then?'

'I do. And I'll have to answer to St Peter for it one day, but I can't find it in my heart to condemn her, or not very much. He was an evil man from his youth upwards, and he was so rich he was insulated from the usual punishment. Did we tell you what he did to Silas Varner, years ago?'

'John said you'd heard a remarkable story from Silas, but he didn't say what.'

'In a nutshell, Hartford destroyed Silas's life.' Alan summed it up, in his admirable fashion using about half the words I'd have needed. 'And who knows how many other lives he wrecked along the way? Without knowing, without caring? St Peter may not be too hard on you, Dorothy.'

I got up to set out the food Amy had brought, and she and Alan followed me into the kitchen. 'All right,' she said. 'I won't dispute a word of that. He was all that and more, and I'd be far better off if I'd never laid eyes on him. No, I wouldn't. I wouldn't have Sue, and she's the light of my life. But, given all you say about Hartford, and about Alexis – Alice, whoever – I don't see how she could have killed him, in the midst of all those people. She was right there in the audience, wasn't she, when Paul's body was discovered?'

'No,' said Alan, 'in fact she wasn't. She had left some time before, just when we were all getting ready to converge upon the buffet tables. A young man came up and said something to her, and she left the room.'

'Rushed out,' I said. 'I wondered at the time what was so urgent, and so did Ms Underwood. It was just at the point when people were about to get a bit mellow, ripe for a suggestion that they might like to pony up a little more cash for the Symphony.'

'Who was the man?'

'Well, of course I didn't know – I didn't know anybody. Ms Underwood thought he was one of Alexis's staff.'

'Hmm.'

'Yes,' said Alan. 'I'll bet the police are trying to track him down even as we speak.'

'Right. Because it must have been just about that time . . .'

'How long was she gone?' Amy's voice was tight. This was, after all, the murder of her ex-husband we were talking about. She had loathed him, true, but she had borne him a child, and some fragment of warm feeling must still remain.

I wrenched my thoughts back to the subject under discussion. 'I didn't notice. How long do you suppose it was, Alan, before we heard the scream and everything fell apart?'

'Let's see. We talked to Ms Underwood for a few minutes, and then had some champagne. Waiters were circulating with trays of glasses. Then just as we were about to go to the buffet, the orchestra director came to talk to us, at Ms Underwood's suggestion. Then the soloist came up, with her accompanist, I think to speak to the conductor, but they talked to us for a bit. Accepted our compliments and so on. Then we started again to make a move, when we heard the scream.'

'It seemed ages,' I said, 'because I was hungry and my back ached. But I suppose it must have been half an hour, or a little more. And we didn't see Alexis again. Of course, the way people were milling around, we might not have noticed her.'

'I would have, I think,' said Alan. 'She's a noticeable person.'

'And you're a noticing person.'

He shrugged. 'Training. I can't help it. I'm not going to swear to it, but I'm reasonably certain that Alexis did not return to the banquet hall. Half an hour,' he mused. 'That's very little time. If she did kill him, she must have worked in sped motion.'

'But we could be wrong about the time. Is there any way to check, do you suppose?'

Alan shrugged. 'The caterers might have made a record of the time they were told to stop serving, which would have been only a few minutes after the body was discovered. I presume many of their employees are paid by the hour. And someone might have noted when Alexis left the party. But none of it's very satisfactory.'

Amy said, 'Well, I don't see what anyone except the police can do about it. They need to find her and her friend.'

'Friend?' I frowned.

'That man who came and fetched her from the party. He would know why she left and where she went – and what she did.'

'What she did. Exactly.' Amy sounded grim. 'And that's why both of them may be very hard indeed to find.'

'You think she did it. Alexis.'

'As I am no longer in active police work, and never had any authority in this part of the world, I can violate the usual practice of reticence and say yes, I do believe Alexis killed Paul Hartford. Whether the crime can ever be brought home to her is another question.'

Amy sighed. 'I wish I could figure out whether I want her caught and prosecuted, or not. I keep thinking back to that homily – was it just this morning? Good and evil, light and darkness. He was mostly evil, but he, or his money, did a great deal of good. And she came across, to women anyway, as evil, but she was also a philanthropist.' She shook her head. 'Everything is so complicated and confused. And I have to get back to the library; I left my desk in a terrible mess and with tomorrow a holiday, I don't want to have to come back the next day and find a rat's nest.'

I'm not a huggy sort of person, usually, but I gave Amy a hug. 'Well, don't work any later than you must. And then go home and get some rest. This has been awfully hard for you, and it won't get any easier.'

'It hasn't been a picnic for you, either, has it? Here you come to one of the beauty spots of the world, expecting to figure out a minor problem, and end up neck deep in murder. I hope you were planning to stay for Canada Day.'

'We weren't, originally,' said Alan, 'but as you say, we hadn't quite expected to get involved in something so serious. And it's far too late, now, to get a flight any sooner than the weekend.'

'Unless . . . oh, good grief, is Sue planning to come home for the holiday?'

'Don't fret, Dorothy. She's in Brazil, remember? She'd hardly fly home for one day. No, you're welcome for as long as you care to stay. I *must* go!'

'It's a shame the police are going to miss their holiday,' I said later when we were sitting around the fire, the evening having become chilly, as usual.

'Part of the job description, as you'd know, love.'

'Yes, of course. I hope they won't keep John's nose to the grindstone, anyway. He's retired, for Pete's sake!'

'As am I, for some little time, now.' But he smiled as he said it.

'And here we are, stuck in the middle of a mess. I wish I thought there was something productive we could do about it. Seems like everything now is up to the police, and we might as well go home, as soon as we can book a flight.'

'And leave a problem unsolved? That's not like you, my love. Perhaps it's time for you to make one of your famous lists.'

'It's likely to be a very short one!' I retorted, but I got my notebook out of my purse. 'Well. What do we need to know?'

'The whereabouts of Alice/Alexis and her friend.'

'But that's something the police can do so much better. They have the resources.'

'But we have ideas. At least you often do. Write it down.'

'I don't have a single one this time.' But I wrote it down. 'And another thing we need to know is who killed Elizabeth George. And we do have some ideas about that: one of Hartford's goons, an employee of AIntell, most likely. But there again, the police can do that kind of combing out much better than we can.'

'Write it down.'

I couldn't see that we were making any progress, but we hammered out one more question: Where did the knife come from, the one that killed Elizabeth? 'And while we're at it, what weapon killed Hartford? And where is it? Problems for the forensics people and the detectives, respectively. Alan, there's nothing here to get hold of!'

'What would you do if we were at home?'

'Talk to people. Someone would know something, or have some ideas. But we don't know anyone here.'

'Oh, dear heart, you're tired. Of course we know people here. Not the vast network we have at home, or the Cathedral grapevine, but – write these down: John, Amy, Silas, Laura—'

'Who?'

'The old lady at the shop in Duncan. Harold, the wood carver. Teresa – whom, incidentally, we haven't checked on for a while. We should phone her. Then there's Ms Underwood, various police officers – we've met lots of people. And don't forget Nigel, back home, who has the entire world at his fingertips and can find out a person's life history in a few clicks. Illegally, probably, but at the moment that's not our worry.'

I tapped with my pen at the last name. 'You know, you might have something there. I'll bet Nigel could find out a whole lot more about Alice/Alexis. More, maybe, than the police, because they have to follow the rules. I'll call him.'

'Not just now, love. It's the middle of the night in England.'

'Oh. Right. Nigel probably wouldn't mind, but Inga wouldn't be best pleased if we woke the children. Well, first thing in the morning, then. Meanwhile, I suppose we'd better call Teresa and see how she's doing.'

'That can wait until morning, too. If she's cried herself to sleep, we don't want to wake her. Let's get some sleep ourselves and tackle the problems tomorrow.'

TWENTY-NINE

We had an early night, and a good thing, too. My phone rang at 6:15 the next morning.

'Hello,' I croaked.

'Mrs Martin?'

The voice at the other end didn't sound at all certain. At that hour I wasn't any too certain myself. 'Yes. Who is this, please?'

'Varner. Silas Varner.'

That woke me up. 'Silas! Oh, sorry, I mean Mr Varner.'

'"Silas" will do. I found something.'

I still wasn't firing on all cylinders. 'Found something?'

'About that man. The city slicker. I think it's important. You said to call.'

'Yes. Yes, I did. Hold on a minute, Silas.' I poked Alan awake and put my phone on speaker. 'Okay, go ahead. What did you find?'

'A credit card receipt. I think that's what it is. Been a while since I've seen one, but I'm pretty sure. From a hobby shop. They sell knives.'

Alan sat straight up. 'Mr Varner, don't tell anyone else. Where are you?'

'Duncan. A coffee shop. Came straight here.'

'Could anyone have heard what you just said?'

'Nope. Borrowed the man's mobile and came out to my truck. Got to take it back.'

'You do that, and go straight home. We'll be there as soon as we can.'

Alan made some instant coffee, which we both loathe, but there was no time to be fussy. The traffic was already building, but we found an A & W that didn't have a long line, picked up a couple of breakfast sandwiches, and munched as we headed for the highway.

'If it has the number on it, we've got him!'

'It probably won't. They usually have only the last four digits, if that. And there's no proof at all that the thing is even relevant to the issue at hand. Anyone might have dropped it, at any time, and it might not be for a knife at all. Et cetera.'

'Yes, of course, your policeman's mind has to think that way. But we'll soon know.'

Alan had become confident about driving on the wrong side of the road, so he was at the wheel. We took the most direct route, but it seemed to take a long time, especially the last few minutes when we had to crawl along Silas's horrible road.

He was waiting for us at the end of his drive. 'Come in,' he said. 'Bit of a wind out here. Wouldn't want to lose it.'

As we walked to his door, he explained. 'Went for a walk. Do that most mornings. Walked up to where the girl was killed. No reason. Just . . . no reason.' His voice had become even raspier than usual. He cleared his throat. 'Saw this paper blowin' around. Don't like that sort of thing spoilin' the woods. Chased it and picked it up. Looked at it, thought it might be important, went to Duncan and called you.'

'And we are very grateful that you did! Yes, this could be very important indeed.' Alan scanned it. 'From a hobby shop in Victoria. No description of what was purchased, only a number, probably a stock number. And four digits of a Visa card number. Where exactly did you find it?'

''Bout ten yards from where the girl was killed. Just where the feller was hidin' that day.'

'And it hasn't been there long; it's reasonably clean. Of course, there's been no rain.'

'Get some fog up there now and then, though. Thick one just before it happened. The paper couldn't't've been there then.'

'Mr Varner . . . Silas. It was so very good of you to leave your . . . your comfort zone to call and tell us about this. It was a great inconvenience, I know, and we deeply appreciate it. You . . . you're quite sure you don't want to have a phone put in here? Alan and I would be glad to pay to have it installed.'

He barked a single raspy laugh. 'Don't need one. Never gonna get mixed up with murder again.'

'Then please think about getting a dog,' said Alan. 'There must be some breed that wouldn't bother your birds. You're not getting any younger, Mr Varner—'

'Silas.'

'Thank you. Silas. You live alone. If something happened to you, you could lie here a long time before any help came.'

'Think about it,' Silas muttered, in the sort of tone that dismissed the subject.

'I hope you will,' I said, without much hope. 'We have to get back to town and give this to John. Sorry to spend so little time with you.'

'I got to fly my birds. Let me know if you catch the feller.'

The trip back to Victoria took quite a lot longer than the trip out. Holiday traffic jammed the roads. 'Is it legal in Canada to make a call on your mobile if you're not driving?' I asked.

Alan shrugged. 'I've no idea. Try it and see. A traffic cop would have a hard time getting to us in this mess.'

So I called John. For a wonder, he answered, sounding a little less harried than in recent days. I told him what Silas had found.

'Good grief! Where are you?'

'I don't know. On the road somewhere south of Duncan. Oh, there's a road sign. Chapman Road is coming up. It's awfully slow going, I'm afraid.'

'Alan's driving, I hope.'

'Yes, of course. I wouldn't use my phone if—'

John interrupted. 'Tell him to pull off on Chapman Road and wait for me. I can get to you a lot quicker. Traffic's mostly coming in to the city. I'll be there as soon as I can.'

'John, bring some sandwiches or something,' I said, but it was too late; he was gone.

'I wish you hadn't mentioned food,' said Alan.

'Me, too. I don't suppose . . . no.' Chapman Road turned out to lead not much of anywhere, and there were certainly no shops or fast-food outlets, just what looked like a used-car lot. I was getting thirsty, too, but I decided not to mention that. And the sun was getting very warm. I rummaged in my purse and found the remains of the pack of gum I'd bought to alleviate ear problems while flying. It was pretty dry. I took a stick and handed one to Alan, who took it without comment.

John got there before we quite perished, and bless the man, he had some bottles of water. 'They're not cold, I'm afraid, but I thought you might be feeling a bit dry, baking here in your car. Now let's see Silas's treasure. Ah, yes. Yes, the old boy's done us proud. This is going to let us nail one case.'

'Perhaps,' said Alan cautiously, but John paid him no attention.

He called the details in to the RCMP. 'Because,' he said, 'I'm not going to get back very fast. Even if I had my old police car with lights and siren, other cars can't get out of my way when there's no place to go. In fact, now that they've got the information at headquarters, there's no real need to hurry. How about some lunch? I know a little place around here, nothing posh, but the food's quite acceptable.'

I would have eaten raw oysters by that time, and they are the one food I detest. Fish and chips were more than 'acceptable'. The little café was crowded enough that we could talk in reasonable privacy.

'Have they had any luck yet in finding Alexis and/or her friend?' I asked. 'Oh!'

Both men looked at me quizzically.

'I just remembered something I meant to do first thing this morning, and Silas knocked it out of my head. Alan, don't let me forget when we've finished eating.'

John looked as if he wanted to ask what I was talking about, and I decided there was no reason he shouldn't know. 'I'm going to call my friend Nigel, back in Sherebury, and given the time difference, I need to do it soon. I want him to do some research on Alexis.'

'We're doing that, you know.'

'I know. But Nigel's approach might be . . . um . . . slightly different from yours.'

John looked at me over the tops of his glasses. 'Slightly less legal, you mean. I thought you said he was "strictly legit".'

'And he is. He would never hack into anyone's files in order to steal anything.' I left it at that, and John sighed.

'Okay, I don't want to know. Information obtained illegally can't be used in court, you know.'

'I do know. But it can be useful, all the same. Would you pass the vinegar, please?'

We spent the rest of the meal talking about the various Canada Day celebrations, and then I excused myself to call Nigel.

'No, I wasn't in bed. It's only a little after nine here; we've just got the kids in bed. What's up?'

'First, I need to catch you up to date.' I told him that Alexis and Alice had been identified as one and the same, and as Alexis had had the opportunity and a whopping motive to kill Hartford, they were looking for her. 'But she seems to have vanished from the face of the earth. I want you to find her.'

'Oh, right, I'll hop on the next plane.'

'Not that way – as you know perfectly well. I want you to get into her computer and come up with some likely places she might go.'

There was a pause. 'And you'll pay my bail?'

'Anything. But you won't get caught. And Nigel, it's urgent! She's got to be found.'

'Yes. Well, no promises, but I'll do my best. Any ideas about a password?'

'None that you couldn't guess as well as I. Permutations on birth date, addresses, names of friends. Oh . . . you might try some variation of Lucia, since that was her obsession.'

'Right. I'll be in touch.'

And we went home by a leisurely route John had suggested to Sadie, and if it took at least as long as the main highway would have done, at least we weren't breathing exhaust fumes all the way.

We got back home in time to see some native dancing (very impressive) and hear some music and eat a good deal of picnic-style food and, when the sun finally set, to watch fireworks over the harbour from our balcony, before we fell into bed at the end of a very long day.

I was not best pleased to be awakened, for the second day in a row, by the telephone. This time I didn't even speak when I answered.

'Dorothy? Are you there?'

'Mph.' I tried to focus on the display. 'Do you know what time it is?'

'Oh. Did I wake you?'

'Of course not. I'm always awake at 4:37 in the morning.'

'You did say it was urgent.'

I yawned hugely. 'I did. It's just that yesterday . . . oh, well. Never mind. Hang on a minute while I get up and go to the kitchen.'

'This is costing a lot, you know,' Nigel complained when I spoke again.

'Send us the bill. I had to get to the coffee. Now, what have you got that justified getting an old lady out of bed at this ungodly hour?'

'It's worth it, I promise. I haven't found her, though I do have some leads. But I got into her computer and found a piece of dynamite. A-a-and – wait for it – I wasn't the first hacker to find it.'

'How do you know?'

'There are footprints, if you know how to look for them. Anyway, I found a document that will set your sweet little community over there on fire. It's a press release, written a couple of weeks ago and due to be sent to the media yesterday. It details, chapter and verse, all the dirty tricks Paul Hartford had been playing for months – all those petty crimes. Then it goes on to explain why he was doing all this – a ploy to create a problem which he then could promise to solve, once he was elected.'

'But that's exactly what we thought was happening. Why would Alexis . . .? Oh.'

'Yes. Her revenge. Brilliant, actually. The release doesn't actually say so, but it's pretty obvious that her planning was behind all this.'

'But then, why would she kill him? This plan was much worse. Build him up, lead him on, and then destroy him. That massive ego torn to bits. What a diabolical woman! Though one admits he deserved it. But murder? Where does that fit into the plan?'

'It doesn't. Which is why I thought you'd find this interesting. I'm going to send it to you. You have, of course, no idea where it came from. I'll keep looking for her hideaway. Go back to bed, darling,' he added sweetly, and ended the call.

I wished I could do as he suggested, but my body was too full of caffeine and my mind too full of conflicting thoughts.

It was too early to call John. It was too early to wake Alan. I sat with my own tangled thoughts, drinking cup after cup of coffee and trying to work out a reason for Hartford's murder.

I jumped when Alan walked into the room, and knocked my cup off the table. He started to apologize. 'It's all right. That's about my fifth cup, and I certainly don't need it. Did it break?'

'No, tough stoneware. Why so much coffee?' He got paper towels and cleaned up the mess while I started another pot for him.

'I've been up for hours. Nigel called, and I have a tale to relate.'

I told him, briefly. 'Nigel's going to send the press release to us, maybe has already. Does it make any sense to you?'

He shook his head. 'I see why you needed so much coffee. No, it doesn't make sense. The plot to take him down is understandable. Brilliant, in fact. We had worked out that he was creating a problem in order to solve it – but we didn't go the next step and sweep the whole thing out from under his feet. That I see. But why, with that plan almost to fruition, she would murder him – no.'

'Maybe she didn't. Maybe we're all wrong. Maybe he – oh, I don't know – committed suicide. Had an accident.'

'And then, while dead, moved to a different location to be found.'

'Maybe he wasn't quite dead.'

'With a severed aorta.'

'You see, that's the trouble. I've been thinking all those things, hoping coffee would clear my head, but all it's done is give me the shakes. And I've thought maybe someone else murdered him, after all, but why? And why, in that case, has Alexis disappeared?'

Alan looked at his watch. 'I overslept. John must be up and about by now. I'll call him.'

But his phone rang before he could pick it up. 'Yes? Oh, I was about to phone you. Yes? Good! Well done! We have some things to tell you, too. Have you had breakfast? Well, then, come over and have it with us.' He clicked off. 'They've got Elizabeth's killer, one of Hartford's employees, as we suspected. The receipt led them straight to him. John's coming to tell us all about it. What would you like for breakfast, French toast?'

'Good heavens, no! All I need is a sugar high on top of the caffeine high. You'd have to scrape me off the ceiling.'

'Ah. Well then, how about a nice surfeit of cholesterol? The fat should buffer the caffeine, don't you think?'

'I don't know. If caffeine is the antidote to alcohol, is the opposite true? Maybe what I need is a good shot of bourbon.'

'Maybe what you need is some fresh air. Go out and enjoy the beautiful morning. I'll call you when breakfast is ready.'

The fresh air didn't help much, but breakfast did, I had to admit. Maybe part of the shakiness was just plain hunger. And it was good to talk things over with John, but he didn't have any solution to our conundrum, either. Nigel had sent the press release; John read it and shook his head.

'That woman belongs in a Greek play. An *ancient* Greek play. The idea of waiting that long for her revenge, of planning out such an elaborate scheme – whew! I wouldn't want her mad at me.'

'John, we've got to find her. How can such a conspicuous person vanish so completely?'

'Well, there's one way.'

'Yes. I thought of that. There's plenty of nice deep water around. But would someone who could be that wrapped up in revenge even consider surrender? Because that's what suicide is – surrender to one's troubles.'

'I agree it doesn't seem in character. Well, I'd best take this to the police. Might as well make them as confused as we are.'

'Anyway, we've got one murderer by the heels. How did you do that, by the way? I never had a chance to ask.'

'Just routine police work, once we had that receipt. When we talked to the guy – his name's Sam Ellis – he couldn't confess fast enough. I think he was afraid Hartford would be blamed, and even though the man's dead . . .' John sighed. 'Loyalty sometimes settles in strange places. Sam told us he knew Elizabeth wasn't responding to Hartford's advances, and he thought he could teach her a lesson and give Silas some trouble at the same time, but it all went wrong. She tried to fight him and he got carried away.'

I was too appalled to speak.

'It won't be a murder charge, probably,' John went on. 'Homicide, certainly, but the guy's pretty convincing when he says he never meant to kill her. He also says, and I believe this, too, that Hartford never ordered that little piece of mayhem. It was his own sweet little idea.' He shook his head. 'Some of those geeks – they know everything there is to know about electronics. Show them a computer, and they can make it fire a rocket to the moon. They can create Artificial Intelligence till the cows come home. But as far as ordinary human intelligence, ordinary common sense and compassion . . .' He spread his hands in the universal 'no way' gesture. 'Nothing, nada, zilch. I really must go.'

THIRTY

'Come, love,' said Alan, when the door had closed behind John, 'let's go for a walk. Most of this lovely city remains unexplored. I think we need a fresh outlook.'

'I have a better idea. We'll probably be going home soon. I'd like to see Butchart Gardens one more time and remind ourselves why this is the Garden City, rather than remember it for all the awful things that have been going on here.'

'Are you up to it, on very little sleep and too much coffee?'

'I want to forget all about crime and misery for a while, and there are lots of benches.'

'And if you fall asleep on one of them, doubtless one of those stalwart groundskeepers will help me haul you back to the car. Very well. Shall we take a picnic lunch or eat in the café?'

'It had better be the café. Our food supply is running low, and I don't want to buy a lot more.'

'Right you are. And I hate to mention it, dear heart, but were you planning to get dressed?'

The day was, of course, perfect. The weather had become monotonous. 'I'd love a nice thunderstorm about now,' I said as I negotiated downtown Victoria traffic.

'Not now. After we've had our little outing.'

The gardens were crowded, as I should have expected. 'I suppose a lot of people took the whole week off,' I said after we finally found a parking place.

But once we got into the gardens proper, the crowds weren't bothersome. The place is big enough to accommodate a lot of people. And the flowers . . . 'Alan, it's all different, and only a couple of weeks later.'

Many more roses were in bloom, and their fragrance filled the air. I found it impossible to dwell on bitterness and revenge in such a place. Those old storytellers who envisioned Eden as a garden were right on the money.

But Alan was right, as he so often is. I ran out of energy suddenly, as we approached the Italian Garden. I sagged onto a bench and gulped from my water bottle. 'Lunchtime, do you think?' Alan asked.

I nodded. 'If we can get in. Maybe we should have brought that picnic after all.'

'It's early. We can but try.'

The nearest eatery was the smallest and most expensive, the Dining Room, housed in the original home of the Butcharts. It was barely past eleven, when they opened, but the place was already full. 'I'm afraid, at this time of year, you really do need to make a reservation,' said the hostess, sounding genuinely sorry. 'You might try the Blue Poppy, but I imagine there's quite a line.'

'Oh, dear. I . . . is there someplace where I could buy a candy bar or something? I feel foolish, but I think I really do need food quickly.'

The woman looked alarmed. 'You're not diabetic, are you? Because I could get you some orange juice . . .'

'It's Mrs Martin, isn't it?' The woman had come up behind us. 'And Mr Nesbitt. Do you remember me?'

'Yes, of course – at the gala – but . . . oh! Ms Underwood, isn't it?'

'Yes, indeed. I'm afraid I overheard part of your conversation. I have a table for three booked here, but I just heard that the other two can't make it. If you don't mind sharing a table, I'd love to have you join me.'

'Oh, we wouldn't want to intrude . . .' I trailed off.

'Nonsense. I hate eating alone, and you're white as a sheet. Come and sit down before you fall down. My usual table, Kathleen?'

We were seated and Ms Underwood had made me eat a crusty roll, lavish with butter, before she would let me say anything. 'That's better. Are you in fact diabetic?'

'No. Just very, very tired and hungry. I didn't get much sleep last night.'

'And you've been having a trying time. I may say I know most of what you've been going through. Amy is a good friend. Have another roll.'

While my mouth was full, Alan gently probed Ms Underwood's knowledge.

'Yes, Amy told me you'd learned who Alexis really was. And her tragic story. Oh, yes, please, iced tea for all of us, and we'll start with the vichyssoise. I hope you don't mind my ordering – if you'd rather have something else – it's just that they're so busy, and I didn't want to keep anyone waiting.'

I started to say that vichyssoise sounded fine, but Ms Underwood swept on. 'I never warmed to Alexis, I must say, but now that I know what that disgusting man did to her – and I'm going to be just like the dean and say what I think about him – and I'm so glad he'll never be our MP, but poor Alexis – or Alice, as I suppose I should call her—'

Alan interrupted her. 'Ms Underwood, do you have any idea where she might be? She seems to have disappeared, and the police are rather interested in talking with her.'

'They think she did it, don't they?'

'There's a good deal of evidence that way, although it's not conclusive.' I tried to say it gently. 'I have a good deal of sympathy for her, too, but private vengeance can't be condoned.'

'No. Ah, here's our soup.'

We worked our way through the soup and a huge Caesar salad and a chocolate mousse to die for, and Alan told her about the arrest of Elizabeth's killer. 'He's confessed, so I'm not spreading tales.' He didn't talk about Nigel's discovery of the press release; that information wasn't yet public.

Alan tried to pick up the bill when it came, but Ms Underwood wouldn't let him. 'You're doing a public service here in Victoria, and not getting a cent for it. I can certainly buy you lunch. And there's something else I can do for you. I've made up my mind. Alice Ingram is staying with me. Here's my address and landline number. And my name, by the way, is Pat.'

And she was gone before we could do more than gape at her.

We tried to call John, of course, but got voice mail. 'Alan, we can't just turn this over to the police. She trusts us. Let's go over and talk to Alice.'

Alan shrugged. 'Who may be a murderer.'

'But may not.'

He shrugged again and led the way to the car.

Sadie got us there easily. As we might have expected, Ms Underwood – Pat – lived in a big, beautiful house in a beautiful neighbourhood. We pulled into the drive, and before we got to the door a vaguely familiar-looking woman opened it and stood there framed in the doorway.

'Pat said you were coming,' said an expressionless voice. 'I'm Alice Ingram. Come in.'

We walked into a room right out of *House Beautiful*, except it looked lived-in. No designer had 'done' this room, just a person with lots of money and excellent taste. Books and magazines lay here and there; a yoga mat lay in front of a window with a view of a gorgeous garden. And a young man got up from a couch as we entered.

'This is my cousin Andrew,' said the woman, strange and yet not strange. 'Andrew, some friends of Pat's. They're helping the police, and they want to know what happened last Wednesday.'

'We're not in any way official, Ms Ingram,' said Alan hastily. 'We have no legal right to ask you questions. And in any case, I'm sure you have here the same right not to respond that you would in England or America.'

'It doesn't matter. Please sit down. We want to tell you about it.' She and her cousin took seats and we did the same, uneasily, for my part.

'Pat tells me you know about my sister.'

We nodded.

'I never wanted that man dead. That was too easy, too kind. I wanted him humiliated. For years I've waited and planned, waited for his ego to lead him into politics, as it inevitably would. I changed my name, not that it would have mattered. He had certainly forgotten all about a grieving sister. I changed my appearance, again needlessly, because he had never met me.'

'But you needed to make sure of attracting his attention.'

'You see a good deal, don't you, Mrs Martin? Yes, I turned myself into the kind of woman that man enjoyed. I led him on. I teased him. I was despicable, and I didn't even hate myself, because he was even more despicable.'

I couldn't bear her anguish. 'Alice, we know most of the rest. You planned a campaign of harassment, suggested a problem he could create and then promise, as MP, to solve. Brilliant idea, actually.'

'And then,' Alan said, taking up the narrative, 'you planned to reveal what he had done. That would have been the coup de grâce, the end of his political ambitions, of his social acclaim. Why then did you decide to kill him?'

'I didn't. Let me go on. Andrew is one of my staff, and goes with me to many charitable functions, working backstage, as it were, to make sure everything goes smoothly. As I said that evening, that man was in Ottawa, or was supposed to be, greasing some palms. So when Andrew came in and told me he was in the back, asking for me, I was surprised and not pleased. But I had to keep up the façade a little longer, pretend for a few more days that I was completely under his spell. I wasn't prepared to find him in a flaming rage.'

'Alice, let me tell them. Don't upset yourself any more than you have to. I took her to where Hartford was waiting for her, in the back hallway. He began to shout, so we pushed him out the back door onto the loading dock. He was quite literally foaming at the mouth; spittle was spraying everywhere. He had hacked into Alice's computer and found the press release she had prepared, detailing every nasty thing he had done, including the death of her sister. It was to go out the next day.'

I nodded to Alan. Nigel had known that someone else had been in the file.

'He started to try to assault her physically, as well, but I wasn't having any of that. Someone was getting close, in a car, so I opened that overhead door thing and shoved him into the pantry where we wouldn't be seen. The lights weren't on, but before I shut the door again I saw a big pair of scissors lying on the counter. Hartford saw them, too. He picked them up and came at me. I'm younger than he was, and in better shape. I grabbed them, trying to twist the scissors out of his hand – and I don't know yet quite what happened, but he sort of lunged at me, and the next thing I knew, he was lying on the floor and there was blood everywhere.'

'Including all over you, I imagine.'

'Yes, of course. I didn't know what had happened, but he was obviously losing far too much blood. Alice was the one who kept her head. She found a tablecloth in a drawer somewhere and tried to stop the blood, but it just kept spurting out. It was . . .

Mr Nesbitt, I've seen combat. I've seen men die. But nothing was as horrible as that room, with the blood—'

He stopped, and Alice went on, pale but determined. 'We were very stupid then. We should have called the police and explained what had happened. But there were so many things we couldn't prove. We'd moved to where no one could hear his tantrum. No one saw what happened at the end. He was a wealthy and influential man. We decided to cover it up. I knew about the storage room, of course; I've often had events in that hall. Another tablecloth served to slide him around the outside of the building and into that little stage hallway. We left him there for the moment while we did a fast clean-up of the pantry, and then went back to put him in the storage room, but someone was coming. We had to leave him where he was, and get out.'

'Of course. There were your bloodstained clothes to deal with.'

'And . . . our bloodstained souls. The clothes were easy. We jumped in the fountain in the park. You know cold water takes out most bloodstains. That meant we wouldn't get much blood in the car. Of course we burned our clothes later.'

'And the weapon? The scissors?'

'In the harbour. I'm sure the Event Centre people missed them. They were heavy duty ones, meant I suppose for opening canvas bags of flour and rice and the like. But scissors are always going missing.'

Alice heaved a great sigh. 'I don't know if anyone will believe us. I'm not sure I care, except for Andrew's sake. The world is rid of that man, and I can't even feel any satisfaction. I don't feel anything. I think I'm dead, too.'

'Accidental death,' said Alan as we drove slowly home. 'We were all wrong. All our elaborate scenarios, and we were wrong. What are we going to do about it?'

'I don't know. Andrew is young. This could blight his life, and he did nothing wrong. Alice committed no crime, only the corrosive sin of hatred. She may recover. She may not. Did you notice she couldn't even speak his name?'

We drove the rest of the way in silence.

I badly needed sleep, but I knew it wouldn't come. I paced. Out to the balcony, in again. Washed my face in cold water. Paced.

My phone rang. I almost didn't answer, but it might be important.

'Mrs Martin, Pat Underwood. I got your number from Amy. They told you.'

'Yes.'

'What are you going to do?'

'I don't know. Everything I think of is the wrong thing.'

'Yes. But I'll tell you what I'm going to do. I'm sending them away. I'm not going to tell you, or anyone else, where they're going. It may not be enough to give them a new life, but it's all I can do.'

'Yes.'

I ended the call, took out of my purse the slip of paper with Pat's address and phone number, and slowly tore it into tiny bits.

Finally making a decision, we told John everything except Pat's name. Somewhat to our surprise, he was philosophical about it. 'There's no proof of anything. They could be found, but to what purpose? In the end, it was an accident.'

'Or perhaps a judgement,' I suggested.

'Perhaps. I'll say a quiet word to the DCC, and he'll quietly ramp down the investigation. It's going to be one of those high-profile cases that never get solved.'

'The media will crucify the police.'

'Yes, but they'll get tired of it eventually. Something new will crop up. All in a day's work.'

'Teresa will be devastated,' I mourned. 'She wants his murderer caught and punished, but there is no murderer.'

'I've told her about identifying Elizabeth's killer. Not his name, but the fact of his arrest. That helped her a bit. She went straight up to Duncan to talk to the family. Dorothy, I'll keep a look-out for her. I think she might move to Duncan to be near the Cowichan people; I can try to find her a job there. Closer to her roots, I think she'll heal. In time.'

He drove us to the airport two days later. 'It's a pity we never solved the murder,' he said loudly and cheerfully as he left us. There were several bystanders. 'But we will, eventually. We're still trying to trace Alice Ingram and her friend, but it's as if they've vanished into thin air. I still think she may be dead.'

'You may be right.' I meant it.

'And I'm sorry we never had that tea at the Empress. Next time.'

'Next time.' But Alan and I both knew it might be a very long time before we wanted to come back.

Our flight was booked straight to London without a stopover, though we had to change planes in Toronto. As we took off and passed into American air space, Alan pointed out the window. 'Fireworks.'

'Oh. Oh! Alan, it's the Fourth of July!'

He smiled, understanding my mixed feelings, and said nothing.

Stiff and tired, we landed hours later at Heathrow, where Nigel met us and drove us home. Home to our dogs and cat, our garden, the friends we loved. Home, where we could begin to forget.